boilerplate C000124991

DESTINY: ASCENSION SAGA - BOOKS 7-9

INTERSTELLAR BRIDES®: ASCENSION SAGA

GRACE GOODWIN

PREQUEL

Twenty-seven years ago Queen Celene was forced to flee Alera with her unborn child. Read the story of her escape to Earth in The Ascension Saga prequel — for free!

Click now to find out how the adventure began...
www.ascensionsaga.com

BOOK 7

PROLOGUE

Q ueen Celene, Aleran Dungeon

DAYS WENT BY. There were no windows, so I could only tell the passing of time based on the delivery of my meals. My cousin, Lord Wyse, had not returned since his visit days ago, since my captors had transferred me here—wherever here was. He'd said I was no longer his problem, and I now believed it. Yes, he wanted royal power, a privilege that didn't belong to him. He'd been bent on that for decades. But I had no idea his bitterness had festered and grown into such focused evil.

He might have been the one who ordered men to Earth to kidnap me, drag me out of bed after nearly three decades, but he must not have been the only one involved in hunting me down. He couldn't be. If he were, I'd either be dead, or he'd still be using me for his own purposes.

Instead, he'd just... walked away.

Then who wanted me here, and why? Had they known about my daughters when they took me?

No. They must not have known. Otherwise, they would have killed my three girls: Trinity, Faith and Destiny. Or kidnapped them as well. Locked them up, as they'd done to me.

Where was I, exactly? I could see enough to know that I was in a prisoner block somewhere. The guards all wore clerics' uniforms. But there were only a handful, and they rotated four times a day. There was never anyone else. No foot traffic. I never heard them talk to one another or question who they were guarding.

I wasn't supposed to see any of them, the black hood they'd placed over my head had made that very clear. They'd shoved it over my head, blinding me, and then transported me, marched me, moved me so many times I'd lost count. By the time they'd shoved me into this cell and slammed the door, I had no idea if I was still on Alera or on the other side of the galaxy.

The lack of buzzing and engine noise under my feet assured me that I was, in fact, on solid ground and not in a spaceship. But that was all I knew. Based on the cleric guard uniforms I could see—thanks to the gift I'd been blessed with by the citadel all those years ago—I assumed I was still on my home planet.

And for some unknown reason, I was alive. They didn't want me dead or they'd have killed me on Earth. Save everyone so much time and trouble. If they wanted me broken and destroyed, they would have kept the torture going. Instead, I was fully healed. Clothed, fed, kept in reasonably restful accommodations. I had a real bed. Fresh water. Food. Comfortable clothing and warm shoes. It wasn't the Ritz, but I wasn't suffering any longer either.

Still, with every quiet slide of my prison door, I feared what might come next. Like now, when the Aleran I called Scarface entered. For the first time, he wasn't alone. A cleric followed behind, his cape swirling around his knees. He was no one special. A low-ranking member of the guard. The insignia on his chest, which had not changed since I'd been gone, made that clear. But he came inside and remained by the door, which closed behind the two of them, locking all of us into the small space together.

Scarface loomed in my tiny cell, the damaged skin on his cheek and along his jaw stark in the glaring light. I refused to rise from the bed, to give him any bit of respect. He'd earned none and he knew it. I lifted my chin, my hands folded in my lap.

Waited.

"I am sure you would like to hear an update regarding your family," he said, his raspy voice lacking all feeling. Just like his soul. Black. Empty.

I did. I wanted to see Trinity on the throne, ruling. A natural leader, she would be an amazing queen. It had been a dream for years, but was something now I feared I'd never see. Normally, she could only rule Alera if I were already dead or had officially stepped down. But my capture and disappearance was a loophole to that ruling I'd never imagined.

And Faith. The poisoning inside the Jax house. There was a story there and I wanted to hear it. Desperately. Surely it wasn't true. I'd spun possibilities in my head since Wyse had shared that bit of information. But it was all speculation on my part. I knew nothing.

And Destiny. Wyse knew of her existence, knew her name. But did he know nothing else? Had she been discovered?

I waited in silence and Scarface grinned.

"I am sorry to report that there has been a death in your family."

I felt the blood drain from my face. Saw little white spots dance across the room. My palms began to sweat and I was hot all over. Scarface was speaking but I couldn't hear him, blood rushing in my ears.

One of them had died. Oh god! Who? When? How?

Why was I safely tucked in this stupid prison cell while my babies were in danger? Why?

"He was no longer any use, and so he was eliminated. A risk. Gone."

Scarface spoke in sentences but I only heard words. I could barely process, barely think.

One of my girls was dead.

But then I realized Scarface had said *he*.

With numb lips, I said, "He?"

"Your dearest cousin, Lord Wyse, is dead."

Relief coursed through me so quickly I became nauseated. A laugh bubbled out of me. Escaped.

Scarface's dark brow winged up, but he said nothing.

I was smiling. Broadly. None of the girls were dead. Thank goddess. "He deserved whatever happened to him," I replied. "I assume whoever is keeping me here wanted him dead."

Scarface nodded.

"Why are you telling me this?" I asked. Coburt was nothing to me but the memory of a skulking, somber boy from my youth, and more recently, my captor. A traitor. He was less than nothing to me.

"Lord Wyse was the Inspector Optimi, father of Radella, the reigning royal, prior to your daughters' return. He was powerful. Connected. Cunning.

"He's dead. All that means is he was a puppet, nothing more."

His smile turned coy, as if I'd figured out something important. "Yes. A pawn. As are you," he replied. He may have acted in a deferential manner to Lord Wyse when he was alive, but it was now obvious he'd held no true allegiance to my cousin. That was very clear.

So much melodrama. Why bother telling me that Lord Wyse was not the mastermind behind my abduction? He'd been a boy not much older than me when the attack had occurred at the palace. We'd both been little more than children. So, what was this really about? "What do you want? You know I don't care about Lord Wyse. I'm not afraid of you. But you, on the other hand, should be very afraid of me."

His laugh was cold, so cold it made me shiver. "We have plans for you, my queen."

"You mean your *real* master has plans for me." I stated it as fact. I'd been sitting in this cell long enough to figure that out, and he knew it. "So take me to him. Or her. Let's get this done. Why keep me here?"

"Your usefulness will have a time and place," he replied. "When the k—"

The sound of ion fire filled the room. Scarface's sneering lips opened in shock as he fell to his knees, then onto the floor.

He never finished his sentence. The cleric, who I'd completely forgotten since he'd stood so motionless until now, lifted his arm. The long sleeve fell back to reveal the ion pistol. Before I could even blink, he had shot Scarface in the back.

My mouth fell open as my torturer, my warden since I'd been kidnapped, rolled on the floor. His eyes remained open and fixed on the ceiling, unseeing. Dead. Blood slowly pooled about him. No ReGen wand or pod was going to save him.

Belatedly, I gasped, the shock catching up to me. I stood then, slowly, watching the cleric as I did so. I had to be next.

But instead of firing, he lowered his weapon, the sleeve hiding it once again as if it had never happened.

"*His* usefulness had a time and place. And it is over."

The cleric's voice was slow and deep. Calm. He was no cleric, at least no peacefully minded student of the order that I'd ever met.

Coburt Wyse was dead. Scarface was dead. Lord and Lady Jax were dead. Someone was getting rid of loose ends. Killing off everyone who knew about me, or the ultimate plan here.

Who was the puppet master?

As I watched the cleric drag the dead body out of my cell, I had a feeling I would find out soon enough.

1

D estiny, *Cleric Fortress, Mountains Near the Capital City of Mytikas*

BACK HOME, on Earth, they call midnight the witching hour. But here, inside the walls of the clerical order, it's more like the chanting hour. In almost every room up and down the long hallways there is a gathering of clerics—either in training or not—chanting. They just didn't shut up. And when they did, the meditating started. Clerics stayed up late, their bodies somehow becoming in tune to the shimmering glow of moonlight on the Aleran flowers that grew outside the citadel. It was all very communal and hippie-like. Irritating as all hell for those of us who didn't do very much communing in life. They had more patience in a pinky finger than I did in my entire body.

But since Faith had announced herself to the world, there had been less chanting and more gossiping, and that was just what I'd hoped for. A bunch of introverts *finally* letting it all out. Discussing the miraculous return of the royal princesses

Trinity and Faith, and speculating about the third newly lit spire and the location of their queen.

What was actually bonkers was that the third princess they were all gabbing about was me. If I were caught right now, I'd be in their dungeon before I was given a chance to explain. Or dead. It was possible they'd just kill me on sight.

Breaking into the elder cleric's office was strictly forbidden.

I'd heard—again from all that pent-up gossip—that a few hundreds years ago, the offense was punishable by death. Since no one had been caught since, I had no way of knowing whether they'd updated their policy or if no one had ever tried.

"Guess I'll just have to be very, very careful." I whispered the words to no one in particular as I clung to the vines that grew along the tallest tower within the fortress walls. I was like Romeo seeking his Juliet in the high school play.

Glancing left and right to make sure no one saw me... or for maybe one last moment before I did something execution-worthy, I opened a window and pulled myself up, slung my leg, then knee, then the rest of me, through the opening. The office was at least three stories off the ground, but the vines were thick, and I was small. They almost made it too easy.

I landed with barely a sound on the thin carpeting and noticed the room was still nice and warm. The old woman who ran the show had old bones, and she did not like the cold up here in the mountains that surrounded the royal city. But then, with the fortress built eons ago, she didn't have much of a choice but to deal with the weather. The clerical order had formed when the royal bloodline did. The first queen recognized by the citadel had accepted the oath of the first cleric, and so it had begun. Generation after generation, the clerics had served Alera in the matters of law and protection for the realm. They were the scribes and record keepers, and trusted with knowledge known only to a few. Both the clerical order and the royal bloodline were linked to the citadel somehow, but each chose to keep their secrets. The clerics had served the royal family—my family—for millennia.

"Bunch of fucking traitors." Not *all* of them were bad. I'd been training with them, eating with them, pretending to be one of them for two weeks now. I was a novice. A new initiate. And they'd welcomed me into the fold. Most of them were good, solid people. Kind. Friendly. Supportive.

But not all of them. No, someone—or *someones*—within was rotten to the core. Yeah, there was a really bad apple spoiling the whole dang bunch. And I would hunt down the traitors if I died doing it. They still had Mom. They'd tried to kill Trinity and my twin, Faith, more than once.

If they knew who I was, no doubt they'd try to kill me as well. It was obvious we were wanted dead. I grinned, thinking our arrival on Alera must have totally fucked up their plans. Ha!

Moving forward swiftly in the dark, I stubbed my toe on an unexpected outcropping from a chair. I hissed and hopped about. "Damn it." The words were barely more than a grunt, but I heard something move in answer outside. Below me. On the ground.

Then a rustling.

The vines.

Oh, shit.

Someone was climbing the vines. Romeo, himself, this time? I was no Juliet waiting to be whisked away. And fuck it all, they were moving even faster than I had. I didn't have time to go anywhere, and the room's door—which normal people used to come in—would be solidly locked. I had to hide and hope whoever was coming would lead me to another clue about my mother. I knew the clerics had her. Somewhere. The rumor mill was buzzing with whispers and speculation about a very top-secret prisoner. It had to be Mom, or to Alerans, Queen Celene. It just had to be.

Because if it weren't, I'd run into a dead end and we were all screwed. Mom would die. And I just couldn't live with myself if that happened.

Hobbling on my aching toe, I dashed to a corner so dark with shadows it looked black. There I stood, immobile, and waited to see who my unexpected visitor might be. What were the chances of there being two snooping initiates?

The waiting was an agony all its own. I was in tune with my body, keeping my breathing quiet, to try and still my racing heart—yeah, right—and stand as still as possible. The Aleran half of my DNA had decided last week that it was a good time to go into full-blown Ardor. I knew what it was because Trinity'd had it when we'd arrived. Every inch of my skin was sensitive. My nipples ached, the lobes of my breasts felt too full and heavy. They were small, which suited me just fine for fighting. But they felt double their normal size. My pussy was constantly wet and my hearing seemed to have kicked up into some kind of superpower level annoying. Like I was the Bionic Woman all of a sudden. The horny Bionic Woman.

I could hear insects crawling in the walls. Conversations all over the fortress; that was why I knew every bit of gossip that had been circling about. My own heartbeat had sounded like a conga drum inside my head until I'd learned how to ignore it and somehow, that had helped me figure out how to pay attention to what I was hearing when I wanted to, and feel somewhat normal the rest of the time.

Trinity hadn't mentioned super-hearing as being part of her Ardor, but she'd been pretty distracted with Leo, as in naked and having screaming orgasms. Stupid Ardor, screwing with me. It was as if I had no control over my own body any longer. And I wasn't getting off. Damn it.

I was so horny I was close to coming by just rubbing my thighs together. And I heard everything that went on in the place. Everything. Including a few rather sexy encounters that had me squirming and wishing taking care of things myself would actually work. But no. Every orgasm I gave myself just made it worse. I'd quit after two and curled into a ball for a few hours, waiting for the need wrecking me to back off.

It didn't. But I'd been coping. I wasn't sure how much longer I would last before I went insane with lust.

Which was why I'd decided to take this last, desperate chance and break into the elder's office. If I didn't find anything, I'd have to go to the palace and find one of those consort men to take the edge off. Right now, I just *needed* and I was nearly to the point that I didn't much care whose cock I was riding as long as it was hot, hard, and lasted all damn night. Oh yeah. *Hot and hard.*

I was panting when two large, very masculine hands appeared on the window ledge. Nice hands. Long, thick fingers. Inside me. Rubbing me. Fucking me.

Shit. I had to get myself together.

Focusing on my breath, I slowed things down and waited. My eyes had already adjusted to the darkness, so I watched the intruder slide through the window like a cat.

God, for such a large man, he could move. He was strong, that was obvious by the way he handled his entire body weight with just his arms and swung silently to the floor. He landed crouched low, one knee bent as if he were kneeling before a queen. But he wasn't kneeling, his chin was up, his breathing silent—even with my incredible hearing.

He was holding his breath. Listening.

For what?

"Destiny? I know you are in here." His voice was deep. Sensual. The low timbre slid over my skin and I shivered, literally shivered, the tone going straight to my clit and zinging through my body as if he had his mouth on me.

What. The. Fuck?

I didn't move. I didn't dare. And I didn't breathe, either. Holding the air in my lungs as if my life depended on it. I knew that voice. Somehow, I knew it. But from where?

He rose, but didn't step in any direction, still as a statue. He whispered, but his voice was full volume to my sensitive hearing. "Destiny. I know you are here. Your sisters sent me. In the conversation you shared, you said you were in danger. Let me help you. I am getting you out of here."

My sisters? Oh, hell no. This had to be the voice of the man on that comm call with Trin and Faith. The one who'd point blank asked me if I was in danger. And I'd given two taps to reply yes.

I should have lied, but something about that damn voice had made me want to tell him the truth. More than that, it had made me want to claw my way through the comm channel and rub my naked all over his naked. Not that he was naked right now. Oh, it would have been great if he were, but no.

That thought was the last straw. I was losing my mind. Romeo didn't climb through the window naked.

"Be quiet or you'll get us both killed," I hissed.

Instantly, his head turned and I watched as he zeroed in on my exact location. Before I could move, or even think, he was close. Too close. Inches. I could feel his body heat. Smell the musky, male scent of him. My nipples hardened and I swear I had a little mini-orgasm. I stifled a whimper.

"Destiny, come with me. I will take you back to the palace where you will be safe."

"Not happening," I countered. "But you should leave. You're going to get me killed. You move like a giant; big and heavy and slow." Lies. Lies. Lies. But I needed him to go. Right now. Before I did something really, really stupid. Like breathe in again. Smell him. Climb him like a tree. God help me if he touched me. I was holding onto my control by a thread. And he was hot. Navy SEAL, superhero, movie star hot. I could see his face. Strong jaw. Full lips. Eyes focused on me with such intensity I couldn't look away. Everything about him, from the way he moved, to the way he gazed at me said he was a predator. A hunter. A protector. He was a soldier.

Fuck. Fuck. Fuck. If ever I lusted, it was after a stud in a uniform.

"You are in danger here," he repeated.

"No shit, Sherlock."

He frowned. "My name is not Sherlock and he will not keep you safe as I will. You need to come with me. Let me handle this. I will find your mother. I give you my word." His words melted into my skin, warming me like he'd just dipped me in melted caramel. Jesus, he was dangerous. Stupid, eff-ing Ardor.

I was turning into a lunatic.

When I remained silent, his heartbeat sped up. So did his breathing; I could hear both changes easily. A shudder moved through him and I watched, in awe, as he closed his eyes. Clenched his jaw, as if he were in pain. He was in my space. Too close.

"Who are you?" I shouldn't have asked. I knew it. But I wanted to know. Maybe after I got this job done, and this Ardor business handled, I'd ask Trinity about him. Look him up. *Look him up.* Ha. I didn't want to do that. I wanted to slam him up against the wall and take him for a ride. Right fucking now.

2

V ennix Blyndar, Cleric Fortress, Mountains Near the
Capital City of Mytikas

"I AM VENNIX BLYNDAR, Captain of the Interstellar Fleet,
Captain of the Queen's Guard, and sworn to serve you,
Princess. You may call me Nix."

"Jesus. Are you trying to kill me?"

She was panting, as if she were in pain. I needed more light
to see her, to look into her eyes. To try to figure out what she
was thinking.

"No. I am here to serve you. To protect you. Let me take you
home."

"Go away." She moaned as if I'd injured her. Her scent filled
my head and her small body put off enough heat to pull at me
like a magnet.

No. Terrible fucking idea. More light would destroy me. I
was hanging onto my control by a thread when all I wanted to
do was *lean* forward, just a few inches, trap her between my
body and the wall. Lift her up. Taste...

Holy fuck. This was insane.

Trinity and Faith were both royal. Both beautiful. But I'd felt nothing more than protective instincts. I'd been protecting people my entire life. Fighting the Hive. Killing our enemies. Hunting traitors.

This time? I'd known the queen's daughter, or Princess Destiny, was in the room as soon as my feet touched the floor. I couldn't see her, hell, I could barely see my own hand. But I'd sensed her. I could actually *smell* her.

Not flowers. Not... something feminine. Just unique and it had made my cock twitch. It had never done that before. Ever. And yet, in the middle of a rescue mission, it had swelled with blood and had been what pointed me right to her.

She'd spoken and my cock had swelled, pressed painfully against my pants. But when I was able to see her face, a slight pale bit of moonlight highlighting her features, I actually spurted pre-cum. A ripple of pleasure had coursed through me unlike anything I'd ever known.

In the past minute, I'd been Awakened. I'd imagined it happening to me many times over the years. In my daydreams, I would see my mate across a room, go to her and then whisk her off to some private spot to claim her for the first time, to sink deep into her waiting, wet pussy.

But not like this. Oh, I'd crossed a room all right and found her. I wanted to toss her over my shoulder and carry her off to my quarters where I could pin her beneath me until my cock was soothed.

But not inside the fortress. Not in some high-ranking cleric's office. Not with the fucking princess of Alera.

The goddess was having a laugh at my expense right now. Surely, Thor and Leo would too when they learned the truth.

"I'm not leaving without you, Princess. I can't."

"Why? Just climb out the window and go back. Tell my sisters I'm fine. Because I am. Just... go." She looked away when she spoke, her gaze falling to my lips. I could see that much. Was it possible she wanted me as badly as I needed her?

"No."

"Why not? I am a princess, and I am ordering you to leave."

"I will never leave you, Destiny. Not now. Not ever. I am your mate."

"Bullshit. I don't believe this." I heard a little huff of a laugh in response and that pissed me off. Everything about this female made me angry. And riled. How dare she put herself in danger hunting some cleric who might have her mother? How dare she climb in a fucking window in the middle of the night? How dare she do one fucking thing that put her life at risk?

My mate needed guidance, a stern hand that didn't hesitate to turn her ass red for impetuousness. For rash decisions. Oh, I'd spank Princess Destiny if she needed it. But that would be after I fucked her into submission. No, I'd get her on her hands and knees and spank her upturned ass, then grip her hips as I fucked her pussy so deep she wouldn't know where she ended and I began. I'd come seeing my handprints marking her pale skin. And then my seed would mark her, coat her so thoroughly she'd know she was mine.

"I. Am. Your. Mate," I bit out through clenched teeth. "I'm getting you out of here."

She crossed her arms over her chest, and I saw her eyes flare. They were dark, that was all I could tell. She had high cheekbones, a pert nose and full lips.

More pre-cum seeped out at the thought of those lips stretched wide around my cock. Oh, I might be a virgin and her pussy would be the one I'd sink into for the first time, but that didn't mean I didn't know what to do with her, what I wanted to do *to* her.

"No."

That one-word reply made me fucking hot, and angry.

"No?" I countered.

She shook her head, her long, dark hair swinging. There was that scent again. I fisted my hands, tried not to grab her.

"I'm here to find my mother."

"I know, but someone could come in at any time."

She shook her head again, the temptress. "They won't. This is the administration building and the elder's office is locked because she attends evening meditation and chanting at six. They keep her office locked until dawn. I've been keeping track of her schedule for two weeks."

That was true. I'd learned that from an informant. I'd spotted Destiny outside, at the start of her climb. But I'd been too late to stop her ascent up the side of the building and through the window. I'd watched from below, ready to catch her if she fell, my heart in my throat every moment. And that had been *before* I knew what she was to me.

Mine.

Indeed, it was the best of luck. Instead of this confrontation happening below, on the lawn, we were safer here. If the lights remained off, our presence would be undetected as long as we were gone before dawn.

"You believe this room holds the answers you seek?"

I saw her shoulder rise in a small shrug. "I'm not sure, but the gossip is that a high-level prisoner is being held. I want to know who arranged it, and where, exactly, they are holding her."

"It could be anyone."

The look she gave me made my blood turn to molten lava. Challenge. "It's got to be her and you know it."

Thank the goddess she hadn't stormed into the dungeons and demanded to see the queen. Based on what I'd heard from her sisters, and the fight I'd seen in the apartment the day she had arrived on Alera, she was ballsy enough to do it. She'd been magnificent that day. Deadly. Efficient. A skilled fighter.

Good thing I hadn't scented her that night, had only caught a quick glimpse of a male and female fighting, the female winning. Had no idea she would awaken my dormant cock, that my body would belong to her for all time. I didn't want her doing anything with those strong legs right now but wrapping them around my back and holding on for the ride.

"You will stop your searching and return with me to the palace. I will investigate with others who are properly trained to do so." Yes, she would be safe and protected while others saw to the dangerous work.

"I've been here almost two weeks, you asshat. I might not be *properly trained*"—she raised her hands and made weird curling motions with her fingers—"but I've been doing just fine. This place is huge and they aren't the most talkative bunch. Besides, you think I'm going to trust someone else to find my mother? No fucking way, caveman. Trust me, I can take care of myself."

"No. I will take care of you." I put my hand to my chest, over my heart, which now belonged to her.

"What are you, a Neanderthal, thinking women are only good for one thing?" Her question had bite to it. Astonishment and anger, too.

I was not used to someone talking back. If it were a subordinate, they'd be on kitchen duty for a month. With her, I was at an impasse. Technically, as a member of the queen's guard, I had to obey her commands. But as her mate? As a male who needed to strip her naked and fill her with my aching cock, I had to tread very carefully. She was a hunter, a fighter, like me. I'd seen it in the way her body moved as she climbed the vines to this room. I'd witnessed her ferocity that very first night when she'd battled my men to protect her sisters. She was magnificent. Beautiful. And deadly. I had to proceed with caution, but she would be mine. "As princess, you may say what you wish, and I will bow to your commands. But you are my *mate,* and you will bend to my will."

It sounded as if she actually growled. I could barely see her hands come up, and she pushed me, hard, in the chest. I only moved back a step, but I was stunned. I'd never been manhandled by a woman before, and it... it made me so fucking hot.

"Your will?" she hissed. "Get the hell out of my way."

"No." I moved in closer, so close her heaving chest brushed mine when she inhaled. And it was then I felt her need, her body so desperate for mine that even now she drained my energy, my strength, across the distance, the slightest touch shooting through me like a rocket. The sensation was heady, providing for this female. Giving her what she needed. She would take my energy and feed her Ardor with me. Only me. No one else would touch her. "You need me right now, Princess, and we both know it."

"I don't need you." She shuddered and her eyes closed as I felt a surge of my strength move to pour into her.

Oh fuck. She was desperate. Dying of Aleran Ardor and she hadn't said a thing. I'd never heard of a female being this close to death, her body this starved for bonding energy, out of pure stubborn will. But if anyone would push her body too hard, fight the Ardor no matter the cost, it was this stubborn mate of mine. But I could not allow her to do this to herself. Not when I was here to provide.

I lifted my hand slowly and touched her face. Wrapped my big hand around her small cheek, fragile neck, moaned as our connection clicked into place, the magic of the Ardor mixing her life force and mine. She held completely still, frozen in shock perhaps. Or lust. Heat poured from my hand to her, the pleasure so intense my knees nearly buckled. "You need me right now, Destiny. Let me take care of you. Let me strip you naked and fuck you raw. Let me touch you."

"Why? Why you?" she whispered.

"Because you're mine and I'm yours. I know you feel it, too. You're my mate, Destiny. Mine." The darkness closed in around us like a blanket, like we were the only two people in the universe. Like we were alone. Totally. Completely. Alone.

"Mate, my ass. I don't even know you," she countered, continuing to fight what her body needed, what I could give her. Always a fighter, it seemed. "You followed me like a stalker and climbed in here to attack me. I've asked you to leave. I ordered you to leave. You are stubborn and annoying and it's obvious that you only see me as useful for one thing."

"Oh, what is that, Princess?" I spoke slowly, each word whispered against the skin of her neck, my lips hovering at the edge of her perception, teasing her. Teasing both of us. I should have kept my distance. This wasn't the best place to take her for the first time, but I couldn't let her leave. Not like this. She was too close to the edge. Pushing herself too hard. Every instinct I had insisted I take care of her. Feed her body with mine. She needed me, and no one had ever needed me before. Not like this.

"Sex. Just sex. That's all you want."

That was it. Her sass, her scent, everything, pushed me over the edge. She was making me insane. Why didn't my cock rise for a biddable, mild female? Why did it have to want *her?*

And it wanted her now. Right. Fucking. Now.

I reached out, gripped her about the waist and lifted her off her feet. Hands gripping her round ass, I leaned in so our foreheads touched. Our faces close. Breath mingling. I watched as her mouth opened in surprise, her lids lowered and her gaze fell to my mouth.

3

N *ix*

I KISSED HER THEN. As if I could stop it. There was no fucking way I *couldn't* kiss her.

She tasted like sunshine and fire, so bright and hot my blood all but boiled. My cock was so big my pants were sure to rip. My balls ached, filled with cum that wanted out. That needed to be deep inside Destiny.

Her hands went to my shirt, tugged at it and pulled it from my pants, her fingers then settling on my belt.

"Yes," she murmured against my lips. Her breathing was ragged, which completely matched mine.

Lowering her to her feet, I tugged her shirt off over her head. I pulled her black pants down and off over a pair of the smallest feet I'd ever seen, her boots not much larger than a pair of slippers, they remained on her feet. She tugged at my belt, freeing my cock and then ignoring the rest. I'd never had another hand on my cock before. She couldn't close her grip; I was too big. I looked down, saw how huge I was now. I'd never seen my cock like this. Full. Ripe. Engorged. Oh, I'd worked it before, tried to soothe the subtle need that had simmered for years, but it had only raged to life now, with Destiny. She had truly awakened me. It was a miracle.

She pumped me a few times, but I gripped her wrist, tugged it away. I was going to come, but I wasn't going to do it for the first time all over her hand.

I lifted my hands to her breasts, small and firm, and I felt the hard nipples against my palms. I wanted to spend time playing, sucking, tugging, but my cock had other plans. It wanted inside her. Now.

Five minutes ago.

I lifted her up, her back to the wall. She clung to me, her legs wrapping around my thighs, her hips undulating, searching for my hard cock. She locked her mouth on mine, taking what she wanted. Goddess, she was intense. Demanding. Every touch urgent and desperate and full of need.

I couldn't fucking get enough. She buried her hands in my hair and pulled, using the leverage to lift herself and settle her wet core over the tip of my hard length. Mouth still locked on mine. Nibbling my lips. Sucking. Biting gently, just enough to sting. Just enough to make my entire body shiver with the urge to fuck her so hard and fast she'd forget to breathe.

She was nearly naked, her bare chest touching mine. Her legs locked around me. Claiming me as her lips did, as her hands did. She said she didn't want me, didn't need me, but her body had other ideas.

Before she could lower her body and take me, I gripped her hips, hard, and pressed her to the wall, my cock hovering at the opening of her wet pussy, and held her there. Drank her in. Enjoyed the moment I knew would never come again, the moment I made her mine. I couldn't miss the pale glimmer of her in the soft moonlight. Yes, her breasts were small. High. Her waist trim, her hips wide. And her pussy. Fuck.

"Hurry up. What are you doing?"

"You're mine."

She moaned, the sound so raw and hungry I nearly gave in and gave her what she wanted. But this was too important. She was too damn stubborn. She was mine. I needed to hear it. I needed to know that she knew exactly what I wanted, what I needed from her. She. Was. Mine.

"Are we going to talk about this now?" she asked as she wiggled her hips, her wet folds sliding back and forth over the sensitive tip of my cock.

"Oh fuck."

I saw a grin spread on her face just before my eyes fell closed. I kissed her. Hard. Deep. Thrusting with my tongue the way I wanted to fuck her with my cock. When I pulled back, she whimpered, pulled my hair hard enough to keep my lips hovering above hers. Her breath was my breath. Her heat was mine.

"God, just do it. Please. I need you."

I need you. The words were like an arrow in my heart and I groaned, kissed her again. Gently this time. But I couldn't give in. This was too important. "Destiny, you're mine. Say it. You're my mate."

"God dammit." I felt her pussy lips part, as if opening in invitation. I watched every expression, savored the way she writhed in my arms. Her need was as great as mine. "Fine. You're mine. You're fucking mine."

Pushing deep, I watched her face as I filled her, one slow inch at a time. She tilted her head back, her long neck open and exposed in an unconscious sign of trust I wasn't sure she knew she was making. But I pushed deep. Fucked her. Filled her.

"Miiiine." Her cry sounded like that of a wounded animal. Primal. Instinctive. She was claiming me. Riding my cock. Taking my energy and easing her Ardor the way she was meant to. I didn't even try to stop the massive force of heat swirling between us. Giving to her like this was erotic. Intimate. So much more than fucking. I would be part of her forever. Locked in her very cells, making her strong. Me. No one else.

"Mine." My word was clear. Short. A demand.

In response, she pulled my lips to hers and invaded me again. Taking. Demanding. Needing me.

She was hot. Wet. Tight. Her walls clenched and rippled around me, as if she'd never taken anything so big, so thick before. I bottomed out, my hips slapping against her ass.

"Holy fuck." I was going to come. Just like that. The pleasure was so intense, the sizzle of my orgasm simmered already, on the edge, at the base of my spine.

"Please," she moaned. "Move."

I pulled back, thrust deep. Hard. She moved up and down along the wall but I held her thighs, spread them wide. Took her again. And again.

Her pussy clenched down on me like a fist, swelling around me until her core was so tight I couldn't breathe. She bucked, biting her lip to keep in a scream as her pussy spasmed around me, milking me of seed and energy at the same time, the sensation like nothing I'd ever imagined.

I came unexpectedly, as if the pleasure were too intense and my body knew what to do before I did, knew exactly what she needed. I gripped her tightly as I held myself deep. Filled her, hot pulse after pulse. Like an animal, I fought down a primal yell of victory as my seed pumped from me for the first time, filled her. Mine. My seed. My energy. My cock. She needed and I provided. No other male would ever touch her. I'd kill them. Skin them alive and enjoy the screams.

Mine.

She remained still, but only for a few seconds. Her breathing still ragged, her skin coated in a sheen of sweat as I returned to myself. Barely.

"More."

"Your wish is my command, Princess." I grinned at her, never feeling so fucking good in my life. I wasn't done. Not even close. My cock was still hard as a rock. I had no idea how long I could keep this up, but I would fuck her as long as I could. As long as she needed me, her pussy a little piece of heaven on Alera and all mine. But now that I'd gotten that initial release out of the way, I was determined to give her so much fucking pleasure she'd never doubt who she belonged to. Hell, I wouldn't relent until she blacked out and I could carry her back to the palace, unconscious. Sated. Safe.

She tilted her hips, grinding her clit on my body. She moaned, reached for me... and froze.

"Fuck. Someone's coming."

I listened. Heard nothing. Pushed deep. Kissed her.

She tore her lips from mine, panting. "Someone's coming. Shit. Move. We can't be here."

I didn't hear anything, but she was distracted, which was not what I wanted. Grinning, I held her body impaled on mine and kicked her clothes around the corner into a dark side room. It was some sort of library, with books lining every wall. I found a dark corner, nearly black, and pressed her to the wall there, buried deep. Breathing her breath. I couldn't find the will to leave her body, leave this paradise. Not when I had heard nothing. We were alone, and I wasn't finished with my mate. Not even close.

Destiny

GOD. He was going to kill me. His cock was so big. So deep. So fucking perfect. Muscles on muscles. So strong. Hot. So hot. His heat poured into me and my body gobbled it up like I'd been stuck in the Arctic for a week with no coat. I was *starving* for him.

Aleran Ardor sucked.

And it was fucking amazing, at least now that I was riding a nice, big cock. He felt so good. I never wanted to stop. Never.

And then my weirdo ears heard Elder Cleric Amandine and one of her aides talking quietly as they made their way to her office.

This office.

Shit. "Someone's coming."

He listened, then ignored the warning and kissed me. Deep. Rough. Exactly the way I wanted it.

But those damn voices intruded. Again. The elder's voice. What was she doing back up here? And with Crayden? I'd seen him around, always within a few feet of the elder and with a bored expression on his face. He was another set of eyes and ears. Protection. Although, if he had to take on a real threat— like me—I wasn't sure he'd be much help to the older female he protected.

There were more of them, the clerics, both male and female who watched over the planet's elder. They were security. I recognized their true purpose despite their ordinary uniforms and unassuming presence. But they were not like Leo, or his father. They didn't strike me as real soldiers. More like rent-a-cop variety security.

The elder's next words made me tense, which didn't help my situation, making Nix's cock rub harder against my rigid body.

"I want to know what's going on with the Optimus Unit. Do you understand? I know you've heard the rumors, that Lord and Lady Jax are dead, that Lord Wyse is as well. I need you to investigate, Crayden." Elder Cleric Amandine's voice was matter of fact, but what she spoke of weren't rumors but reality. She was in her seventies and sharp as a tack. No one wanted to mess with her. Including me. I just had to wonder why she was here, in a building that was supposed to be locked down for the night. She didn't work late. Ever. Well, not once in the two weeks I'd been stalking everyone in this fortress.

I was one to talk, being out in the middle of the night. But I was breaking in. The two of them were here on purpose.

"I don't know where to start, my lady." That male voice belonged to Crayden. "With Wyse dead, they've closed ranks."

Wyse? Why were they talking about the asshole who tried to kill Faith? And Trinity? And who was closing ranks?

"I can give you a contact, on the inside." The elder cleric's voice was easy to recognize. I'd been listening to her sermons every morning for two weeks. Well, not sermons, exactly, but *reminders*—that's what they called them—reminders of the responsibilities of the clerics on Alera, their duties and the honor they carried in serving the royal family and all of Alera. They weren't a religious order as I'd first assumed, but something else almost holier. Strangely reverent in their devotion.

The voices were coming closer.

Dammit. I didn't want to stop. I needed more. More of this man. More of his energy. More kisses. More cock. Just more.

But as my dad liked to say, *Want in one hand and shit in the other. See which hand fills up first.*

Homegrown, small town wisdom of the first order. And he was right. He was always right. I tore my mouth from Nix's and grasped at enough air to talk. "Someone's coming. Shit. Move. We can't be here."

He didn't let me go, as I'd expected. Instead, he kicked at my clothes, moving the discarded things into the elder's study. Once my clothes were gone—he still had his on because I'd been so damn impatient—he carried me into the study and pressed my back to the wall in a dark corner. And he'd stayed nice and deep the entire time.

I should insist he let me go. Get dressed. Get the hell out of here.

But damn. I needed more. All of his movement, the kicking, the walking—my pussy was riding the edge of another orgasm. I wasn't calming down. I was spinning up. Out of control.

And the closer the voices got, the more I liked it. The

danger of being caught heightened my senses, made my pussy clamp down even harder. Tighter.

One thrust. He moaned and pushed deep. That was it. I came apart in his arms, the orgasm even more intense than the first, his hand covering my mouth to keep me quiet. His seed filled me, and it was as if my body craved him like it needed food or air or an essential nutrient. I hungered for him. For his body. For his heat. For his kiss. His touch. His seed.

I was out of control, and I hated being out of control.

Nix was the most dangerous man I'd ever met, and here I was impaled on his cock, naked, risking my life for a quickie. And every orgasm made me worse, not better.

I'd lost my damn mind.

The outer door opened and Nix froze, pressed me harder into the wall once he realized the danger was real.

"Told you," I whispered.

"Hush." He whispered the word back, his lips lingering over my ear. He inhaled deeply, taking the scent of my hair into his body. It was erotic and I imagined his face somewhere else. Inhaling *something* else.

My pussy tightened again, the muscles clenching in preparation for another orgasm, for his cock was still hard, still deep, even though we'd both just come.

God. No. I needed to listen.

The lights came on in the next room and the elder cleric and her guard entered the outer office. I heard the creak of her chair as she took a seat, the soft padding of his feet as he paced in front of her desk. She spoke first.

"They are keeping an unauthorized prisoner on Optimus Cell Level C. I want to know who it is and who authorized it. Do you understand? The queen is still missing. Her daughters, the revered princesses, aren't talking, and we don't know anything about the third female who entered the citadel. I assume it's another one of Celene's daughters. But we can't protect them if we can't find them. And neither Princess Faith nor Princess Trinity trust me enough to talk. The fact that they have reason to suspect the clerics is not acceptable. I will not allow our order to fall, is that clear? The role of the clerics is to protect the queen, and her daughters now that we know they exist, whether they trust us or not. Which means I need answers. At any cost. Do you have any questions?"

"Are you authorizing the use of deadly force?" The question was quiet, but not alarmed, and my opinion of the man in the other room shifted. He was not what I'd thought he was... which hadn't been all that much. I had assumed he was a standard mall-cop. Mild. Not much more than a pencil pushing assistant who checked video feeds and followed the elder around so she was never alone. If he were this deadly, that meant none of the elder's guards were as harmless as they seemed. He sounded like a soldier. A hunter.

"Yes," the elder replied. "You have one day because the triad is coming."

I heard Crayden's swift intake of breath. Who the hell was the triad and why was he surprised?

"Here?" he asked.

"Yes. Elder Clerics Marna, Forge and Severil want updates about the queen in person. Since Princess Faith announced the queen had been kidnapped—and not just missing—they want answers. They are demanding I set up an audience with Princess Trinity for them."

"Doesn't Elder Cleric Forge live in Corseran?"

"Yes, and if she's coming from that great a distance, then you know the trip is not an idle one. Having the queen *missing* was one thing, but knowing she's been kidnapped and at someone's mercy is another. It goes against every principle of the clerics. I want answers and I don't care what you have to do to get them. I must give the triad something. They are militant and unforgiving in the wilder regions. They won't be satisfied until we have answers. And neither will I."

Damn. The old woman's tone was hard and unforgiving,

full of rage. In one breath, she spoke of the principles of being a cleric. Peaceful and full of reverence for the crown. Eons of protection and honor, and in the next, carte blanche to do whatever was necessary to learn the truth, even violence. And yet, I was reassured. She was one of the good guys.

"I'll kill them all if I have to," came the male's reply, confirming they would not remain passive to find their queen, or at least answers.

But kill who? I wasn't sure. But his tone held no mercy and I could respect that. More danger.

My pulse skyrocketed. Excited. My pussy fluttered, and I held back the orgasm with a force of will. Big. Hard. Cock.

Nix shifted. His cock slid deeper. Opened me up. Wide.

Fuck.

Too late. I came. My body lost control, draining Nix dry in every way I could. Skin on skin, taking his energy, his heat. His seed pumped into me and he threw his hand over my mouth again to muffle the small sound I hadn't realized I was making. We were insane. Hard core insane to be fucking like this. Coming like this. Who came from just standing still? No thrusting, rubbing, moving?

After a few minutes that felt like hours, the elder and her guard left. Turning off the light and locking the door behind her. We were safe.

I kissed Nix again, thanking him the only way I could at the moment, with slow, deep kisses. Gentle kisses. *Thank you* kisses. I felt almost... human again. Sexy. And the fact that the energy pouring off his body and into mine was like a drug didn't hurt either. I could do this for hours. Hell, for days. But I knew what he was going to do. He was going to insist I go with him so he could keep me 'safe' and feed my Ardor again.

I'd come three times and he hadn't even *tried*. I could only imagine what he could do to me if we weren't interrupted and had a bed. If he was this skilled just wielding his big cock, what could he do with his hands... or mouth? My pussy clenched at the thought. But, I felt better. Cooler, calmer. My mind was clearer. Yeah, I was thinking about Nix's head between my thighs and his tongue on my clit, but I wasn't feeling the Ardor haze I'd been in for days.

Well, this hot sex fix would be enough to keep my body under control for a while, and safe was a word I had no interest in, not with my mother still missing and Lord Wyse dead. Not after hearing the elder mention someone important was kept in Optimus Cell Level C. I had no idea where that was, but I was going to find out. And find Mom.

"I need to get dressed, Nix. We can't stay here."

"Agreed." Slowly, he pulled out of my body and set me on my feet. We both moaned when he slid free, my pussy grasping after him like a greedy little bitch. I mentally told her to get herself together—that Nix wasn't *that* hot. But as he stepped back I got a good look at those pecs and abs peeking at me through his open shirt, at that big, hard cock—glistening with cum and my arousal—still straining forward as if it was reaching for me. Chiseled jaw. Dark eyes. Silky hair I loved to pull. Not that hot?

Oh, hell yes he was.

And if I were being completely honest with myself, I loved his alpha male, chest pounding, mine-mine-mine business, too.

Talk about messed up in the head. I didn't need a man. Didn't want a man. Not for more than hot sex, anyway. I did *not* need a man trying to run my life, telling me what to do, trying to keep me *safe.* No. No fucking way. And Nix had proved he was all for doing that. He wanted me safe and secure and eating chocolate bon-bons and giving my sisters pedicures, while the *men* went out and saved the world. As if.

I had to get out of here. And if I crawled out the window and down those vines he'd be right on my tail. Which meant that was not an option. I needed another way out of here, a way he couldn't follow.

I pulled on my black cleric's uniform as quickly as I could, ignoring the sensual glide of the smooth black pants over my thighs and hips. My skin was sensitive. Too sensitive. Worse than it had been before. But at least my pussy was temporarily satisfied—albeit dripping with his seed—and my body didn't feel weak and lethargic. I had probably pushed the Ardor thing too far. I'd have to be careful in the future and not let it get that bad.

But then, that's what the royal consort was for. All I'd have to do was sneak into the palace, ask Trinity for a hookup, get my fix, and sneak back out. That would be the easy thing to do. No strings. No complications. No expectations or Neanderthal claims on my person.

But the thought of another male touching me made me nauseated. And if that was Nix's fault, I might have to strangle him later. Being dependent on a man was not my thing. Not now. Not ever.

"I'll check the door and make sure it's locked." I moved away before he could answer, using my speed to my advantage when he reached for me. If he kissed me—hell, if he even touched me—I'd never want to leave this stupid room.

Once I reached the door, I held perfectly still and *listened*. My new ability was uncanny, and I felt like a bat, but that didn't stop me from using it to my advantage. I listened for footsteps and tried not to imagine what was going on in the other room as the rustle of Nix's clothing sent all kinds of naughty images into my mind. I didn't want his pants closed or his shirt covering that meaty man chest. The only thing that should be covering all that magnificent male was *me*.

Terrible damn timing. That's what this was.

Once I was sure no one else was outside the door, or even on this floor, I slipped into the hallway, leaving Nix behind.

4

D *estiny*

I HEARD his quick footsteps toward the closed door and his nearly silent cursing. He could not follow. Too many patrols on the lower levels of the building. He was not a cleric. Not one of us. Well, I wasn't really one either, but after all this time in hiding, *pretending* to be one, I felt like I'd earned the title. Besides, he had no uniform and would stand out—not only because he looked like a sex god on long, muscled legs, but he was dressed like a queen's guardsman.

I moved like a shadow and slipped into another room within seconds, the door unlocked. It closed behind me without so much as a whisper of sound.

Crazy caveman. Despite the risks of not leaving the way he snuck in, through the window and down the trellis, I heard him open the elder's door and step into the hallway. Too late. I was gone. Twenty doors on this floor alone. He'd have to check them all if he wanted to find me, and I was already through a servant's small side door in the adjoining room. He could either take his chances with the patrols that came randomly on the lower floors, or escape out the window and back down the vines.

Not my problem. Nix was a big boy... all over. He let himself in. He could let himself out, too.

With a grin, I disappeared into the shadows to make my way back to my quarters. I'd rather risk being caught here than try to get away from the possessive male I'd left behind. No doubt if he got his hands on me, he'd most likely toss me over his broad shoulder and carry me back to the palace.

He might get caught, but if he pulled that *mate* stuff with the guards, they'd probably let him go. His cock hadn't gone down at all after our little sexy bout of fucking, so that would be all the proof they'd need. And, if he did get me over his shoulder, my Ardor would most likely start up again, and I'd want to bite his ass instead of kicking it.

Fortunately, I was new enough to claim getting lost if I were caught out here, alone. And I didn't want to argue with Nix, nor try to fight him. For some perverse reason, the thought of hurting him was horrifying to me. And he'd fight. Argue, until he did actually toss me over his shoulder like Leo had with Trinity. So, I'd take my chances on the inside. If I were caught on the upper floors, I'd just say I got lost.

I wasn't in the elder's office. I was out roaming. I'd have to figure out how to explain that one, and I might get extra kitchen duty, but they didn't kill people for wandering at night. And Elder Amandine was on my side, although she just didn't know it. She'd ordered 'all force necessary,' but not with me.

My mind returned to thoughts of Nix. His scent, the feel of his cock, even the growl of his voice. Man, he had to be pissed. I had no doubt he'd be beside himself with... fury that I'd slipped away. Perhaps he'd expected me to just docilely follow him since he'd soothed my Ardor a little. But no. I didn't need him. His cock would come in handy now and again until this Ardor was all gone, but I had a mission to complete and he'd just have to deal. So would my pussy. I just had to hope he wouldn't be too pissed when I saw him again. And that my pussy could survive without him inside me.

I had a job to do. Find Mom. *Chicks before dicks* and all that.

Moving like a shadow, I made my way to the lowest level, found the laundry room, grabbed an initiate's formal robe, put it on over my sex-stained uniform and quietly slipped into the back of one of the chanting sessions. Ten minutes later, I had a firm alibi for the evening as multiple other initiates and clerics wished me a good night once the session was over. I'd been seen. That was all I wanted.

Tomorrow, I'd tail Crayden and find out who the elder's contact was inside the Optimus Unit. I needed to get into the place called Cell Level C, or at least find the thing. I'd have to alert Trinity, of course. Just in case I didn't make it back out. At least that way she could send in the Neanderthals to follow up on the lead.

I made it to my room and literally passed out, a smile on my face, my pussy sore and aching.

Visions of Nix swirled like sugarplums in my head. The scent of him eddied around me. God, I smelled of sex and hot Aleran male.

Dangerous, deadly, Nix.

I wanted more. Did I ever.

MORNING *REMINDERS* WERE CUT SHORT the next day, the elder cleric distracted in a way I doubted anyone else noticed. As always, Crayden and another guard stood at her back, keeping watch on the crazy, chanting clerics.

If anyone in this room was capable of the patience and political skill required to pull off a three decades' long coup and chase my mother across the galaxy, I would eat my boots. No way. Nothing here but children playing in grown up clothes, waiting to be told what to do. I mean, chanting? How was that going to save the world? It might as well have been *Kumbaya*. I sighed. But, they'd been around for eons, and as far as I knew of Aleran history, Mom was the only queen to have had 'problems'.

When Crayden exited the room through a small rear door, I followed, keeping to the edges, moving like a shadow myself. Adrenaline pumped through my body, and with the fresh supply of energy I'd sucked off Nix like a vampire last night, I felt better than I had in days. I hadn't exactly *sucked* anything from him, but I started thinking about what I could *suck* on him. Yet, I felt good. Revived, better since I'd arrived on this planet.

But the hunger was building again. I could feel it at the base of my spine, an ache that would become a burn, then stabbing pain. The pressure behind my eyeballs would increase until it hurt to see. My head would pound. My skin would hurt. Ache. My clit would throb with the need to come, but not be assuaged. Oh, I'd tried with my hand, and while I'd come, it had done nothing to soothe me. It had only made it worse. And now, I knew what I could have, and I began to hunger for a specific touch and heat. Dammit, it was all *him*.

I felt odd. *Alien*. For the first time in my life, I had to come to grips with the fact that I was not completely human, and that was a mind trip all its own. Earth was only half of me. A damn good half, but only half. And despite being told for years, hell, my whole life, hearing it from my mother and *knowing* I was not 'Earth' normal were two different things.

The Ardor wasn't finished with me yet. And since I'd had a few hours of relief from a few incredible male-given orgasms, I was not eager to go back to where I'd been before Nix. I could go back to Plan A, which was a consort at the palace, but the thought made me cringe. Just, no. I didn't want a complete stranger getting anywhere near me with his cock.

Nix had been a complete stranger, too, if I was going to get technical, and he'd gotten more than just near me with his cock. He'd gotten *in* me. In me so deep I hadn't known where I ended and he began. But my pussy was *not* interested in technicalities. And neither, apparently, was the rest of me. Too bad. No more naughty time until we had Mom back, and I could keep Nix inside me for a week. Work now, sexy times later.

"Suck it up, Princess," I scolded myself and slipped through the door into a very dark, very quiet tunnel behind Crayden I'd never seen before. It was cool, every surface—floor, walls, ceiling—made of a smooth gray and pink stone. The sensation of being underground was strong, but I knew that was not the case. Still, I wondered how much stone was in the arches over my head to create the deep quiet I'd only ever experienced below ground on Earth.

Once the door slid shut behind me, I closed my eyes and *listened* with my new bat hearing. I didn't know exactly what the citadel had done to my sisters, but Mom had told us about the royal 'gifts'. Seeing things no one else could see. Speed. Brain power. Fighting skills. Psychic stuff that would give us an edge over the general population. Nothing crazy. We weren't like *Wonder Woman* or anything, according to her. Just... more. And I had to admit this super-powerful, vampire level hearing had come in very, very handy.

I used it now, focused like I'd practiced during all those meditation sessions. I'd gotten pretty good, able to focus on one beating heart in the room over all the others, then move on to the next. Listen to that heartbeat while I listened to the kitchen staff talk about dinner on the floor beneath us. All that meditation and focusing had worked wonders, and I could control it most of the time, as long as I wasn't freaked out or I wasn't in too much of a hurry. I zeroed in on what I needed and heard the soft sound of Crayden's feet as he moved steadily away on my right.

Moving that way, I followed. Lost the sound. Heard muffled grunts.

Fighting? I knew the sound of hand-to-hand combat. Of fists striking flesh. Of kicks landing solidly on an opponent's back or thighs.

Running now, I kept going and going and going. Crayden had been fast, dammit. And a lot farther ahead of me than I'd given him credit for. And, my hearing was better than I'd ever imagined.

I was out of breath when I reached another door. I pushed it open and blinked at the bright daylight. The tunnel led to a large park within the fortress. Tall trees, bushes and trails for walking surrounded the area. And this one was used fairly often, a gathering place for initiates, when the weather wasn't blistering cold. After being in the tunnel, I rubbed my arms against the chill. It hadn't been cold in the city, but up here in the mountains. God, I was ready for a Hawaiian vacation.

I caught sight of steam, which rose oddly from the ground behind a short bush. I walked around the corner to find that it wasn't steam... exactly. Crayden lay sprawled on the hard ground in a pool of blood, the cold air causing the soft wisps of heat to rise from the pools of hot red liquid like fog from a stream.

I winced and looked away. "Shit." I didn't need to feel for a pulse to know he was good and dead, the slice across his throat big enough to take down a lion, let alone a man. Still, I went over to him and knelt, blood soaking through the knees of my pants, coating my palms as I felt around for a pulse, tried to officially determine if he was well and truly gone. Beyond saving.

Nothing. The ReGen wands and pods they had out here in space were amazing, but dead was dead. And Crayden was gone. I had no idea how a pod could heal having his carotids severed.

I squeezed my eyes closed and tried to listen again, to find the sound of someone running away. Breathing hard. Or laughing. Anything. All I needed was a noise, a direction to go. Something.

A scream sounded at a distance. Then another. The pounding of at least a dozen feet. Shouts.

I stood slowly, paralyzed for a few heartbeats, anger beating inside me. They were ruining everything. A fleeing killer was lost in all the racket.

Shut up! Shut up! Shut up!

I couldn't hear a damn thing with them all carrying on like panicked idiots. The murderer was going to get away.

A hand closed around my upper arm, a big hand. My heart leapt into my throat. My instinct was to spin around, karate chop him in self-defense. Do anything to keep my head attached to my body. The instinct was there, but for a split second, I thought it might be Nix.

Whipping my head around, I looked up into the eyes of a fortress guard. My hand flew to my chest as I tried to calm down.

"Are you all right?" His gaze looked me over, then scanned the area, as if the killer may still be about. "Did you see anything?"

I shook my head, held my hands out in front of me, saw the blood covering them. "No. God, the poor man. I came out of the fortress and found him like this."

The guard looked up and around the walls of the building. "I've been on patrol. You didn't see or hear anything?"

"Did you?" I countered.

The guard frowned, staring down at me like I was a child. "Cleric Crayden exited. I saw him when he stepped out. He does this often and we see him here after morning meditation and reminders, so I thought nothing of it."

He spoke into his comms unit, announcing the murder and requesting backup and a sweep of the area.

"You saw him get killed then?" I asked when he was done, wiping my hands on my pants, leaving streaks of damp.

He shook his head. "No. I walk patrol along the top turret on the south corner. I saw him, walked around, and when I came back to this side, I saw you exit and kneel down. It was then I saw his body. You are the one who had an opportunity to witness the killing. Or hear it."

He didn't say I'd done it. If he suspected me, we wouldn't be standing about, idly chit chatting. "Did you see anyone? Hear voices? The sounds of a fight?"

I had, but nothing useful. "From the tunnel I heard muffled noises, like fighting, but no talking. I ran this way, but when I came out the door, he was dead and alone."

His frown told me in no uncertain terms that he was not satisfied with my answer. It wasn't thorough, but again, I wasn't in handcuffs. "I'm sure Elder Amandine will want to speak with you."

Other guards appeared, knelt before the body.

"As will the rest of her guard," he continued. With the body attended to, he continued, "Come with me."

"But—"

"I said, come. Now." He pulled me, none too gently away from the guards and Crayden's dead body. The concern I'd first seen in his eyes completely gone, replaced with resolve and anger. I couldn't blame him. I'd followed Crayden out of the building and now had his blood all over me. It didn't look very good.

"I don't know anything," I insisted.

He ignored me and pulled. I curled my bloodied hands into fists and walked with him. I had nothing to hide.

Well, that wasn't exactly true, but I had nothing to hide in regards to this murder.

Thank god this guy had seen me the moment I walked outside. If not, I'd have to call Trinity and beg for royal intervention. I wasn't sure what the clerical order did to cold-blooded murderers, but if they executed someone for walking into the elder's office without permission, I knew I didn't want to find out.

And since the clerics ran the Optimus units, the legal side of things on Alera, I didn't want to get locked in a cell before I could break Mom out of hers. Although, I could end up on Cell Level C, but this wasn't the way I'd considered getting in there.

Who had killed Crayden? And why? Because he was digging around on behalf of Elder Amandine? If so, she'd just given him his orders last night. That was awfully fast for things to move from zero to murder. Because he knew something and had to be eliminated like it seemed everyone else I'd heard about on the news? Lord and Lady Jax, Lord Wyse. Had Crayden been next?

If so, then perhaps I was closer to the truth than I'd ever thought.

The guard pulled me along until I was in the very same office I'd been hiding in the night before. He pushed me down into the chair opposite the elder female, and I stared at the caked blood on my hands. Crayden was dead. I was pretty sure he was one of the good guys, so that really stunk. Or had he been? Had he been like a double agent, working for the bad guys and cozying up to Elder Amandine?

God, so many questions. And *zero* answers.

The guard updated Elder Amandine on what had happened. When he announced Crayden had been murdered, her lips pursed and her cheeks went pale, but she gave no other outward response.

When he was done, her gaze turned to me. "What were you doing this morning, Initiate? Why were you in the elder tunnels? Those areas are restricted to my personal guard."

Oh, shit. The elder did not sound amused. She'd really freak if she knew what I'd been doing with Nix up against the corner right behind me. And also in the other room.

I crossed my legs, looked up and tried not to blush as memories flooded me, memories of Nix's hard cock, my orgasms, the hot sex I'd stolen from him in this very room just a few hours ago. Staring into the elder's eyes was like trying to lie to a very wise grandmother—or at least that's how I imagined it.

Still, I was a princess. And now, thanks to that very same midnight escapade and overhearing her conversation with Crayden, I was confident that this woman was firmly on my mother's side of things. Loyal to Queen Celene. Which meant loyal to my sisters.

And me.

We could use a few more allies. And I was tired of chanting and praying and sneaking around. That was soooooo not my style. I was more the smash and grab type.

"Young woman, you will answer me. Now."

Oh, yes. Total pissed off mom voice. If she knew all three of my names, no doubt she'd be scolding me with every syllable right now.

"All right, but just a moment. I need to make sure we are truly alone," I said.

"I dismissed my guard. I assure you—"

I held up my hand, pointer finger up in the *just a minute* signal as I rose slowly and walked along the walls in her inner office, listening. *Listening.*

"What are you doing?" she asked.

"Checking. Please, don't make any noise. Just for a couple moments. I know there are no guards nearby. Which was foolish of you, by the way." The Aleran language flew off my tongue easily, as it had for as long as I could remember. But I saw her eyes narrow at my implied threat.

"I may look helpless, child, but I am far from it," she scolded.

That made me grin. "Same."

Perhaps out of sheer curiosity, she watched me silently as I continued my journey around her office. I was less concerned with the outer rooms, as she and Crayden had spoken quietly.

No, if someone had a listening device in here, it would be close to her desk. As close as they could get.

When I had circled the room, I asked her to stand. Looking annoyed, she did and I walked around her desk at a snail's pace.

There. A buzzing so slight the bee making it would have been the size of a grain of sand. But I could hear it. Freaking amazing. I could hear *everything*. And the more I used it, the better I got at controlling what came into my head and what didn't.

Sliding my fingernail beneath what looked like a natural whorl in the wood-like surface, I lifted a flake from the bottom edge of her desktop, midway between her chair and the desk's corner. I began to peel the glue flake from the back of the small transmitter, but her wrinkled hand wrapped around my fingers and I looked up to see her shaking her head.

"Too small."

I held it out to her with my finger over my lips.

She nodded and then pointed to a place on her desk and I set it down there, gently, in case anyone was listening. Speaking in a normal voice, I stepped away and sat back down in the chair opposite her desk. "I was just curious about the tunnels, Elder. I am new here. I am sorry. I didn't mean to cause any trouble."

"And yet, you witnessed the murder of Cleric Crayden."

I shook my head. "Oh, no. I didn't. I didn't see anything. Just found the body. That's all. You can ask the guard who brought me here. It was all a big misunderstanding."

"You are coated in his blood."

"I had to check. You know. Just in case I could help him." I stared down at the caked blood on my clothes and hands. I wasn't acting now. The shiver that raced through my body was very real. As was the sadness I felt in my eyes.

"Check what?"

"For a pulse. I touched him. I'm sorry. That's where all the blood came from."

"I see." She swiveled in her chair and stood, motioning for me to follow her to the door. "I will confirm your story with the guard. You are free to go, for now."

"Thank you. I'm so sorry. Thank you."

She opened the door to her office. Loudly. "Don't leave the fortress. I may have more questions for you later."

"Of course not. I have nowhere to go."

That caused her to raise a brow, but she waved me into the hallway and I went. To my surprise, she followed, and made a production of slamming her door closed. "Are there more transmitters out here?" she asked in a quiet voice.

I closed my eyes. Listened. Nothing. No guards. No buzzing. Nothing. "I don't hear any."

"Good." She crossed her arms and looked me over like she'd never seen me before. Too damn smart. Reminded me of Trinity. "So, you're the third princess."

I gasped. How the hell did she know that? "I'm no one. Just an initiate."

The old woman actually rolled her eyes. "Right. You've been here less than two weeks, appearing in my fortress the day after three mysterious females disappeared inside the citadel. There are no records of you from your previous years of life. No birth records. Nothing. And you can hear the microscopic buzzing of a comm transmitter, which means you and your sisters already received your gifts from the citadel."

"What?" No one knew about the gifts. No one outside the royal bloodline. That was what Mom had always told us. It was too dangerous for outsiders to know. Then how?

"Don't worry. I am loyal to your mother, Queen Celene. I have been protecting her throne for nearly thirty years, waiting for this day."

"How did you know she wasn't dead?" I asked, then

groaned. Stupid question. I already knew the answer. So did all of Alera.

"The spire, of course. It never dimmed."

"Right. Sorry. I forgot." I lifted my hand to rub my face, saw the blood and dropped it. I took a deep breath. Allies. We needed allies. "All right. Look, I know you are loyal. And I know you sent Crayden to find out about the mysterious prisoner in Cell Level C in the Optimus Unit."

It was her turn to frown. Ha!

"How could you possibly know that? Unless you are the one who placed the comm transmitter in my office."

"No. I was... well"—I blushed. I couldn't stop it this time —"I broke into your office last night to look for clues. Heard the two of you talking."

"That's impossible."

I shrugged. "Not really. You've got a really strong vine outside that window. I highly recommend you cut it."

She studied me closely, her lips pursing. "I see. What else did you hear?"

"Enough to know you aren't my enemy. Or an enemy of my family."

"So, you truly are the third princess?"

I nodded. "Yes. My name is Destiny. Faith is my twin sister and Trinity is older than both of us, and the only full-blooded Aleran." I held out my hand, Earth style, and she smiled kindly as she took it, dried blood and all. Squeezing, not shaking up and down, but it wasn't unpleasant.

"An honor and a pleasure, Your Highness. Now, tell me why you are hiding here, and how I can help you."

"I'm not sure yet. I'm very sorry about Crayden. I think the first thing we need to do is find out who put that bug in your office."

"Agreed. I will give it to my people."

That worked for me. It wasn't something I could tackle, and

since she didn't seem too surprised her office had been bugged, had evidently been through this before.

"And I will keep your identity a secret. It is the only way you will remain safe within the fortress."

"Thank you. I'm going to contact Trinity and catch her up to speed on things. Then, once we know who set that bug, we can make a plan. Someone kidnapped our mother, and we've tracked the traitors to the clerics, and the Optimus Unit. I believe the mystery prisoner you mentioned is the queen."

She stared at me wide-eyed. It was one thing to have the queen missing for twenty-seven years, another that she was in one specific place and could be saved. "Do you have proof?"

"No. Just gut instinct."

She smiled at me. "My gut agrees." She chuckled, as if this was incredible fun, an adventure, not life and death.

"This is serious."

"Of course it is. Life is always serious for people with power and responsibilities. But that does not mean you can't take moments and make them more, even after what happened with Crayden. Life is too short to pass by an opportunity to laugh. You are young, but you will learn. Steal laughter. Steal joy. Steal love. If you don't, you'll never have it."

How did this go from a cool spy mission to a lecture? Sheesh. I didn't need more of that. Between Nix and Trinity, I'd heard enough for a while.

"I'll contact my sister. With your permission, I would like you to meet me back here in the morning."

She nodded, even patted my arm. "Go. Get cleaned up. I will discover what I can while you rest and recover."

"Thank you." I didn't mean to run, but I was suddenly in a hurry to get back to my room. The blood was gross. The memory was disturbing. And now that I had the most powerful female in the clerical order on our side, I felt just safe enough to let my guard down and drown in the shower for a solid hour and wash off the smell of death clinging to me.

5

D *estiny*

ONCE SECURELY IN MY ROOM, I pulled a stolen comm unit out from the hiding place I'd made and called my sister. The bossy one. I'd had the comm since coming here, but this was the first time I'd used it. She'd reached out to me twice through my NPU, which had seemed completely unnecessary for translating since Mom had taught the three of us Aleran and we were all fluent, but the connection had been useful, and reassuring. It had also come in handy when Warden Egara had been talking to that giant Prillon warrior on the comm screen when we'd still been on Earth. So, the warden had been right to jab all three of us with that giant needle. Hearing Trinity's voice, and then later, Faith's as well, had been so *nice*.

Trinity answered immediately, the frown on her face and the worry in her eyes a bit annoying. I loved her, but she was way too overprotective. Kind of like someone else I knew and had recently left behind. "Destiny, are you okay? Why are you calling? What's going on?"

I shrugged. "Oh, you know, just a murder here and there."

"Is that your blood?" She was holding in a scream, I could see it in her eyes and the stiffness of her shoulders.

I didn't mind getting her riled up, that was definitely a sister's job, but not like this. "No. It's not."

She slumped and put a hand to her chest. "Thank god. Now tell me what the hell is going on?"

"I sneaked into the elder cleric's office last night."

"That's why you're covered in blood?"

I shrugged. "Not exactly." I explained what I overheard, leaving out the fact that I'd been nicely impaled on Nix's cock at the time.

"God, that poor man," she replied, looking down, probably at her lap or the floor or something. "He died, you think, because he'd been tasked with looking into Mom? Because this... this triad wanted answers?"

I just stared at her because... duh. I didn't want to feel like a wimp, but seeing Crayden's head nearly cut free from his body had been a bit much. I was tough, but apparently, a still bleeding decapitation was near the edge of my mental limits.

"Okay, sorry. Of course he was killed because of that. So we look into this triad, these three clerics... Marna, Forge and Severil?"

"Elder Amandine says they want answers, not that they were the masterminds. They're just higher ups or something," I replied. "Have Nix look into them."

She laughed. "Yeah, right. You might have ditched him, but I'm sure he's not far."

I hadn't seen anything of him since last night, but I wanted him. Now. I wanted his big body and his heat and I wanted him to wrap me up and make me forget everything but him. And his kiss. And his cock. My pussy clenched at the reminder. I was sure there was a big wet spot on my pants again, just from thinking about him. We'd both come, what, three times last night?

And now? I wasn't covered in his scent or his seed. I'd washed all that off this morning. Now I was covered in death and pain and secrets. Blood.

Elder Amandine had turned into my ally. She would do her thing while I did mine, which was talking to Trinity.

I really needed another shower, but she needed to know what the hell was going on first. Crayden hadn't survived twelve hours after his orders to look into Mom's kidnapping. Which meant whoever had killed him had people on the inside, who knew where she was. Perhaps even knew who and where I was, especially after talking with Elder Amandine for so long. Some asshole could be stalking me right now, waiting for his chance to slit my throat, too.

Why I assumed the killer was a man, I wasn't sure. But it seemed the violence and strength needed to cut someone's neck that deep, with such raw rage? Just felt male to me. Pissed off, vengeful, hate-fueled male.

"Destiny?" Trinity prompted.

"I'm fine," I replied.

"You don't look fine."

"If not Nix, then have someone else look into this. I can do some of it from here, especially now that I've got an ally in Elder Amandine, but things just went from meditating to murder around here."

The way she pursed her lips, Trinity didn't look happy about that.

"Did you send that Neanderthal here?" I asked, then cursed myself for a fool. With everything that had just happened, I had to ask about Nix? Really? I was pathetic.

"You know I didn't," she replied, rolling her eyes. "You were the one who said you were in danger. That *Neanderthal* just decided he'd go after you." *That* was my big sister. She didn't back down and she gave as good as she got. Damn lawyers. Her and Dad. I could never argue my way around either one of them. "And what did you do to your hair?"

I reached up, touched the long strands. I'd forgotten I'd dyed it black before I joined the clerics. "I had to color it. It's not like a purple-haired woman wouldn't stand out around here." I hadn't seen anyone with colored hair since we'd transported to Alera. Not a one. And purple? Not happening. But black? So boring. I hated boring hair.

"Trin, forget my hair. That conversation was so two days ago. I'm sorry I scared you, but I'm fine. I just wanted to give you a heads up... and to see your ugly face."

"Ha ha," she said, waving her finger at me.

"As for Nix, I don't need him lurking around like an overly protective caveman. He's just going to get in my way. Again."

Or get me naked and riding his cock. That would probably be an even more dangerous problem.

"How did he get in your way before?" Trinity asked, the question slyly. Her grin contained the question I refused to answer.

"He followed me, then cornered me," I said evenly, leaving out everything after he climbed through the window. Hell, I even left that out and how exactly he *cornered* me. "And now he's gone. Don't let him come back here. Don't do that to me again."

"Gone? He just left you?" she asked, sounding stunned. "Is he dead?"

"Dead?" I laughed. "Of course not." I shook my head. "I'm not *that* bad."

"Destiny Jones, what did you do with Nix?"

She knew me too well.

"Nothing. I didn't do anything *to* him." Except fuck his brains out. "I only left him locked in the admin building. I'm sure he's fine."

"Fine? You think he's *fine* you ditched him? He's a queen's guard. You just waved a red cape at a bull."

Bull, definitely. Oh, his cock had been huge and with all the cum still seeping from me, huge balls. I squirmed at the thought. I needed to change the subject. Nix was not my problem. "Whatever."

The once-locked door to my room opened and Nix walked in, closing it—and locking it again—behind him. "Yes. I want to hear all about this bull."

My jaw dropped and I tucked my hands between my legs to hide the blood.

I'd only seen him in the dark. In heat. Inside my room, with anger simmering in his gaze and the lights on his high cheekbones and cut jawline, I went from annoyed to horny in about two seconds flat. Shit. My body roared like I hadn't had sex in years instead of the night before. Like I was going to die if I didn't get more. Now. Right now.

"What are you doing here?" I asked him.

He crossed his arms over his formidable chest. "A locked door won't stop me, Princess." It was a statement, but also a warning. He wasn't going to be deterred from his own mission. I glanced down at the front of his pants, saw the thick—huge—bulge of his cock.

"Destiny?" Trinity's voice broke the hypnotic pull of him and I tore my gaze away, looked at the small screen where my sister was eyeing me like a worried mother hen.

"See, he's not dead," I told her, and swung the screen to Nix so Trinity could see him.

He bowed low. "Princess Trinity," he said to my comms unit. "I am here and your sister is safe."

"Oh, thank god," she replied. "Thank you, Nix. Don't let her do anything too dangerous."

Now she sounded like my mother and not my sister.

He grinned at the order, his smile diabolical, and I knew I was screwed. Anything I said now, he would ignore. Pull rank. He had orders from Trinity. The future queen. I was two steps down the royal ladder and she'd just handed me to him on a silver platter.

I turned the screen back and glared at her. "You take that back, Trin. Right now."

"Nope. He's going to keep you safe. You're the one that did that tap-tap thing and said you were in danger. Which reminds me, why didn't I ever get to know about that secret twin stuff? Totally not cool."

"Really, Trin? You ask that now? We were kids."

"Fine. But enough of you being all alone." She shook her head. "About what you told me. I'll send Leo and the queen's guard to check it out."

"I can take care of it myself," I countered. Leo and the queen's guard? They'd be too obvious, make too much noise. One hint that I was on to them and they'd move Mom somewhere else. I would do it.

Nix stirred and took a step toward me. I wanted to stay angry, but he knelt in front of me. *Knelt.* As in On. His. Knees. Like I mattered. God, he was dangerous. "Tell her, Destiny, or I will. I heard the conversation as well."

He was right. He had. Thankfully, he'd left off the part that he'd been buried deep inside me at the time.

He grabbed my wrists and lifted them up. "Are you hurt? Why the fuck are you covered in blood?" His gaze raked over me as if he expected to find a spurting artery.

"It's not mine. It's that guy's. Crayden's."

His dark brows winged up. "From the office last night?"

I nodded.

"Speak," he commanded.

"Fine." I sighed. "Elder Cleric Amandine is not involved, as you heard last night, Nix." I turned from him to the comm unit and Trinity. "She's pissed someone went after you and Faith. She sent Crayden to find out about Optimus Cell Level C. He's now dead, which makes his searching, well, a dead end. I have no idea where that is, but that's pretty darn specific. She said they're keeping an unauthorized prisoner there. A high priority, top-secret prisoner and she sent someone to find out what the hell is going on. She's an ally."

Trinity sucked in a breath. "I've heard of that place before. That's where Wyse tried to send Faith. You think it could be Mom?"

"Based on the fact that I'm now wearing that guard's blood, yeah, I think that's a safe bet. Elder Amandine does, too."

"Shit."

"That's what I said."

"Get back to the palace," she ordered. "Now. Let Leo and his dad handle this. Get the hell out of there."

"I don't think so, Trin," I replied. "Someone here killed Crayden. Someone here knew he was asking questions. We have enemies here, and I intend to find them. I said I would meet with Elder Amandine in the morning." It felt a little odd talking with Nix kneeling before me, staring at me like I was a work of art. A fascinating, sexy, goddess. No one looked at me like that. Ever. I had to clear my throat and tear my gaze from his face. "If it's not Mom in that cell, I'm betting someone here still knows something about her disappearance." I had a gut feeling about this one. It was Mom locked up. I knew it. But I didn't want to get Trinity's hopes up. Or mine, for that matter. Somehow, not saying it made it easier to keep moving.

"Okay. I'm on it," she replied.

"No."

"You can't stop me and I can't stop you."

I grinned. Couldn't stop myself. "Sounds like old times."

Trinity laughed. "Come on. Come back to the palace. You said yourself Elder Amandine isn't in on it. You should come in now. It's too dangerous for you there."

"No, it's not. I'm fine. And with Crayden dead, someone's got to watch her back."

"And who is going to watch yours?" she countered.

"I will, of course," Nix replied.

I eyed him, knowing now I wasn't going to get away from

him so easily. From the gleam I saw, the clenched jaw, I had a feeling I wasn't breathing without him next to me.

"No." I raised a bloody hand. "I'm not finished. This is a big place, Trin. There are more players than just the one elder. Since she's a good guy, then someone else has to be in on it. I'm in deep here and I've got help from a head elder. I dyed my freaking hair," I replied, eyeing her carefully. She knew that was a big deal. "I can learn more."

I wasn't sure how I was going to do that with Nix here, but I had to get Trinity satisfied and off the call and then I could deal with him.

She sighed and I knew I had won. I ignored the caveman kneeling before me, looking up at me, staring at me like he'd never seen anything so beautiful. He lifted a hand to my hair and ran his fingers through the black strands as if he'd never seen hair before. I was waiting for him to grasp my neck and strangle me for how I'd gotten away from him.

What was *wrong* with this guy? Why did he think I was his mate? I mean, I was so-so, at least average in looks. Maybe. My eyes were too narrow and my nose had a weird bump near the top. My lips were too thin and I had no boobs to speak of. For being a twin, Faith got it all in the looks department. What the hell was he looking at like *that*?

His hands slid under the long hem of the tunic I wore; the heat of his hands seeped through the material of my pants. Higher and higher he moved, not slowly and not with too much haste, as if he were savoring the journey, until he cupped me.

His eyes flared, his jaw clenched as I knew he felt how damp the fabric was and what that indicated.

I moaned because his hand felt *soooooo* good.

"Trin, I've got to go."

"But, I need to—"

I disconnected, let the comm fall to the floor.

Yeah, I needed to do something too, and it was Nix.

I didn't want him here. Obviously, the stubborn Aleran male had zero intention of letting me just go about my business. And now he would hover, with Trinity's blessing. I had no chance of getting him to see reason. And based on how quickly he'd tracked me down, he wouldn't be easy to shake off my trail.

But, at the moment he was working my pants off and that was more important than anything else in the world. Thank god he'd closed the door behind him.

"You're in big trouble, mate," he said as he worked my small boots off, then my pants.

I grabbed the hem of my tunic and pulled, tossed it over my head. It was in my way, dammit.

"You're going to be in big trouble if you're found in my room," I countered, tugging off my undershirt next. I needed to be naked. Now. "God, this is insane. I need you again."

Nix stood and began to strip. One piece of clothing at a time, with a confidence mastered by a Chippendales dancer. And what he revealed. Hell, he wrecked those exotic dancers. Muscles on top of muscles. Broad shoulders, rippling abs, bountiful biceps, narrow waist. Thick thighs and that gorgeous V that led to his... god, that had fit?

His cock was huge, and gorgeous. Not usually so, but his was a soft shade of pink, thick and almost pulsing with need. The crown was wide and smooth and pre-cum already dripped from the slit. Below, his balls hung heavily, as if he hadn't already come in me three times.

I pointed there. "Are you always like this? Are you a consort or something?" I wouldn't have put it past Trinity to send me a consort to ease my Ardor. But a queen's guard who was a consort? Who could sneak into buildings with stealth and a hard-on? And I'd never told anyone I had the Ardor.

"I am the male who's cum is going to be sliding down your thighs."

I glanced down at my nearly naked body, imagined him smeared all over my skin. Fuck, that was hot.

"I'm no consort. I'm your mate and you awakened me."

I frowned, thinking. "Are you saying you've never, that I was, that you—"

"Never had a hard cock before? That's correct. Never fucked before? That's also correct."

"You were a virgin?" I asked.

"Yes."

"Holy shit. You're really good for a virgin."

That only stroked his male ego. His shoulders rolled back and his cock swelled even more.

"We should... I mean, don't you think we should wait? Take this back to the palace?"

"Now you wish to go to the palace?" he countered. Slowly, he shook his head and stepped toward me.

6

D*estiny*

I RETREATED toward my en suite bathroom. It wasn't fancy, but it worked. I never realized how small it was until Nix took up most of the space.

Unhooking the Aleran version of a bra and undies, I dropped both at my feet. I had now stripped out of every blood-stained, nasty bit of clothing I had. Even my boots. Nix had seen it all before, and I couldn't stand to have the blood touching my skin for another moment. I'd had dead guy on me for *hours*.

Gross.

Naked now, I couldn't quite stomach covering up with the robe either. I was still filthy. Blood caked on my palms. On my knees where it had soaked through my pants. I turned the faucet on and scrubbed my hands under the running water like my life depended on it. Soap. Wash. Rinse. Repeat. Twice. Three times. I'd never be clean.

Nix reached over my shoulder and turned off the water,

waited until I turned toward him and reached for a towel, gently drying my hands as he spoke. All towel. No skin.

"You made my cock awaken. We fucked, then you ran away from me last night. You are the one who put us here instead of in a private bedroom at the palace. We could have done this in a large, comfortable bed. Instead, you're going to get the spanking and fucking you deserve right here in your shower tube."

A shudder went through me at his words. Holy hell, I hated to be bossed around, but Nix's dominance hit every one of my hot buttons. That didn't mean I would give in though. No way in hell.

"As if."

The corner of his mouth tipped up. "You may have gotten away before, Princess, but not this time."

"I'm not a princess," I countered. "At least, I am, but I'm not. Not really."

"You mean spoiled and used to getting her own way?" He reached past me again, this time to press the wall to turn the shower on. He had yet to touch *me* and it left every single nerve ending wide awake. "A man had his throat severed, you're covered in his blood and you think I will allow this? That I will allow my mate to take such risks?"

"Nix," I said, not exactly sure why. Was I saying his name to have him touch me, to warn him that we would be too loud in a dorm-style building? To tell him he was being unreasonable? That he was absolutely right and I just wanted to be in the palace in a big bed and beneath him, all the bad stuff just... gone? Poof! I had no idea. My mind was scattering like leaves in a fall wind.

I mean, I was in a confined space with the hottest man in the entire universe and he was naked. His cock had gotten hard for me. Only me. I knew about the Aleran males' awakening. How they might search for years for the right woman to turn them on and wake them up. It was like instant puberty. From zero to hero instantly. And for Nix, that one in a million woman was me.

No wonder he looked like he wanted to eat me alive.

If that wasn't hot as fuck, I had no idea what was.

And what was I waiting for? I wanted him inside me giving me orgasms. By the dozen.

"You doubt I'm your mate?" he asked, glancing down our bodies at his cock, which bobbed between us. When he stepped closer, it pressed hot and heavy against my belly. "That this is just... fucking to you?"

Yes, I wanted to fuck him. I'd had sex before, but never like this? God, it had *never* been like this. I wanted *him*.

"Nix."

Reaching out, I grasped his cock, stroked the full, ridiculously long length of it. His eyes fell closed and his hips jerked. I felt powerful, knowing what I did to someone so serious, so in control all the time. Leave it to me to turn on someone so uptight and rigid. He just *had* to be a queen's guard.

"I'm supposed to be finding my mother's kidnapper," I said randomly. "Not going at it like a rabbit with a man I don't know."

He stilled my hand by gently gripping my wrist. "You know me," he said, his eyes meeting mine. Holding me pinned just as much with his gaze as with his grip. "I am yours, Destiny. That is all you need to know. To feel. But as to the rest? Your hand is on my cock and you're thinking of your mother?"

I bit my lip, said nothing. He was right. My body was melting and my mind was screaming at the rest of me to get a fucking grip and get back to work. I didn't have time to take care of myself. I had to find Mom. She needed me. Trinity needed me. Faith needed me.

Nix cupped my face with a gentle touch and angled my head so I looked up at him. "Destiny, there is nothing else you can do tonight. You neglect your health, push your body to the point of starvation. Tempt death to take you. You do not take care of yourself. That is what happens when you're in charge."

"Nix." God, his eyes were dark. And the emotion I saw there scared the hell out of me. Shit. He was right. How had a man I'd just met known that much already? I did push too hard. I broke things. Bones. Skin. I had scars. I'd kept the emergency room back home well-stocked in casts when I was a teen.

And this Ardor? I had waited too long, but I hadn't realized just how close I was to the edge until Nix had shown up and set my body on fire. Who knows? Maybe I would have been fine. Maybe I could have held on for another week. Or two. "I'm fine."

"I hear that word a lot from you, yet I find you covered in a dead man's blood. I do not believe you are using it properly."

"I don't think—"

Nix interrupted, placing his thumb over my lips. I wanted to lick and nip and suck him into my mouth. "Thinking. Too much thinking. I might have been a virgin before you, but even I know that right now what my mate needs is to be a sweaty, screaming mess from a good, hard fuck, from my energy pouring into you, feeding your Ardor, taking me inside you forever. That's what you need and I'm going to give it to you."

Forever? What the hell was he—

His free hand cupped my pussy, slid over my wet folds. Over my clit. Back and forth. Teasing me.

I never finished that thought. No longer cared.

"I love the feel of my cum in you. Knowing I've been here, taken you."

I whimpered, circled my hips as he slipped two fingers inside.

His hand moved away and he turned me around, pressed my breasts to the cold, smooth wall of the shower tube. "Nix!" I cried.

His answer was to kiss me. My shoulder. The back of my neck. The side of my face. Luring me into trusting him, he raised my hands over my head and locked one large hand around both of my wrists as water poured down on both of us.

"You need to take better care of yourself, mate." He washed my body with one hand, making quick work of the job, making sure all traces of the earlier violence were gone. It wasn't sexual, but his touch made me feel cared for. Pampered. That was before the sharp slap landed on my ass. The sting had me gasping, then coming a little as the fire spread and his hard cock slid up and down the small of my back, the curve of my ass.

Holy shit. Hot. "I'm fine."

Another swat, the sweet sting moved through me like liquid heat and my pussy clenched around nothing. Empty. Hungry. My core twitched and spasmed in the beginnings of an orgasm. I tugged at my wrists, tested his hold. He wasn't hurting me, but there was no give. His heat was like an inferno at my back as he towered over me.

Hot. So fucking hot. I wanted more.

With a sound bordering on a growl, he leaned down and moved his lips over my cheek, making me shiver despite the hot water. "I'm in charge now. Your pleasure is mine. That little bite of pain, you like that? You just came, didn't you, mate?"

Gone was the gentle lover. Well, he'd never been gentle, but he'd also never been like this. Dark, controlling, maybe a little bit of the Doms I'd read about in romance books coming off him.

But that bite of pain had been delicious and I wanted more. I widened my stance in the hopes of him giving me another stinging swat with that deliciously large hand. On my ass. Making me burn. Then he could lift me, fill me from behind. Fuck me again.

I didn't ask. Didn't say a word. Speaking those kinds of thoughts out loud was completely different from *thinking* them. Telling him what I wanted made me too... vulnerable. I couldn't go there with him. I couldn't give in.

He pulled back, that free hand of his roaming up and down my spine with a touch so gentle it made me shake.

"Nix," I said, sobbing his name, needing more but unable to ask.

"Do you know why I got you all cleaned up?" he asked.

I didn't care, but he kept talking anyway.

"So I can get you filthy dirty again." He slipped his arm around my hips and lifted me, his knees coming between mine from behind. Opening my legs. Lifting my ass. He filled me in one smooth stroke, pinned me to the wall of the shower as he pumped into my body over and over again. "Later, we will find your mother. Fuck, we will save the fucking planet. But right now, I will save you. From yourself."

I cried out his name again, needing this, needing everything he'd give me. Everything he'd take. I didn't have to think, didn't have to do anything but feel.

It was liberating. Freeing. For the first time since I'd arrived on Alera, I was free. Protected. Safe.

And later, when he finally, *finally,* laid me down in the bed and fucked me, slowly, kissing me, watching my face as I came apart in his arms, I let him have me. I hid nothing. I took him deep and clung and kissed and whimpered when he pulled out, separating us. My body needed his in a way I'd never even imagined. The pleasure of pulling his essence into myself as he came inside me made my eyes roll into my head like I was taking a hit of the deadliest, most seductive drug. I couldn't stop touching him. Wanting more energy. More touching. More. Just more. Needing him.

And he gave himself to me. He thrust and groaned and worked his body to the verge of collapse. I watched his muscles shake with fatigue and his veins strain with exertion. I stared at his face as he came inside me, his expression—as I drained his strength and his seed—a mixture of pleasure and pain. Agony and triumph. And I couldn't stop. My body had a will of its own. A *hunger* unlike anything I'd ever imagined.

He didn't try to stop me. Didn't ask me to stop. I took and took and took. And he gave.

When we both finally collapsed, unable to move, I knew I was in big trouble.

When I snuggled into his embrace and pressed every inch of my skin to his warmth? When I pulled his arm tightly around me and cuddled into him like he was mine? When he covered us both with a blanket and I trusted him enough to fall asleep in his arms?

Trouble.

Really *big* trouble.

7

I WAS on my feet blocking the ion blasters pointed at my mate before the door to Destiny's room flew open and hit the wall. Or at least, I thought I was.

I expected to find her snuggled in the blankets behind me, still warm from our slumber. Sated. Looking at me with the sleepy eyes of a well-fucked female in the pre-dawn light. Like I was her world. Like she *cared*. Wanted me. Was happy that it was me in her bed and not some other male.

Instead, my deadly mate was crouched on the end of her bed, naked and beautiful, her own weapon pointed at the intruders. I'd had no idea she even had a blaster. "Get out of my room."

Three clerics stood there, scowling, ion pistols pointed right at me. They ignored her, apparently assuming she was no threat. Idiots.

"Get out. You have violated the sanctity of these grounds

with your fornication and broken the initiate's oath. You are henceforth banished from theses premises."

The grin spreading on my face was impossible to contain. The young guard looked like he was about to piss himself. But the male behind him was ogling my mate, and that was not acceptable. "I am not an initiate," I said.

"Not you," he countered and pointed. "Her."

Clearly these were not guards Elder Amandine had sent. They knew nothing of her meeting with the elder. Someone on the floor must have heard us and complained. These guys were the morals police.

"That *her* you are referring to is my mate. If you do not stop eyeing *my mate*, I will pluck your eyes from your skull and make you choke on them. Show her some respect."

The leader of the three, a young man who looked barely old enough to be weaned from his mother's breast, and completely incapable of killing, puffed up his chest like a bird with ruffled feathers and lifted his blaster a bit higher. His gaze, however, shifted lower, to my engorged cock. There was no lying, not about this. An Aleran male's cock did not become fully functional until his mate awakened him. And my body, despite the hours I'd spent lost in the pleasure of Destiny's soft, warm sex, was very, very *awake*. And hard. And ready for another round.

And these three were keeping me from that.

The guard cleared his throat and stopped looking at my obvious erection. "Mate or not, she is an initiate of the clerical order."

"It is Aleran law that you can't separate me from my mate."

"We are not separating a mated pair. Both of you are expelled from the property. Take your mate and get out. Both of you. Fornication is not allowed on sacred ground. You should have taken it somewhere else. You are banished."

DESTINY, The Palace, Two Hours Later

THE LOOK on Nix's face had been hilarious. I doubted he'd ever had three women shut the door in his face before. Well, not three women, but Trinity. It wasn't as if he was going to stop her. She was the reigning royal and she was a princess. And, as a member of the queen's guard, he took commands from her.

So if she wanted to yank me out of his arms, pull me into her bedroom and slam the door in his face, he wasn't going to say a word.

But his look? Half horror at being separated from me—and half painful desperation. I guessed his cock had been the source of the agonized expression because anyone with eyes could see that it was still hard and straining... for me.

Not that I was eager to be away from him either, but the hard-core craving my body was dealing me was not okay. And neither was the emotional attachment I was feeling to that warrior. Possessive. Needy. Desperate.

Desperate. Had I really just applied that word to myself?

My pussy clenched and my skin ached for his touch.

Yes. I had. And I didn't like being this needy, dependent, weak-willed freak.

Women ruled the world here. Literally. Maybe this was the universe's way of laughing at us. Since the society was more matriarchal, perhaps this was the males' revenge.

Ardor.

A biological necessity to keep the males and females together for breeding.

Breeding. Fucking. Clinging. Screaming. Orgasms.

"Don't worry, Des. He'll get over it." Trinity locked the door and walked to me, putting her arm through mine and pulling me to a sitting area that looked like it belonged on one of those billionaire home showcases. And this was just her *bedroom suite?*

What did the rest of the palace look like?

Did I care? No. Not really. Other than to get Nix into one of those giant beds, like the one in the next room I couldn't take my eyes from.

"I know. He's a big boy. He'll deal." But I doubted a woman had ever had the balls to shut him out before. Not a big, brawny guy like him. What woman would want to? He was gorgeous, sexy as hell and wickedly skilled in the sack. What woman in her right mind would ignore him? Well, I had. With frequency.

Faith laughed. "Your mate looked like a puppy that just got kicked to the curb."

I bit my lip to stifle a smile. She was right. I wanted to open the door and hug him and kiss the top of his head and tell him it was all right. He was just outside the door. I had no doubt of that. He wasn't going anywhere. Although, he was probably freaking out because he knew about all of the secret passages inside the palace. In fact, that's how he'd sneaked me in here.

Right at this moment, he was probably ordering guards to stand in them so that there was no chance someone could get inside, or more likely, that I could get away. He had made it very clear that he did not want me *gallivanting* around and placing myself in danger. Whatever. I can handle myself.

And I do *not* gallivant.

"I knew he was into you," Trinity said, tugging me down onto the sofa. Her bedroom suite was enormous. And there was that super-sized bed again. Maybe I should get up and close the door, so I didn't have to look at it. The bed was against one wall, all beautifully decorated, although in colors not quite her style. It wasn't as if she'd had time to put her personal stamp on things. Fabric shopping and paint swatches weren't high on her priority list.

"What about you?" I asked. "The last time I saw you, Leo was definitely *in* you."

"Leo is mine."

"I think he would say the opposite, that you belong to him."

She rolled her eyes. "Ha ha. Faith's totally in love with Thor and now you're totally falling for Nix. Mom is going to be so happy for all of us."

I held up my hand. "Don't count your chickens, Trin. I am not falling anywhere," I countered.

"But he's your mate." Faith wrapped her arms around herself and curled up on the couch like a sleepy, pink kitten. So cute, my twin. She got all the fluff and I got all the fire.

"He's not my anything. Not yet." We hadn't had all that much time talking about the whole mating thing. He'd said often enough I was his mate. He'd tossed out the word 'mine' frequently, even made me say it a time or two, but his cock had been buried deep inside me at the time. If he'd told me to shout 'squirrel feathers' I would have.

"Well, he's *had* you, multiple times, unless I miss my guess," Faith countered. She wore soft pajamas in pale pink. They were cute and comfy and totally her. "Destiny's first walk-of-shame. Mom will be so proud." Her soft laughter was so familiar and full of love and sisterhood and everything I'd missed that tears gathered in my eyes. Stupid.

"Oh, shut up." So what? Yes, Nix and I had woken everyone up after our dawn walk of shame from the fortress. But what else were we supposed to do? The only tunnel he knew how to crawl around in was the one that ended up in this very room. Trinity and Leo's bedroom. I'd just been thankful they'd been sleeping and not sexing it up when we knocked on the hidden door.

"What the hell are you wearing?" I asked Trin, finally getting to take a moment to eye her.

She glanced down at herself. "Unlike your twin, I don't have the inclination or time to figure out the S-Gen machine. So this is what I end up with." She tugged at the gray sweats that looked like they came from a women's penitentiary.

"I'm surprised Leo's still with you in a get-up like that," I countered. It was pretty ugly.

She angled her head, gave me the stink eye. "You think he lets me wear clothes when we're alone?"

"Good point," I conceded. I'd known Leo for a few days, tucked away in his quarters after the incident with assassins jumping through windows and fighting with Jax guards. What a cluster fuck that had been.

Turned out, the good guys had been the bad guys and the bad guys, at least one of them, had been Nix. The male now claiming I was his one and only mate.

Insane.

"Why aren't you asking about Faith's sex life? I mean, she's mated to Thor."

I glanced at my twin, who blushed hotly.

"Who wants hot chocolate with lots of marshmallows?" Faith asked.

My mouth fell open. "Here? Now? I'd think we all needed some whiskey or something." With all the danger and chaos and death, fluffy marshmallows weren't high on my list. But they did sound good.

She hopped up from the couch. "Whatever. We always have cocoa and extra marshmallows when we have slumber parties."

"This isn't a slumber party," Trinity countered, tucking her feet up beneath her, but she didn't say no to the hot drink.

"I think our slumber party days are over," Faith agreed. "I mean, they're fun and all, but I'd rather sleep in Thor's arms than in a Wonder Woman sleeping bag."

"I doubt Leo would let me sleep anywhere but with him," Trinity added.

They looked to me. "What? You think I'd let Nix decide where I sleep?" I laughed. "Please. I'd kick his ass before he bossed me around."

They stared at me, wide-eyed.

"What?"

"I'd think your ass would be red for thoughts like that."

I blushed. I couldn't help it. He'd spanked me in the shower the night before. But we'd also been naked and wet—me from more than just the water raining down—and it had also been hot as hell. The stinging swats had only amped my desire for him. Who knew I had a spanking fetish?

I'd never expected that, but with Nix... oh yeah. I'd come and come hard from his dominance.

Not that I was going to tell him that. Or admit it to my sisters. "You two might be into the alpha male bossiness thing your mates have going on. Not me."

They continued to stare at me.

"What?" I asked again. I began to feel uncomfortable as they kept doing it. "Is it my hair?" I ran my hand over the black strands, totally messy from being wet from the shower and then a wild bout of fucking in my bed, then being tossed out of the fortress without even a comb. "The black washes out after a while. It'll be purple again before you know it."

Faith shook her head. "The black looks good. It's not that. Destiny, seriously woman, I knew Nix before he laid eyes on you and now... god, that man is pussy-whipped."

Was he? Truly? That would imply that I had some kind of mystical, feminine hold over him. No man had ever wanted me enough to let me so much as comment on his clothes. I couldn't help but smile at the thought that Nix might be different. Did he really care that much? I might not mind that at all.

"You're his mate. You've got to cut him some slack," Trinity added.

"Me?" I put my hand to my chest. "He's the one who came to the fortress and tracked me down. He's the one who didn't take the brush off and leave me alone. He's the one who was found in my bed and got us both kicked out before I could talk to Elder Amandine again. God, that was embarrassing."

"He was grinning when he came in here behind you," Trinity said.

I stood, paced. "That's because he's got me where he wants me. Back at the palace, safe. His guards are doing the dangerous work while we sit here and talk marshmallows."

"Speaking of." Faith hopped up and went over to the S-Gen unit on the wall and began pushing all kinds of buttons.

"It's been, what? Two days? There's no way his Awakening can be... resolved in that time. Especially if he's been separated from you. And you—" Trinity pointed at me, completely ignoring whatever Faith was doing with the S-Gen unit. "You're flushed and antsy."

"I'm always antsy," I countered.

"You've got Ardor."

Faith turned and looked me over.

I crossed my arms over my chest. "So?"

"Sooooo, you should be having a sex marathon right now," Faith offered.

"Yes. Getting to know each other. Learn that Nix is just as bossy and alpha male as our two men." Trinity leaned back into the cushions and grinned. "Trust us, it's not all that bad, having a bossy man in bed."

God. I knew *that*. And thinking about bossy, alpha male, spank my ass Nix was making my pussy wetter, not calming me down. I pointed at Trinity. "You're the one who shut the door in his face. I'm sure he was thinking we'd be having a sex marathon right about now himself."

Faith came back balancing three mugs of steaming beverages. When she sat them on the large coffee table, I could see the heaping piles of marshmallows melting on the surface.

My mouth watered at the sight.

"None of us should be having sex marathons with Mom missing." There. I said it. That was the one truth that was holding me back from a no-holds-barred sexual marathon with the sexiest man I'd ever seen. Guilt.

Faith sat back down on the couch, frowned. "Take love where you can get it, twin. Everyone keeps dying."

I thought of Crayden and his slit throat, and of how very odd it was that my sister's words so closely mirrored what the elder had said to me just a few hours before. But I arched a brow at her to get her to talk. "Mom is not dead. None of us are going anywhere. You hear me?"

"You heard about Lord and Lady Jax?" she asked.

I shrugged. "Only that they died honorably."

Faith laughed, although she didn't sound—or look—amused. "It was like this..."

She filled me in on what had happened with her. How Thor had literally rescued her from the brink of Lord Wyse's clutches. Not that she—or any of us—knew he was evil at the time. A quick and not-so-dirty recap of her mating with Thor, her dinner at the Jax house and how Lady Jax had tried to kill her. All of it. By the time she was done, I'd drunk half my hot chocolate and all the marshmallows were gone.

"Holy shit, Faith." What else was I to say?

"Everyone's dying all around us," Trinity murmured.

"Mom's still alive," I said, with fervor.

Both sisters nodded. "Yes, she is. We'll find her and catch whoever's behind all of this," Faith said.

"One thing I've learned, being the reigning royal, is that I can't do everything myself." Trinity set her mug down, completely empty, I noticed.

I didn't like that thought. I liked to do everything myself.

"I'm the ruler until Mom gets back, but I can't do everything. Not even close. The guards won't allow it and it's not as if I can just go to the grocery store and snoop around. Everyone knows who I am. I'm a target."

"Obviously," Faith added. "So am I."

Trinity held my gaze, perhaps trying to make sure her words were sinking in to my thick skull. "We have to let the guards do their jobs. I hate it, Des, but we're targets. Famous. Everyone knows what we look like."

"Not me, they don't." And no. My skull bones were functioning at optimal levels.

"But you have Ardor. How long can you hold out this time? A day? Two? You need to take care of yourself and let Leo and the other warriors do their jobs. They want to protect us, and find Mom."

"I don't want to wait," I replied. "I can find her. No one knows I'm here. No one but you guys and Cleric Amandine know I'm a princess. And now that I've got her on my side, she can help us."

"Help you what?" Faith asked.

"Break into the Optimus Unit and storm the hallways like a berserker?" Trinity always thought she was so damn funny.

"Not funny."

Faith touched my hand. "Nix won't let you go, Des. I saw him. He's in way too deep with you."

"Exactly. You think he's going to let you run off again?" Trinity glanced at a clock on the wall. "I'm surprised he hasn't burst in here by now to take you away."

As if Trinity were a prophet, not a princess, the door was kicked open and I jumped to my feet, ready to fight. But it was Faith who, in the blink of an eye, leapt over the back of the couch and crouched, arms raised.

What the hell? When had she turned from a soft, passive kitten into a ninja?

There, in the doorway, was Nix. Cheeks flushed, cock thick and tenting his uniform pants.

"Jesus, Faith. I thought you hated those classes I dragged you to."

Faith relaxed as Nix stormed over to me. There was no other word for it.

"Sixty minutes, mate. I allowed you your time with your sisters, but that is all I can stand. Your Ardor needs soothing."

Oh, he just knew how to push my buttons. "My Ardor

needs soothing? Don't you mean your Awakening? That huge cock is practically busting out of your pants."

He grinned then. Unabashedly. "You noticed that my cock is hard. Just for you, mate. It is proudly weeping pre-cum in eagerness for your pussy."

I flushed hotly. "Jesus, Nix," I choked out. Faith and Trinity giggled behind me.

"You need a good hard fuck—and a spanking for your sass —and I'm going to give you both."

I stared into his eyes, those impenetrable, dark as sin eyes, and knew I wasn't going to say no. Not now. Maybe not ever. Not to him.

Leo, my inconvenient brother-in-law, chose that moment to knock on the door like a gentleman.

Why did I get the caveman?

"Trinity? We've got a message here for Destiny."

"What is it?" I turned away from the walking sex god in front of me and made my way to the door. I grabbed the envelope and grinned when I saw the unbroken seal on the back. I recognized that stamp.

"Who's it from?" Trinity asked.

"Elder Cleric Amandine." I tore open the paper, Nix leaning over my shoulder. I tried to resist, but his heat was too damn close, and my body was too needy. I leaned backward, pressing myself to him as I pulled the handwritten note free and unfolded the crisp linen paper.

Nix wrapped his arm around me, and I sighed in pleasure before I could stop myself.

I had to get a grip. I was sending all the wrong signals. Weak-willed. Needy. Sex-starved... well, technically, that part was actually true.

"Destiny?" Nix's deep rumble forced me to focus on the note and not on him.

"She knows where the meeting is going to be."

"What meeting?" Leo asked.

I looked up and let the fury pour out of my eyes. "The secret meeting of traitors. I'm quite sure they'll be discussing the fate of our mother."

"When?" Nix asked.

"Three days."

He sighed and took the note from my hand. I would have protested, but he handed it to Trinity and she smiled.

Nix leaned down and whispered in my ear. "Three days. Let's go, mate. That pussy is mine for at least two of them."

He picked me up and cradled me in his arms, leaving the others gawking. The only sound I heard behind us was laughter.

BOOK 8

PROLOGUE

Q ueen Celene, Planet Alera, Optimus Unit Prison, Cell
Level C

I HEARD them before the door to my cell swung open. Heavy
boots. Two males and one female. All three wore clerics'
uniforms, the emblem on their chests that of the clerical order
itself, rather than from one of the noble families.

Orphans then. Which explained why they would be so
fervently loyal to this mysterious master I'd heard so much
about over the last few days. The master who was responsible
for my first husband's death, for the attempt on my life, for the
hunters who had searched for me for twenty-seven long years
and stolen me from my home on Earth to bring me... here.

On one hand, I was glad they were finally talking about
him. On the other? I knew that any information I gained now
was most likely because they would kill me soon.

Whatever they had wanted from my daughters, they had
been sorely disappointed. As far as I knew, they still lived. But
that meant they'd switched their focus back to me.

"Good morning, Celene. Stay warm enough last night?" The eldest cleric spoke for all three of them. She always did. I'd been in this cell for several days now, and other than the male who'd killed the man I thought of as Scarface right in front of me, hers was the only voice I'd heard.

"You know I didn't." She'd made sure of it, taking my blankets and leaving me to shiver and sicken each of the last three nights. It had been cold in Mytikas, our capital city. Cold in the mountains surrounding us. Even in the depths of the cell block, inside the building, it was cold. I hated the cold.

"Yes, well, you have not earned the privilege of comfort." She was close to my age, nearing fifty if she was a day. Her long brown hair was streaked with gray and pulled up into a rather severe bun on top of her head, the tight pull causing her cheeks to thin and lines to fan out from the corners of her eyes to her temples. She was fit, her muscles outlined by the cleric uniform's tight black pants and fitted tunic. I had never seen her before and did not recall her from my youth. But she'd been close to my age when the attack happened at the palace, when my beloved had been taken from me and I'd been forced to flee to Earth with my unborn child.

"I am the queen of Alera. This building belongs to me. As does the blood running in your veins and the clothing on your backs. Claiming otherwise does not make it so," I stated.

Her dark blue eyes narrowed and the young male behind her stepped forward as if to strike me with his fist, but she placed a hand on his shoulder and shook her head. "Our master arrives in a few days. I thought you would want to know. You are running out of time."

When I'd first been kidnapped, I'd been beaten and tortured for answers. They'd given up on that. Then I'd been held in warmth and comfort. Now, the comfort was lacking. It seemed I was at the whims of my latest personal warden. Clearly, *she* didn't like me and wanted me as miserable as possible. All of them had been pawns to this *master*. They were all dead. This female, she too, was a pawn. I had to wonder if she would be dead within a few days as well. She had a purpose... now.

Finally. *Finally*, I would know who was behind everything. Who'd masterminded so much evil. Why I was still being held. What he truly wanted.

"Time for what?" This female elder, this *pawn*, was bat-shit crazy. The old Earth term jumped to mind, and I applied it happily. The fervor in her gaze was alarming. There was no logic there, no analysis or contemplation. Pure devotion. Obedience. She was like a trained dog. To *him*. My impatience to know the truth made me antsy.

"When he arrives, he will use you as bait. You will be the one to help him kill your daughters."

I frowned. I hadn't been kidnapped so my daughters could die. No, this *master* had gotten more than he bargained for. A queen with three daughters.

"That's not possible," I told her. "I know what he wants. He wants the royal jewels so he can take the throne." I stood, despite the fact that my knees were shaky. If nothing else, I needed to keep moving to stay warm. I hadn't slept more than a few minutes in days. It was too damn cold. "But it won't matter. The truth will come out. The people will reject him. Jewels or not."

"You are a fool." Her cackling laughter made the hair on the back of my neck raise in alarm. "He doesn't need the jewels. He never needed the jewels. What would he need with such worthless relics?"

I thought of the way Wyse had wanted them so desperately. So it hadn't been for their master, but for himself.

"He needs me alive," I countered.

Her laughter died off to a smirk that I wanted to punch right off her face. But the knowing grins on the faces of her two young attendants alarmed me more. They were not of her caliber, too young and stupid to feign such contempt. "For now.

But not for long. And once your daughters are dead, everything will be exactly as he requires."

"Requires for what?"

"To finally kill you and assume the throne. Try to stay alive until then. We wouldn't want you to die prematurely, now would we?" She nodded at the guard next to her and he tossed a blanket at my feet. "Tonight you'll be warm, but you won't eat."

Fine. Fucking fine. I refused to answer her, protest, or rise to the bait. So, this *master* thought he was going to use me to lure my daughters into the open. Away from their protectors, into a trap. To murder them?

Was it his plan to starve me into giving him what he wanted or was this female just a stone-cold bitch?

Apparently, *he* believed the best bait to catch a royal princess would be me.

Over my dead body.

I knew enough now. It was time to stop sitting here and letting these people fuck around. No one was coming for me. I'd waited patiently for the hopes of rescue, but the queen's guard either didn't know where I was or couldn't find me.

My daughters had settled in, Trinity and Faith had taken mates, but they had not been able to find me either. It seemed when they'd moved me about, from one prison to another, they'd been careful. Smarter than I'd thought.

Enough.

I had to rely solely on myself now. As my girls would say, I was so fucking tired of this shit. It was time to get the hell out of here.

1

D estiny, *Planet Alera, The Royal Palace*

"Harder."

With my ankles over Nix's shoulders, he was bottoming out in me with every deep thrust. The raw sound of flesh slapping flesh filled the room, mixed with our ragged breathing and a growl from Nix every once in a while. My pussy should have been sore. Hell, it should have been *broken* by now.

We were two days into our little staycation at the palace and my Ardor hadn't been soothed. Our bodies were sweaty, we were covered in cum, because while Nix had put it all deep inside my pussy every time he came, I'd barely let him out of me and it had all slipped free. My thighs, my belly, *his* belly, his balls, his thighs. The sheets. It was everywhere.

I lost track of how many times we'd come. Nix's balls should have shriveled up and fallen off by now. But no. He was still hard, still pounding me with an insatiability that matched my own. Thank God. Because I wanted more.

His hands gripped my ankles and pushed forward—I'd

never doubt a yoga workout ever again—and he did as I requested. Took me harder. He leaned over me, bending me into a pretzel; the new angle had the base of his cock rubbing my clit, pushing me to the brink.

"It's not working," I sobbed, my head thrashing on the sheets.

Nix's jaw clenched and his eyes met mine. "It's working, mate. You should be unconscious by now from all the orgasms."

Tears slid out of the corners of my eyes. "That's just it. I'm not. I need more. How can I need more?"

A wicked grin spread across his handsome face. "Because you're mine. We belong together. Your pussy is mine. It knows me. Needs me."

"Yes, but this much?" I asked.

He pulled back, stilled. I whimpered. What the fuck? He couldn't *stop*.

"If you are thinking and talking in coherent sentences, then I am not doing it right."

He gripped both my ankles in one hand and turned, rolling me unceremoniously onto my stomach. Carefully, he lowered my legs so my toes touched the floor. One hand tucked under my hips and banded about my waist as his foot kicked my own wide. Then wider.

I felt the wide crown of his cock at my entrance and he slid in again.

My eyes fell closed and I groaned at the new position, at the way his cock stroked over new places. My fingers curled into the bedding and held on as he took me even harder.

"You. Are. My. Mate." Each word was punctuated by a deep thrust, fucking me in cadence. "You. Need. Orgasms. And. I. Will. Give. Them. To. You."

My clit rubbed against the mattress and I came, the hard pounding exactly what I needed.

I cried out his name, sobbed through the pleasure, the feel

of him swelling and coming, filling me again with his seed. But that was nothing to the ravenous hunger I had for his skin, his heat. His *energy*. My body pulled at his, that was the only way I could describe it. I drained his heat, absorbed it into my skin. Sucked it up like a sponge.

Somehow, he knew, leaning over me, pressing every inch of his chest to my back, his hips to my ass, his thighs to mine. Contact. Skin. Heat. It was better than any drug I'd ever experimented with on Earth. Better than a hot bath, a massage and hot sex rolled into one. Combined with the orgasm, and his seed, and the megawatt of energy my body was absorbing on the inside—from his cock—I was blissing out.

At once, it was like a drug fix. The clawing need to fuck eased.

I began to count, silently, in my mind. I made it to thirty before the need came back to life inside me, clawing and twisting its way through my cells like a fever. Or a curse. I wanted him again. Needed more. More. *More.* Jesus.

"Fuck." I moaned the word into the bedding, hoping he wouldn't hear me. This damn Aleran Ardor was a relentless bitch. I didn't know how Nix was still walking, let alone feeding my body energy along with his seed. He must be some kind of Superman.

No. He wasn't human. I had to remember that. He was Aleran. He was built for this shit. I was *not*. Being this dependent, this freaking needy was not making me happy. The human half of me was sulky and depressed. Confused and pissed off. I shouldn't be this desolate at the idea of him removing his cock from my body. It was insane.

Nix pulled out and I hissed, not used to feeling empty. His seed trickled down my thighs.

He spanked my ass with the palm of his hand, not hard, but enough to sting. "I thought that's what we just did. Again?"

I climbed up onto the bed, then dropped, sighed. The tangled sheets felt cool on my heated skin. All at once, I was tired. Bone weary. Exhausted. I still felt the tingle beneath my skin, the need that I knew would grow from a smoldering fire to an inferno soon enough. And the worst? I wanted Nix to climb up onto this bed, wrap his arms around me, and hold me. *Hold me?*

Two words I had never spoken to a man in my life. What. The. Fuck? That screamed dependent, needy, weak female. No man would want a woman that clingy. Especially not a warrior like Nix. He was hard core. I knew a soldier when I saw one. A no bullshit, no drama, alpha male. They didn't go for women like me. They wanted control and I refused to be controlled. Which led me in a circle back to my original problem. Ardor.

"Dammit. When's it going to stop? When will I stop needing you?"

Out of the corner of my eye, Nix stilled. His cock was still hard, still a dark plum color and pointed straight at me. It glistened with our combined fluids. God, he was gorgeous.

And pissed.

"You are my mate. You will never stop needing me." His voice was flat. Emotionless.

I closed my eyes, rolled over and tugged at my hair. We'd fucked in more places than just this bed. Against the wall, over the desk, in the shower. My black hair was starting to change back to purple from being washed so often.

"Nix, you're not making it better. It's not going away. It only took Trinity two days to get over her Ardor."

"Are you implying that you would rather have Leo in your bed?" I thought his question was a joke, until I lifted my head and saw the fury simmering in his eyes. And my sister's mate? Gag.

"Hell no. Gross. Sisters do not break the sister code. I can't believe you said that."

"I did not. You did." He prowled closer but did not touch me. "Believe me, Destiny, the only male who will be in your bed is me."

"About this mate thing. We haven't discussed that, Nix. I'm not sure—" I was about to say *I'm not sure I'm the right kind of woman for you,* but he interrupted before I could finish the sentence.

"We spend two days in bed. I give you everything. Soothe your Ardor. Make you mine. Claim you as my mate. Yet you speak as if you will toss me out with the trash once your Ardor is soothed."

I curled up so I faced him, lying on my side. I'd hurt him. But how could I not? I didn't answer to anyone. Sure, I'd had sex before Nix, but not like this. I craved him. I craved more than his cock. I actually *liked* him. A lot. Too much, if I were being honest. And the idea of him in another woman's bed made my blood boil.

But that didn't mean I wanted an alpha male bossing me around. Forever. And once I agreed to this mate business, I was pretty damn sure he was going to get even more bossy than he already was. Not that I minded, in bed. But out of it?

His words from our first night together came back to me often. In fact, they damn near haunted me—*you are my mate and you will bend to my will.* Oh, and the other classic— *You will stop your searching and return with me to the palace.*

Seems he'd won *that* battle, thanks to my traitorous pussy and this alien Ardor business I had going on. Thanks to my body, I was simply not myself. And that fact alone made me nervous. Nix didn't know me. Not really. He knew the sex-starved, submissive, begging version of me. And that wouldn't last.

I was not a wallflower. I was a fighter. And I loved being a fighter. If I had to sit in meetings all day and act the politician or learn to run a household like a bona fide lady, I'd lose my freaking mind. He continued to insist that I would not be *allowed* to be in danger. As if. I wasn't *allowed* to do anything. Hadn't been for years. Even my parents gave up—although I did generally do what they wanted out of respect. But not fear. Never fear.

So. Yes. Nix and I were going to have a problem. A serious problem. Why couldn't he see that?

"You've got a job to do and so do I, a serious one. You can't have me underfoot when you're working, and I can't sit around the palace eating bonbons while my mother is missing—"

He grabbed my ankle, tugged me so I was flat on my back. He dropped his hands so they were on either side of my head and he loomed over me.

All I could see was him. God, what a view. He really was magnificent in every way.

Get a grip, woman. You can't keep him.

"Even after we get Mom back, I'll—" What could I say? I'll go crazy if I have to be locked up in this palace like a prisoner. I wasn't a criminal, I was royalty. But that reality had seemed a lot more romantic and special back on Earth. The Disney princesses in the movies didn't seem to have this kind of problem.

"You'll what?" he asked.

I licked my lips, thought. I had no idea, actually. I just knew I didn't want to be tied down—to my title as princess or to the dictates of a man. And I really didn't want to be addicted to a cock. Since I didn't have a good answer, I chose not to say anything.

"What will you do, Destiny?" he asked again. "Go back to Earth?"

My eyes widened. "What? No!" I'd never been asked that before, never considered it, but my response was immediate. I wanted to stay on Alera. I knew that. Going back to Earth now would be like... well, I didn't know what it would be like. But my sisters were staying here with their mates. My mom would be here. Hopefully my dad could come live at the palace. "There's nothing on Earth for me. I don't want to go back."

"So, you'll continue to sneak into dangerous places you have no business being and risk your life?"

I took objection to that. Faith had snuck into the Jax mansion and pretended to be a maid. She was just as snoopy as I was. "I'll have you know everything that's happened wasn't my fault."

"I know that, mate. But that doesn't answer my question."

I pursed my lips. Duh. *Of course* I was going to get into trouble. That's what I *did*.

"How do you plan to defend yourself, Princess? An army of one out there alone wandering the planet? No guards?"

"No babysitters, you mean." His hips were nestled between my legs, his cock so close to my core all I had to do was lift my hips and he'd slide right in. But he was heavy, and if he didn't cooperate, I'd look like an even bigger fool than I did now. Didn't stop my pussy from clenching like a grasping, greedy little animal. Still, I wanted to try. Angry sex was good. Arguing and fucking was good. Possibly great. Nix made me crazy. I made him crazy, that was obvious. That's all there was to it.

"The queen's guard is dedicated to your safety. As am I. We do not watch over infants, although your stubborn pride is making you sound like a child. You have responsibilities to the people of Alera, and to me."

Now that just made me mad. How dare he lecture me? I pushed against his chest, tried to get him off of me. *Tried.* "Nix, I'll have you know—"

There was a knock on the door. The first sound from outside of this room in two days. "Princess Destiny. Nix," a man shouted.

Nix closed his eyes for a moment. "Not now. Fuck," he growled. Pissed we'd been interrupted. He wanted whatever *this* was between us worked out. I was all for delaying because I had no answers.

"Who is it?" I asked Nix, who obviously had recognized the owner of the voice.

"Captain Turaya. Leo's father." Nix leaned back, away from me, and instantly I shivered with cold. "We can't ignore him. He is my commanding officer, and he knows you are in your Ardor. He would not interrupt us if it was not urgent."

Nix pushed off the bed and grabbed my hand, tugged me so I was standing before him.

"Duty calls, Princess," he replied, all lust or even playfulness gone from his voice.

He walked over to a couch where I'd tossed a robe... yesterday? I contentedly watched the taut play of his ass muscles as he walked away, then took in the sight of his cock as he turned about and returned to me.

"Here, put this on," he told me. "No one needs to see you as I do."

I would have protested the order, but I was not interested in Leo's dad seeing me naked. And the gesture was kinda sweet. And I was kinda cold.

He went to the door, clearly unconcerned for his own modesty. He arched a brow as he looked back at me, hand on the knob as he waited.

I tugged on the silky robe, tied the sash. Only then did he open the door.

The older soldier in the doorway kept his gaze affixed to Nix's. He didn't react to Nix's nakedness, although it appeared he was too professional to gawk. But then, he was a soldier. He'd probably seen more naked men than I could if I took a new man to bed every night for the rest of my life.

Not that I wanted to do that. The only man I was currently interested in having in my bed was a chest-pounding, overly protective Aleran. And I had no idea how we were going to come to terms. Or *if* we would.

Captain Turaya bowed slightly to me, looking over Nix's shoulder. "Princess Destiny, Captain Nix. Princess Trinity requests your immediate presence in the main salon."

I pushed at Nix, trying to get to the door, but he blocked me in a stop short motion of his arm, so I ducked under. "Why?"

Nix's hands settled on my shoulders.

"You have received another notice from Elder Cleric Amandine. The meeting location has moved. And the names of several attendees have been included in the missive."

"She knows who the traitors are?" I asked, excitement pounding through my body like electricity. Finally, I could go kick someone's ass.

He shook his head. "Only Princess Trinity has read the note. She awaits your arrival."

"Okay. Thanks." Nix's hand lowered to rest at the base of my spine, and I wasn't sure if it was meant to offer support or remind me that I wasn't allowed to leave him behind again.

The first would be fantastic, but I was pretty sure it was the second.

"We will be there as soon as possible," Nix told him.

Captain Turaya nodded and turned to leave. Nix closed the door and went to the S-Gen machine on the wall.

"Nix," I said, not sure what to say. He wanted to control my life. I loved the sex, but I didn't want forever with a man who would try to keep me in a bubble. I needed to be able to fight. To protect my sisters. To do... something.

Being a pampered princess mated to a guard who protected them—and me—wasn't the same thing at all.

"Go, Destiny." He cocked his head toward the bathroom. "Take a shower."

"What about you?" I asked. We were both a hot mess. His seed slipped from me and down my thighs even now.

"I will wait until you are done. If I join you, we will keep your sister waiting." The growl in his voice made my body burn, and so did the way his cock was aimed straight for me, but he was right. Duty called. We had to save the world.

Then we could figure out what the hell we would do about... us.

2

N^{ix}

MY STUBBORN, beautiful mate sat beside me, her body inches from mine. And covered, head to toe, in Aleran armor. Guard's armor. Complete with a weapon at her side and a dagger on her opposite hip.

The sight made me both angry that she would defy me and continue to risk her life, and proud that this beautiful female was mine. Every stubborn inch of her.

Swirling inside me was the need to dominate and control, but mostly to protect. Which she refused to allow me to do. Oh, she surrendered to me beautifully in the bedroom, with my cock buried deep, my body feeding hers heat and strength and energy. The drain was orgasmic for me, knowing I was the one sustaining her, that it was my essence soaking into her very cells, my seed filling her pussy. But the moment we were out of bed, she defied me at every turn. Argued with me. Refused to back away from the search for her mother. Refused to admit she was mine.

Infuriating.

Aggravating.

So fucking frustrating.

And it made me want to drag her back to bed, tie her down, and fuck her until she came to her senses.

But she was a fucking princess, so I couldn't do that either. Unless she begged.

"Stop scowling. You'll scare my sisters." Destiny's eyes sparkled with mischief as she wrapped her hand around mine where it rested on my thigh. Instantly the flow of energy connected us, my body heat rising to meet the demands of hers. And for someone so small, her Ardor was incredibly strong. A lesser male would have collapsed by now. A lesser female would have had her Ardor soothed. But no, even subconsciously, she was so stubborn. Her mind, her body. And her heart.

"They should be frightened," I replied, my voice tipped low so only she would hear. "As should you."

She laughed, the sound carefree and happy. The look on her face was one I'd not seen the last two days. Content. At peace. At least for the moment. And I took some small pride in knowing I was the cause. For two solid days, I had cared for her, soothed her Ardor, given her what she needed. She was mine. There was no question. No doubt. It was so fucking obvious that someone should have made a large sign. But why couldn't she see it? *Feel* it? Why did she still fight my claim? Deny me? Resist?

She even refused to eat what I ordered for her, nutritious, healthy Aleran foods, insisting on using the S-Gen machine to order things that were made on Earth. Ice cream. Chocolate cake. They were delicious, especially when licked off her creamy skin, but not meant to sustain an Ardor.

"Glad to see you are feeling better, twin."

Faith reached across the table and Destiny took her hand, squeezing it. They shared a look I couldn't begin to fathom and broke the connection, staring at Trinity as if nothing had passed between them.

Princess Trinity seemed distracted, staring off into the distance, a piece of paper in one hand as she tapped the top of the table with it. The table itself was round, and large enough to hold ten. The seats were solid wood and plain, except for hers. The reigning ruler's chair had a tall back and arms, a throne of sorts. A reminder to anyone who sat at this table exactly who the ruler was.

As if a reminder was needed. Trinity carried herself like a queen already.

I sat to Destiny's right, Leo on her other side. Trinity was next to him. Then Thor and Faith, so that each princess sat next to her mate. Captain Turaya sat on my right, across from his son, the look on his face much more grave than the look on mine could have been. The table had three empty chairs, but it didn't seem as if Trinity was awaiting more people, but just thinking.

"Trin? Can I see the message now?" Destiny leaned forward and put out her free hand. Trust my mate to be the one to get the meeting going. In my mind, starting it meant it would end sooner. We could either go hunt down the mastermind behind all this mess or I could get Destiny beneath me once again. Either option worked.

Trinity handed her the envelope and Destiny released her hold on me to open it and take out the folded message it contained. The envelope was no longer sealed, and I had no doubt Trinity and Leo had already read the handwritten note.

Destiny scanned it, and I read it over her shoulder, but I was not sure what the message referenced. It was short. Two lines.

I had a damn good idea, based on what we'd overheard in Elder Amandine's office, but I'd wait this one out, hear what everyone else had to say, then make my move. Destiny was *not* going to risk her life again. I'd do whatever was necessary to see to that.

"Well? What does it mean?" Trinity asked. Everyone looked at my mate in silence, waiting. While I'd overheard Elder Amandine speaking with Crayden when we'd been hiding in the dark corner of her office, that was the only time I'd been near her. Destiny was the only one who might know what the elder was trying to communicate.

"She said the meeting is at midnight tomorrow, and she gave me an address," she said.

"What meeting?" Faith asked.

Destiny looked at her twin, her voice deep and stern, a voice I didn't recognize. "Amandine told me that she suspected the traitors who planned the attack and tried to kill Mom were gathering in town for a meeting. This meeting."

My mate tossed the note on the table and Captain Turaya leaned forward to pick it up, scanning the address. "This is less than a block from the Optimus unit's prison blocks."

"Is that where Cell Level C is?" Destiny asked. She was in full warrior mode, and I found it fascinating, and erotic. The stronger she was, the more I wanted to dominate her. Fuck her. Hear the sound of sweet surrender on her lips. Goddess, she was magnificent. And mine.

"Yes. It is," the captain confirmed.

"Less than forty-eight hours. That doesn't give us much time to plan," Leo said.

"No, it doesn't." Destiny frowned. "Trinity, did Amandine contact you about setting a meeting with some clerics coming in from out of town? She called them the Triad."

"Yes." Trinity leaned into Leo and he draped his arm around her like it was the most natural thing in the world. She could be reigning ruler of an entire planet and still seek the reassurance and comfort of her mate. Envy. That was this acid-like feeling pouring through my body. "What about it?"

"When is the meeting scheduled?"

"Tomorrow. Midday." Trinity frowned. "Why?"

"They're going to try to kill you." Destiny's voice was monotone, not a hint of worry or excitement in the words.

"That's not funny, Des." Faith shifted in her seat, placed both of her hands on the table, palms down. Her spine was straight, her gaze direct on my mate. "Not even a little bit."

"It's not a joke," Destiny countered. When her sister would have spoken, Destiny held up her hand. "When I was arrested, after Crayden's murder—"

Captain Turaya interrupted and everyone turned to look at him. "Cleric Crayden is dead? Why was I not informed?"

I hadn't realized it wasn't common knowledge. I had thought during the two days of... alone time with Nix, Trinity would have updated the others. Obviously not.

Trinity asked, "Did you know him?"

Captain Turaya nodded. "Yes. Very well. He was one of my best informants and a skilled soldier."

"Soldier? He wore a cleric's uniform."

"And you wear a queen's guard uniform and yet you are not one."

The captain's words made Destiny blush fiercely, a dark pink that matched well with the purplish color of her hair that was becoming more pronounced by the day.

Princess Faith's hand went to her mouth as if she were trying to stifle a smile. "Ouch," she whispered, but everyone at the table heard. "That had to burn."

I had to assume it was an Earth slang term, for Destiny didn't look overheated.

He held up his hand. "I meant no disrespect, Princess, only that you are so much more. Crayden *was* a cleric, but he was also a skilled fighter against the Hive and, as I said, an informant. He kept the lines of communication open between myself and Elder Cleric Amandine. She is not a traitor. I trust her with my life."

"But would you trust her with mine?" Trinity asked.

Captain Turaya didn't hesitate. "Yes. On my honor, she is not a traitor. I have known her since I was a boy. She was one of my mother's best friends. She would never betray the queen."

Destiny pursed her lips and gave the older man a slight nod. Moving on, she said, "Back to Crayden." Her fingers tapped on the table. "Not just a soldier. He was an assassin, wasn't he?"

The captain looked at her, his brows raised in surprise. "Yes. How did you know?"

My mate glanced at me, then away, quickly, as if she didn't want me to notice that she'd paid me any attention. "I can spot a trained killer, that's all."

So was that what she thought of me? That all I did was kill? She was not wrong. I had served the Coalition Fleet, Prime Nial and his father before him, for many years as an assassin in the Fleet's Shadow Unit. But I was not a cold-blooded killer. I killed to protect what was mine. My planet. My people. Innocent children and those too weak to fight the Hive themselves. I killed, but I would never apologize for the things I had done. They may have stained my soul black, but the fact that the sun shone on Alera and children ran the streets was my solace. The Hive had not conquered us. Never would. Not while I was breathing.

Was that why she would not acknowledge my claim as her mate? Did she sense the truth of my past?

Could she not see past the blood on my hands? Hive blood. Prillon blood. I'd killed every race for a hundred different reasons. But I'd done it all to protect my people, for the Coalition Fleet, to win the war. For her. For the promise of her.

I killed, but I wasn't a monster.

Yet, how could she see me as a worthy mate? The first time she'd ever seen me, I had burst through a penthouse window pretending to be an assassin. She'd believed I was there to kill her.

Fuck. Would she never completely trust me? Had I ruined my future with her?

Enough. I tore my gaze from my female and focused on the conversation, not sure how much the Captain had been told. "Crayden was Elder Amandine's most trusted guard," I said. "Just a few hours before he was murdered, she gave him orders to investigate a prisoner held by the Optimus Unit. Apparently, there is a very secret, unauthorized prisoner being held on Optimus Cell Level C. She was not happy about it."

"That was where Wyse wanted to take you," Thor said to Faith. "This Optimus Cell Level C. Is it possible the queen was there then?"

Destiny shook her head. "I heard of a special prisoner arriving there well after that. Days after you made your formal announcement as princess to the planet."

Captain Turaya glanced across the table at his son, then back at me. "So, Elder Amandine ordered Crayden to investigate, and he was dead within a matter of hours."

I nodded. "It appears that way. Yes."

"And I was the one to discover the body, so I was questioned for it," Destiny added. She shivered as she stared off, probably remembering what the poor male had looked like. I knew, by all the blood that had been on Destiny afterward, and what she'd told me, that he'd had his throat slit brutally.

"Which is how you were talking to Elder Amandine, right?" Trinity asked.

"You spoke with her?" the captain asked. Clearly, he knew the kind elder as well.

"Yes. I found Crayden's body, was standing over him, covered in his blood when the other guards found me. They took me directly to her. Not because I wanted to talk with her, the other way around in fact."

"And?" Faith asked, waving her hands in the air in a motion for Destiny to talk faster.

"We talked. But not before I found a transmitter hidden on her desk."

"Someone bugged her office?" Trinity asked.

"Exactly. I have no idea how long it had been in place, but they... the bad guys, would have known anything and everything Elder Amandine discussed, including the conversation she'd had with Crayden. His orders to investigate and search."

Again, my mate's glance slid to me, and I realized she was thinking about us, talking, fucking all the while the transmitter had been there. In that room. I'd called out her name. Told her mine. Told her to return to the palace. They... whoever the fuck they were, knew Destiny was a princess, knew she was in hiding and snooping at the fortress. Fuck! I'd placed her in danger without knowing it.

I didn't dwell on that for long, because the captain stood and began to pace behind the table. "He's not the only one. Two of the queen's guard have been killed in the last two days. I have reports of three dead members of the Optimus Unit, plus Crayden and two clerics from the fortress in Corseran."

"I'm so glad you're safe, Destiny," Faith said, grabbing her twin's hand again. She gave it a squeeze, which was accompanied by a watery smile. Thor put his hand around Faith's shoulder, but I doubted she needed his comfort as much as her sister's. I had to agree with her, for I'd spent the past two days touching, holding and fucking Destiny to assure myself she was whole, well and safe.

"Eight dead in two days? Why wasn't I told?" Leo asked.

"I didn't realize they were connected, son."

Trinity shook her head and tossed up her hands. "Why? Why now?"

"Maybe they were all looking for Mom and someone didn't like it," Faith said.

"In Corseran?" Trinity asked. "The *secret prisoner* is here. In Cell Level C. Not a continent away."

"Amandine and Crayden said that's where your father was from, Trin." Destiny said.

"Yes. I remember the name of his homeland," Trinity

replied. "Mom told me about him. She said she only went there with him once. But he's dead and that was so long ago."

"Well, maybe these dead clerics in Corseran knew something, and the people who have Mom are trying to cover their tracks. Maybe these clerics are the ones who were there the night of the coup?" Faith spoke and my respect for her went up another notch. She was a confusing female, appearing soft and kind, but fighting like a trained killer. And with this suggestion, I realized she was also intuitive and highly intelligent.

But then, she was Destiny's twin, so I should not have been surprised. My mate was all of those things. And more.

"But that was twenty-seven years ago!" Trinity repeated.

"I was there twenty-seven years ago," Captain Turaya added, his jaw tense, voice grim. "I saw what happened. Saw the king stabbed with my own eyes. Your mother in anguish over that, her escape. I was there for all of it. While I would have liked to question those clerics from Corseran, if they were involved all those years ago, I am not saddened by their loss."

Destiny's leg was wiggling under the table, nervous energy pouring off her in waves. I wanted to wrap her in my arms, carry her off, and work off some of that energy, but based on the way this conversation was going, I might not get her naked for quite some time.

Destiny looked to Captain Turaya. "How old were the dead guys? Old enough to have been in on the murder attempt on our mom?"

"Of the eight, they were not all males. And no. Some of them weren't even alive at the time of the coup."

"So much for that theory." Faith blew out a huff and leaned into Thor, who'd remained silent the entire time. But I wasn't fooled. He was a politician and a businessman with interests all over the planet. He was thinking, and I was glad he was on our side.

Destiny bolted out of her chair like a spooked zebcat and

paced on the opposite side of the table from the captain. Two leashed hunters, impatient to be set on their target.

The room remained quiet for several long minutes as we all contemplated possibilities. I, for one, had trouble concentrating with Destiny's Ardor calling me like a moth to a flame.

Thor was the first to break the silence. "Assuming our enemies are trying to cover their tracks, that does not bode well for the queen."

All three princesses froze and stared at him in horror.

"Explain," Trinity ordered.

"They took your mother, yet kept her alive, all this time. Which means they want something from her. *Her* specifically." He spoke slowly, forming thoughts as he went. "However, the lighting of three additional spires was probably not part of their plan."

"Still not getting it, Thor," Trinity said.

"They found your mother and kidnapped her from Earth. They had no idea the three of you existed. Obviously, they'd been searching for her all this time. *She* was the plan all along. And then three new spires lit. Meaning the royal lineage didn't stop with the queen as everyone thought. They have tried to kill you, Trinity, more than once. They tried to kill Faith. They failed. And they have no idea who the third princess is or where to begin their hunt." Thor looked up at Captain Turaya for confirmation. The older male took up where Thor left off.

"And now, we have eight dead in two days, knowledge of a prisoner being leaked to people in positions of power. They are either setting the stage for a new plot, or they are cutting their losses and starting over."

"Oh, shit. Are you saying that since they haven't been able to kill us, they're just going to go ahead and kill our mom?" Faith asked.

Thor raised her hand to his lips and kissed her folded fingers. "I don't know. But whoever planned the coup almost thirty years ago didn't get what they wanted. Sure, the king is dead, but he wasn't the one holding true power. It was the queen who was supposed to die. Instead, she got away. Hid. That mastermind hasn't given up, he's been searching. But she was found and then the plans were all fucked up because of the three of you. If I were planning a final royal coup decades in the making, and I had not one, but four female heirs in the way, a change in strategy would be in order."

I looked at Thor, thinking. Aloud, I said, "What do you believe they wanted from the queen, when they took her from Earth?"

Trinity answered. "We thought it was the royal jewels. Mom always said they were important and that the people wouldn't accept a new ruler without them."

Thor shook his head. "That has already been proven false. Before your arrival, your cousin, Radella, was the reigning royal. She was accepted and respected in that role, and the royal jewels haven't been seen since your mother disappeared. And with your return and no jewels about your neck…"

"Shit. They are eating you up like their favorite new dessert, Trin. Jewels or no jewels." Destiny picked up the pace behind me, moving silently, like a predator. Everything about her made me hard and hungry for more. The fact that she was so dangerous had my cock roaring to be set free. "So, if they didn't bring Mom back to get the jewels, what do they want?"

3

D*estiny*

I FELT like I was coming out of my skin. Like I wanted to climb the walls for some ludicrous reason. I wanted to toss furniture, rip my hair out. Scream.

"Holy shit, Dest, you need to chill out," Faith said.

I was back at the table and looming over her before she could even blink. No, I didn't have speed as the superpower the citadel had magically given me, but I was worried, for the first time since we'd arrived on Alera and seen Mom's spire was still lit. I was worried they might actually *kill her.* But I didn't handle worry well, so I channeled the emotion into anger, and being furious gave me *lots* of energy. I was pissed at my mother for absolutely no reason, the mystery mastermind who was fucking up all of our lives, at Crayden and every other person who had gotten themselves killed. Yeah, it wasn't their fault they'd been shot, had their throat slit or some other horrible ending, but I was pissed they were all dead.

And for what? Why had so many people been killed?

We still had no idea.

Faith held up her hand and stood to face me across the table. "You need to slow your roll, woman."

I leaned forward and used my scary voice, the one I saved for extra special, *I'm-about-to-kick-your-ass* moments. "Okay, then stop getting up in my grill."

"All right, we're done here," Trinity said, all diplomatic and perfect. Calm. Even that made me crazy.

I turned my head and glared. "How are we done? They're going to kill Mom! We don't have a plan in place to get in to Cell Level C. We need to go now. We need to organize and get Mom out of there."

"*We* will work on that. *You* need to go solve your Ardor problem," she countered.

"I'm fine. Nix made sure of that." I put my hands on my hips. "And not all problems can be solved by a man."

"No, but yours can be," she countered.

Out of the corner of my eye, I saw Nix smirk. He wasn't the least bit embarrassed that his body was a tool for my problem. That his cock was just what this specific job required. Me? I was too agitated to be embarrassed. "No. I've done nothing but have wild monkey sex for two days. That should be enough. Don't try to hide me away for another two days while you plan without me. I'm in. All the way."

With those words I glared at Captain Turaya.

He had the gall to look at Nix.

"Hey!" I stared the older man down until he had the good grace to bow his chin, just a touch. I was a princess. He was queen's guard. He worked for *me* and my sisters, not the caveman who wanted to lock me up, keep me barefoot and pregnant for the rest of my life. I ran my hands through my hair. Jesus. Trinity was right. I was coming out of my skin, and I'd only been out of bed for an hour or so.

Nix was a drug. An addiction. Tugging at my dark strands, I spoke slowly and clearly so Leo's father and everyone in the room would understand exactly how serious I was. "I make my own decisions, not Nix."

"He is your mate," the older man countered. "Should you not consider his wishes? Allow him to protect you, as a good mate should?"

It was possible that the top of my head blew off then. Maybe it spun around in circles like one of those horror films because Thor stood and grabbed Faith about the waist, tugged her back out of my reach.

Leo rose to his feet and put his hand on Trinity's shoulder.

"I think your Ardor's made you insane," Trinity said, cocking her head to the side. "I mean that seriously. You like to fight, but not with words. Listen to yourself, Des, you're losing it. Either that, or you've got a hormone rage from hell."

I bit my lip to keep from giving her any more fuel to light her argument fire.

"She's not full Aleran, it's possible her Ardor is... different," Thor commented.

"It wasn't like this for me," Faith added, so I glared at her. Of course her Aleran Ardor had been *perfect*. Nice and tidy and easily resolved with just some wild fucking and then it was over. She shrugged and had the nerve to grin at me. "I was over it in less than two days. But you like to do everything hardcore. You always did have to beat me at everything."

I couldn't help the way my eyes narrowed. "All I've done for days is have sex. This is insane. No one should have to go through this."

Faith made the L shape on her forehead, an indication she thought I was a total loser. "Deal with it. I win. And you need to get naked and roll with it."

"Great, just great. Now I'm the crazy one."

"Destiny," Trinity began. "You're arguing because you're having too much sex. Too. Much. Sex. There is something wrong with you."

Nix slowly stood, but didn't come over to me. Perhaps he

was smarter than I thought, because I had no idea what I would do if he touched me right now, in front of everyone. I felt weak. Vulnerable. Exposed. Hurt. Even though that last one didn't make sense.

Was Nix really with me because he liked me? Me, the smart-mouthed, aggressive, protective fighter? Or was he only with me because I'd die if he didn't stick his cock in me over and over again? I was a princess. He was a queen's guard, sworn to serve my family. Did he actually *like* me? Or was he just doing his job? Was he *serving* me in a very special way?

I mean, fucking for days on end, in every possible position, wouldn't be a hardship for any man I knew back on Earth. Hell, in my experience, that's all they required. Wet pussy and a free pass to do whatever the hell they wanted to my body.

Nix didn't touch me, but he did break the tense silence in the room. "We don't know what is going to happen. We do know that whatever happens, it will be tomorrow. Therefore, mate, we have time to finish your Ardor once and for all. There is no reason for you to suffer."

"You want to have sex, now?" My body was screaming at me, *Yes, please!* But my mouth was all sassy and angry.

"I will always want to touch you, mate. But Thor is correct, the Ardor is breaking the boundaries of desire and moving into other emotions. You need your mind clear for tomorrow. Yes?"

I crossed my arms over my chest, but dropped them because they only rubbed my already sensitive nipples. So I nodded instead.

"Then let's finish it. Then we'll prepare for whatever battle we have to fight tomorrow."

I looked around the room. Everyone was staring at me as if I were a bomb about to explode or a two-year-old who hadn't quite finished her temper tantrum.

"Fine." I snapped my fingers and strode toward the door. "Let's go."

Nix caught up to me in the hallway, took hold of my elbow

and since his legs were much longer, kept right on going, and it was I who had to hurry to keep pace. He turned down a secondary corridor toward our rooms, and then he stopped, pressed me into the wall. All was quiet except for our breathing. I was caught in his stare. It was pure heat, but something more as well. Something I'd never seen before.

"Listen to me, Destiny. Listen and hear me. I'll follow you to the pits of what Earthlings call hell. I'll fuck you at your command. I'll bend for you in any way I can to make you happy, mate, but you will not mistake that for weakness."

I'd never heard him speak like this before, never felt the laser sharp focus of his attention out of bed. Weakness? Never. Nix was the strongest man I knew. "I—"

"You what?" he countered. "You'll use my cock to ease your Ardor and toss me aside like garbage? You'll ignore my desire to protect you and run headlong into battle? You'll deny yourself my help because you are afraid to allow me to stand beside you? Do you not trust me? Do you not understand what you are to me?"

I blinked, licked my lips. Nix in bed was hot enough to make me lose my mind. But like this? My heart was aching, pain slicing through my chest like he was stabbing me with a knife, and I had no idea what to say. "You said I was your mate, Nix. But it wasn't you talking. Not really. It was just your cock. Your body. We are great in bed, but as far as I can tell, you don't like me very much. Everything I do makes you angry."

He leaned his forearms on the wall on either side of my head so we were close. So close I felt his breath on my face. Felt the heat from his body seep into mine. "Only because you insist on doing it alone. And my cock didn't say we were mates. The goddess did. I awakened only for you. Do you think all my life I envisioned a mate who was headstrong and stubborn and willful and disobedient?"

I took a deep breath, narrowed my eyes. "Exactly my point. If you don't want me, that's fine. Just go. Go home, wherever the hell that is. Forget about me. I'm sure the consort is around. He can finish me off and you'll be free."

I didn't want him to go, but I wasn't going to be with a guy who didn't like me just the way I was. He could just go back to being a queen's guard, and he wouldn't have to deal with someone so willful and stubborn. Oh, and headstrong too. I *was* disobedient.

"Free?" He leaned in, pressed his forehead to mine. We shared breath. His heart was pounding. Hard. Like he was running a race, or fucking me raw. "Save me, mate. Don't you understand?"

I pursed my lips. "Obviously, I don't."

He closed his eyes. Breathed. When he looked at me again, I sucked in a breath. I'd never seen him like this, not even when he was deep inside me and at the brink of a climax. "I am free. I am home. With you. Wherever the hell that is. Palace or cleric rooms at the fortress. Mytikas or Earth. *You* are where I belong. I am in love with you, Destiny."

Wow, that had all the feels and that dagger in my heart twisted. Pain flooded my body and tears gathered. I couldn't breathe. Was he trying to kill me? Did he mean it? Truly? "You don't even know me."

"Yes, I do. I want *you.* Your sharp brain, your brilliant brawn, your gorgeous body. I love the way you challenge me and everyone else. I respect you for your power and your strength. Everything about you makes your surrender in my arms all the sweeter. I want you. Your heart. Your trust. Your mind. I want all of it. Yes, we've been fucking like zebcats to soothe your Ardor and I want to end it and soon. I want to be able to prove to you I'm not here just to fuck you senseless, although you won't hear me complain about that."

I cracked a smile. A real smile, with tears. This was torment of the sweetest kind. A pain I'd never felt bloomed in my chest. Love. But not the kind of love I shared with my sisters or my parents. That love was safe. Old. Well worn. No, this was raw and powerful and hurt like a bitch. And I didn't want it to stop. Ever.

"I want every stubborn, willful inch of you."

"Nix." I whispered his name and held his gaze. I didn't try to hide what I was feeling. I didn't know how. My smile grew wider and the tears slid silently down my cheeks as I saw the same agony in his gaze. The same pain. The same raw, vulnerable anguish.

He loved me. Holy shit. He really did.

Before I could even reach out and cup his cheek, he gripped my elbow and tugged me further down the hall to our rooms. "I'm not fucking you in a hallway. We're finishing this in a bed."

Kicking the door closed behind him, he crossed his arms over his chest and leaned back against it, watching me. We faced each other for long moments; neither of us said a word. This time was going to be different. This time was going to hurt in the most elemental of ways. Not physical pain, but raw emotion I'd never imagined.

After this, there would be no going back.

Was I okay with that? I closed my eyes and took my time, pulling air into my lungs, making sure it was me, and not the Ardor, answering that question. Nix. He'd given me everything. Every part of himself. He'd fought in the Hive wars, he killed. He protected. It was part of his DNA. Just like me, he was selfless. Honorable. Sexy. Intelligent. Possessive. Rough. Gentle. Honest. Fearless.

He was fucking perfect. Well, except for the caveman, overprotective, keep me in a bubble mode. But he'd learn.

Opening my eyes, I walked to him, lifted my hands to his cheeks and tilted his face down to mine. "Are you sure, Nix? Really sure? Because after this, I'm not going to be able to let you go."

He sighed then, as if he were a balloon that had deflated. The fight left him and all that was left was Nix. *My Nix.* "I'm yours, mate. I've always been yours. It just took you a while to figure it out."

He was right. I'd been the one holding back, not committing. Afraid to trust that his promises meant anything. But now I knew the truth. He *was* mine. Really mine. Forever. And that changed everything.

Lifting myself up on tiptoes, I kissed him. His hands came up to rest on my waist, but he didn't pull me closer or try to dominate the kiss. He let me have my way, and I wanted to be gentle with him, only now realizing how my rejection must have hurt him. How frustrated and annoyed he'd been. "I'm sorry I was so slow on the uptake, mate."

He groaned and closed his eyes. "Say that again."

I grinned and ran my hands up and down his chest, his magnificent, muscled, perfect chest. Too many clothes. He was wearing too many clothes. "You're mine, Nix. My mate. And I'm never letting you go."

He opened his eyes and looked down at me, held my gaze. "And that's not just the Ardor talking?"

Strangely, the Ardor was on a low simmer, as if it had a mind of its own and knew what was coming, content to wait for this moment to be just right. I shook my head. "It's not the Ardor. It's me. I'm falling in love with you, Nix."

I'd never said those words before. Never loved someone like I loved him.

"Thank the gods, because you were killing me, female." He swung me up into his arms like I was a new bride and carried me to the bed with a huge smile on his face. A happy smile. A smile I'd never seen before and would do almost anything to see again and again.

I wrapped my arms around his neck as he settled me gently on the bed and pulled him down for a kiss. "Maybe I can make it up to you."

He waggled his eyebrows and it made me smile.

"Whatever you need, mate. I will provide."

"So selfless," I replied.

He grinned at my teasing and pulled my uniform tunic up over my head. "Of course I am. I am the most magnificent male on all of Alera."

I watched, biting my lower lip as he pulled his own tunic from his magnificent body and lowered himself over me, his weight on his elbows so I could breathe. I kissed him. Again. "Yes, you are."

His mouth settled over mine, our tongues tangling, our bodies pressed together, chest to chest, skin on skin. Soft kisses. Slow kisses. *I-love-you* kisses. I could have stayed there, pinned beneath him, his mouth on mine for hours. Days.

This was what my Ardor craved. Slow. Gentle. For the first time, we weren't ravaging each other. We weren't frantic or even desperate.

But his cock grew hard, pressed between my hips and my Ardor rose to meet him. Not wild this time. There, but not boiling over, as if even my body had been tamed, gentled by Nix and his feelings for me. Or mine for him. As if since my mind had finally accepted him, my body did, too.

My heart still ached, but the dagger-like pain was gone. Now the hurt filled me with power. With hunger and the need to make this man happy. No one else mattered. Only him. And me. And this heat flaring between us.

"I need you, Nix."

He kissed me with a soft groan, lowering his mouth to my neck. Working his way lower, he took a slow exploratory path across my heated skin to my breasts. He sucked my hard nipple into his mouth, then the other, giving them due attention, as if he had all the time in the world. When I was gasping and writhing beneath him, he smiled and went lower still, kissing my stomach before lifting his head to pull off my boots. The rest of my clothes.

He tried to slide back over me, his pants still on, but no way I was allowing him to get away with that. I wanted skin on skin.

I needed *him*. I put up one foot and placed it square on his chest, but I didn't kick. Just held him back. His eyes met mine. "You are not getting back into this bed until you are naked, mate."

He chuckled, but undressed quickly. "As you wish."

When he came back to me, I spread my knees wide, making room for him. Inviting him in. "Hurry."

His gaze was fixed between my thighs. I'd been bold, but he made me confident in my body, in my sexuality. There was no shame or embarrassment between us. Perhaps that was why we were mates.

"Not this time." He was on me before I could protest, his tongue working my clit as I arched off the bed. He lifted my bottom with one hand and pressed two fingers deep with the other, zeroing in on my G-spot with ruthless precision. My Ardor screamed through my bloodstream like a tsunami of boiling liquid in my veins and I came. Hard. My fingers tugging at his hair as I twisted and tilted my hips, trying to take him deeper. Harder. It felt so good. Exquisite. Bliss.

"More."

I felt his smile in his cheeks as he kissed the inside of my thighs. He moved up my body with kisses, in no particular hurry, and I felt like I was being worshipped. Learned. Not possessed, treasured.

When he reached my lips, I kissed him with tears streaking along my temples and down into my hair. He was killing me slowly, twisting my soul into an aching, needy thing. And I didn't care.

He slid deep, taking me with one slow thrust of his hips and I wrapped my legs around him, locked my ankles around his back. I never wanted this to end.

His body fed me, the Ardor taking energy from him like it had dozens of times before, but this time was different. Slow. Gentle. If energy could be soft, like a warm blanket spreading through my body, this was it. Nix would be part of me forever and the thought made my pussy clamp down in hunger as another orgasm rocked through me.

We kissed. Nix rocked his hips, not pounding into my body as he had in the past, but stroking me. Loving me, now that I had finally let him. It was bliss, his fingers entwined with mine, our mouths connected, chest to chest. Slow. Deep.

He pulled his lips from mine and I felt his cock swell, knew he would come inside me. Fill me with his essence and his seed. And I wanted everything, everything he would give me.

His cock jerked as he filled me, his lips next to my ear, my name like a prayer on his lips. A harsh growl that said... mine.

God help me, I'd never felt anything so intense in my life. I exploded, crying out for him as I came, wrapping every part of me around every part of him. I didn't want to be Destiny, I wanted to be us. Whole.

"I love you, mate." His words caused a flutter of aftershocks, and my Ardor made one final plea for him. Of course, his body responded, filling me with heat. Energy. Power. He made me stronger. He saved me, not just my life, but in every way.

"I love you, Nix. Never leave me. Promise me." I shouldn't have begged, but I did, the insecure part of me refusing to die without a fight. I was too impulsive, too aggressive, not feminine enough. I'd heard it all before. And even though my heart ached with the need to trust him, there was still a part of me that couldn't quite believe this was real.

"Never, Destiny. You're mine. My mate. I will always be at your side." He kissed the wet remnants of my tears from my temple. "I give you my oath, on my honor. I will never leave you."

God, it felt good to hear that. Lying on top of me, I held him as my Ardor fed and then was quenched, the storm easing until there was nothing left. All at once, it stilled. My body was quiet, sated. Complete. Calm. The Ardor was over.

And I didn't want Nix any less.

Nix must have sensed the change, for he pulled his cock

free and rolled us both, tugging me into his arms. His heartbeat was a steady drum beneath my cheek and I was happier and more content than I'd ever been in my life. "I love you."

He kissed the top of my head and pulled the blanket up to cover us. "Sleep, mate. You can fight tomorrow."

I pulled his arms tight around me and nuzzled in as close as I could get. He was mine. Really and truly mine.

The Ardor was over, and I had never been so exhausted in my life. It was as if all the energy had been sapped from me. The Ardor had used it all up and I had to recharge. When my eyelids grew heavy, I trusted my mate to keep me safe and finally... finally let go.

4

N *ix*

I HEARD heavy footfalls outside the door, the murmur of deep voices. My comms unit beeped quietly from my clothes across the room. When I ignored it, a quiet knock sounded on the door. I knew it was Captain Turaya. Perhaps Trinity or Leo had sent him. Had there been a change in plans? New intelligence that would require my mate's input or mine?

We were locked in a life and death struggle for control of this planet. My home. And though Destiny's blood was half human, she belonged here. With me. With the people of Alera. She and her sisters gave the planet stability and hope for a better future. The past three decades of war and political upheaval would come to an end. Either the queen would be found, or she would not. But Trinity was here. Faith. Destiny.

My mate was important to the people. But to no one more so than to me. She was my world now, and I would die or kill to protect her. Without thought or regret.

Mine.

Looking down, I stared at the top of her head. She was sprawled on top of me, her cheek pressing into my chest, one of her legs thrown over mine. A mate blanket.

A sleeping mate. This was a rest of someone finally rid of their Ardor, her body exhausted and recovering, using the energy I had provided to grow strong again. The knowledge that it was my touch that healed her, my seed and my life force making her strong, filled me with a satisfaction so intense I nearly choked on it. I stroked her silky hair, and she murmured something unintelligible, nuzzling me with her lips, kissing my chest—even in her sleep. I marveled at the color of the strands as they slipped through my fingers. A deep purple, as bold as she was.

Another knock, a bit louder this time. Damn it all.

I glanced down at my mate. She hadn't moved at the sound. She was out and it didn't appear that she would wake any time soon. I didn't want to leave the bed, for it was quiet, she was also *quiet,* and I marveled at the feel of her in my arms.

"One minute," I answered so that whoever was on the other side of our door would hear me. Destiny rolled over in protest when I pulled away, one eye peeking up at me.

"Where are you going?"

"Go back to sleep. Someone's at the door."

"Tell them to go away and get back in bed."

I grinned. That was my demanding little mate. "Yes, Princess."

She snuggled back under the covers and closed her eyes, asleep in seconds. I stared, amazed that this female was really mine. It seemed impossible. A miracle. A blessing from the goddess I would do anything to protect.

I knew my mate wasn't safe. Even now, someone plotted to murder her and her sisters. The loss of any member of her family would cause Destiny great pain and could not be allowed.

This secret meeting we'd spoken of was no accident. The

hidden mastermind behind nearly thirty years of Aleran suffering was growing desperate, willing to risk everything in one final play. I sensed we were close to the end, that the Queen would soon be found, the traitor revealed. Until that happened, we would not truly be free to live out the rest of our lives together.

Even as I worried about my mate, I could not bring myself to regret the circumstances that had brought us here. Had Queen Celene never been attacked so long ago, she would not have fled to Earth, met a new male, given birth to my mate. Had she not been kidnapped, my mate may have lived her entire life on another planet. My miracle lost, forever beyond my reach.

I hated to hold gratitude to the traitors behind this mess, but in an odd twist of fate, had they not attacked Celene and killed the king that night, my life would have been empty. Destiny not part of me.

She was now free of the throes of her body, the dangerous Ardor finally complete. I was fully awakened. I'd lost track of how many times we'd fucked over the last few days, but while my cock still rose for her—as it did now just thinking of being inside her again—it wasn't an intense, all-consuming need. And still, there would be no going back. For either of us.

Her Ardor had triggered something in me, something just as wild and edgy. She needed and I provided. That was what my body demanded. No other male would touch her. Kiss her. Fuck her. Give her his essence or his seed.

Truth be told, I was exhausted, my body completely drained in every way, sexually, mentally, physically. But I had never been so content. She was finally mine. She had spoken the words. Claimed me. Spoken of love. I'd seen the raw emotion in her eyes, tasted her tears. She was mine, and even as I lay in bed, every muscle languid and weak, I felt as if my insides were about to jump out of my skin.

Joy. This was joy. I'd never experienced this before, and I was heady with it. Smiling. I couldn't stop smiling.

All because of one spectacular, unique, incredible female.

I kissed the top of her head and made sure she was covered with the blanket. She didn't even stir, her hair fanned out across the pillow and one bare shoulder peeked out from the covers.

Tugging on my clothes, I watched her sleep, reveled in the fact that she was finally at peace, that her body no longer ruled her. I refused to awaken her for another session of arguing and analysis. There were enough people working on finding her mother and ending this mess that she could continue her rest. She'd earned it.

Opening the door to our suite, I looked up and saw the captain, Leo and Thor ten feet down the corridor, talking quietly. They looked my way when I stepped out and I shut the door carefully behind me.

Leo's face was filled with an odd expression. Resignation? Regret? "I apologize, Nix. I know you didn't want to be disturbed, but this couldn't wait."

I joined them. "What has happened?"

It had only been a few hours since Destiny had stormed from the meeting room with a brash snap of her fingers. Oh yeah, that had been a challenge I could not ignore. She might own me, body and soul, but I was not a male to be dominated.

"Cleric Amandine has sent another note." Captain Turaya held an envelope identical to the one Destiny had opened earlier when we'd all been together. "The meeting has been moved up. It happens tonight, not tomorrow."

"The triad is already in Mytikas?" I asked, tempering my voice low to ensure Destiny rested. She needed to recharge. Becoming upset or agitated because of this latest information wasn't what she needed. I needed her restored, energized and ready for what was to come.

"Yes," he replied. "I have men watching them now, following their movements, although it has been a surprisingly simple task. They went directly to the cleric building down-town and have yet to exit."

I looked to Leo. "Do the princesses know?"

Both Leo and Thor shook their heads. Leo spoke. "My father collected this from the messenger, and I read it first. We wanted to discuss this with you, before we informed our mates."

I had no idea what they'd been up to since we'd left the meeting, but since we were standing in a back hallway and not conversing across a meeting table, they seemed to have some ideas on the next steps. "You don't intend to tell them, do you?"

Leo and Thor shook their heads. "No fucking way," Leo said. "We can have this over and done. Every single one of our mates has a giant target on her back. I want Trinity safe and sound, surrounded by as many guards as I can spare."

I looked to Thor who crossed his arms over his chest. "And you?"

His slight smile made it appear he was in pain. "Faith is soft-hearted. She has this magical ability to fight like nothing I've ever seen, but she hates to hurt anyone. And they've already tried to kill her. My parents are dead because of these traitors. I don't want her anywhere near this bloodbath."

I couldn't help but grin. I'd seen Princess Faith in action. She fought better than some of our most experienced, most skilled warriors. But he was right. The idea of the kind female being within three miles, let alone three feet, of a murderer did not sit well with me. And I wasn't her mate. Thor looked barely contained in his feelings about this. And if anything happened to Destiny's twin, my mate would be beside herself.

It appeared these males were as serious about protecting their mates as I was. I nodded in approval. "Agreed. We take care of this ourselves. They will be angry, but I'd rather have my mate furious with me than in danger."

"Trinity is the problem. If she finds out, she'll order us to include them and we won't be able to say no," Leo said.

"Destiny is sleeping off the Ardor."

"Is it done then?" Captain Turaya asked.

I nodded. "Yes."

He slapped me on the shoulder. "Well done, son. I'm surprised you're still standing."

I chuckled, remembering just how exhausted I'd felt before hearing this news. Now adrenaline and action pulsed through me. These males and I would end this. Leo was from the Shadow unit, a skilled hunter and warrior. Captain Turaya was solid. Deadly. And Thor? I had not thought much of him before his mating to Faith, but he was deceptively dangerous, and had obviously received training at the hands of his mother, who had spent years in law enforcement within the Optimus Unit.

We were a force to be reckoned with, and with our mates in danger?

"No mercy." I said the words as much as a vow to myself as an order to the others. I needn't have worried. Both men agreed at once.

Captain Turaya shook his head and grinned. "Are you sure about this?" He looked at each of us in turn, like a father scolding his young sons. "Your mates are not docile females. Earth has shaped them to be... different. *More.* They will not be happy that you have decided to exclude them."

"I'll take my chances," Leo said.

Thor smiled. "A few hours in bed and Faith will forgive me anything."

The captain looked at me, all laughter fading from his gaze. "Your mate is not like the others, Nix. Are you sure you want to do this?"

I gave him a decisive nod. "Yes. She won't allow me to protect her. And so, I will protect her without permission."

"You are all either very brave, or complete fools. The wrath of your females will be severe. I hope you've fucked enough for this lifetime. I doubt your cocks will see relief again."

I didn't like the idea of Destiny turning away from me, but if she was alive to do so, I was willing to pay the price. "She is my life. I will protect her at all costs."

"Very well." The captain shrugged and tucked the note into the pocket of his tunic. "I will meet you in the armory in thirty minutes."

Thirty minutes I would spend holding my mate and praying she could forgive me.

5

D estiny

SHE WON'T ALLOW me to protect her. And so, I will protect her without permission.

Oh. My. God. I felt like one of those mothers accused of having eyes in the back of her head, her kids not understanding how she knew they'd snuck into the cookie jar while she was in the other room.

Oh, I doubted anyone else on the planet, hell, the universe, had bat hearing like I did. But I understood the true nature of the gift now. The men outside the room were talking quietly so they wouldn't disturb my sleep. Ha!

I could hear the cook in the kitchen tell someone that the stove was set too high and the pastry was going to burn. I could hear one of the maids in a far bedroom complaining to herself about a sheet she'd discovered had a hole in it. I could hear *everything.*

Four guys huddled just a few feet away in the hallway trying to keep secrets? Easy pickings.

But Nix's words weren't just idle chatter. No. He actually intended to leave me in bed completely unaware of their plans to confront the traitors at that meeting. Perhaps even to get my mother back. After what we'd just done, how we'd just been... it hurt. A whole hell of a lot.

A cold, burning fury rolled through my blood. This rage was different, not like earlier when my Ardor made me into a berserker. No, this was distinctive. A woman who needed to teach her man a lesson about what would and would not be tolerated. This betrayal went deeper, as if his words and his intended actions were arrows he'd slung purposely to hit their mark.

My heart.

He'd claimed he wanted all of me. The fighter. The protective instincts. He'd *said* he'd never leave me. Well, that lasted all of an hour or two. Now he was standing just outside the door making plans to do exactly that. Finding my mother was not a game. This was not a chess match. This was *my* life. *My* family. I was a royal fucking princess, and he intended to protect me *without permission?* There were exactly three people on this planet I had to answer to—my mother and my older sisters—and he was not one of them.

I had chosen him. Trusted him. I would have asked his opinion and consulted with him as an equal out of respect. I would have included him because I didn't want to hurt him, because I valued his strengths and his knowledge. Because I valued *him.*

That he did not intend to extend me the same courtesy stung, and my eyes filled with tears once more. This time they burned like acid on my cheeks. And so I was, after all, a bed mate and nothing more. He did not want *me* as I was. No. He wanted to hold me back. Change me. Force me to occupy the mold he'd formed for me in his mind.

Damn it to hell. I loved him, which made this hurt ten times worse.

And my sisters? What would they think of these males making choices for them? They didn't have bionic hearing, but they had plenty of girl power. And fury. When they heard what their own men intended... the shit was going to hit the fan.

There was no way I was letting those arrogant cavemen get away with duping my sisters. They were going to go after my mother and lie to us about it. *For our own good*, like we were three years old. This was our mission. Mom had been preparing us to rule Alera since we were born, playing to each of our strengths – Trinity's analytical mind, Faith's compassion, and my protective instincts. She had believed in us from the day we were born, and so we'd always believed in ourselves.

That the men we loved did not was a hurt none of us would easily get over. Yes, my mother's enemies—our enemies—were dangerous, but I'd survived a whole lot of danger since I'd transported to Alera. We all had. And we were even stronger now.

I sat up in bed, propped my elbows on my knees. I felt better. So much better. No fever, no simmering need. I felt like me again. A pissed off me.

Men. What was the saying? *Can't live with them, can't live without them.*

Whatever. Now that my Ardor was over, I could live without Nix if this was how he was going to be. What would he be like later on when something else came up? A bully at school with one of our kids? Okay, so that was pushing it a little far, because we weren't going to have any kids. Not after what I'd just heard. Captain Turaya had been right. Nix was cut off.

My entire being protested the thought. Could I do it? Be near him and not want him? No. I already knew the answer. Knowing Thor was right about that—that I'd probably forgive Nix just about anything if he could get me back in bed—made my rage percolate a bit faster, not with anger at Nix, but at myself. I was stronger than that.

Wasn't I?

Nix planning, even thinking, that I was not going to participate in the plans to raid the meeting tonight, was beyond ridiculous. Ludicrous. And insult to every cell in my body.

I was going. I was finding Mom and then beating the shit out of whoever it was screwing with all of us. I was going to destroy them slowly and with a whole lot of glee. Nix was not going to deny me a reckoning with the people who were trying to destroy my family.

I thought for a few moments as he finished his conversation and an idea formed in my mind. I smiled, mentally preparing myself for the attack of total hotness when he returned. He wanted a biddable, meek mate? He'd get one.

I listened as the other men walked away. I didn't care where they were headed, only that Nix was coming back in the room. When he saw me sitting up, he smiled.

"I'm surprised you're awake," he murmured, coming to sit beside me on the bed. He leaned in and kissed me gently, sweetly, as if he hadn't just been plotting against me.

Two could play that game.

I ran my lips over his, soft and sweet. I felt anything but.

The traitor. He was a mate traitor. We were a team, or so I'd thought. He wanted to be sly and devious? He wanted to leave me out? Fine.

Game on.

"I missed you," I replied. I had, actually. It was why I'd woken up to begin with.

He stroked my hair back from my face. I was sure it was a total wreck, but I didn't care. I wasn't all that much for vanity anyway.

"I know we just... well, fucked a few days away, but I still want you."

He frowned, studied my face. "I thought the Ardor was gone."

I gave a slight shrug and the sheet fell a little bit. With my knees tucked up in front of me, he couldn't see all that much, but I couldn't miss the way his eyes heated.

"It is. I can think clearly now." *Very* clearly. "You've always been the one to dominate, if you know what I mean." I glanced up at him through my lashes, gave him a little smile.

He grinned in return.

"I thought maybe I'd have my way with *you* this time." I slid a finger down his cheek.

"Oh?"

I nodded. "Can I be on top?"

He glanced at the door, even though it was closed, and I could hear no one was there. I knew he was thinking about how much time he had, that he'd promised to meet the others in the armory in a half an hour.

We'd never had a bout of fucking last that long. We'd gone at it one time after another for hours, but I'd been so feverish they'd all been quickies.

He stood, opened his pants, tugged out his glorious cock. "I'm all yours."

I shook my head. "Naked, mate," I replied. I shifted and swung my feet over the bed, the sheet falling away entirely. He took in my nude body for a second, then tugged off his clothes.

I grinned, glad an Aleran male was like all others. None could say no to sex. Ever.

Tilting my head, he moved around the far side and dropped onto the bed, his head on the pillow. I turned, crawled up and straddled him. I intentionally settled onto his length so he parted my slick folds, then rolled my hips.

His hands came to my hips.

"Ah ah," I said, scolding him. "I'm in charge, remember?"

He lowered his hands to the bed, made tight fists.

Leaning forward, I lowered myself so my breast was right over his mouth. He sucked at the hard tip and I gasped. I might be mad at him, but that didn't mean I didn't love what he did to me. He knew exactly how to make me hot.

But I knew how to make him hot, too, because his hands were right back on me again.

I sat up, took his wrists and raised them over his head. He wasn't paying much attention because my breasts were right in front of his face again.

"Hold here," I said. His fingers curled around the slats of the headboard as he continued to suckle and lave at one nipple, then the other.

I rocked my hips again.

"Mate," he growled. "Put me in you."

I shook my head. "Not yet."

During all the time we'd gone at it, I had yet to give him a blow job, both of us being too busy getting his cock in my pussy instead of my mouth. I slowly kissed my way down his lean, hard torso.

I felt his cock bob against my belly, and I looked up at him. His hands went to my hair, pushed me lower. If I hadn't given him oral sex, that meant he'd never done it before, but he knew my intentions.

He didn't, actually. If he did, he wouldn't be so relaxed.

I took his wrists in my grip. Sat up. "You're being bad." I climbed off him, grabbed the utility belt from his uniform, found his wrist restraints. They dangled from my finger as I smiled at him. "It's my turn to play."

His eyes widened, but his cock bobbed, pre-cum seeping from the tip.

"You want to restrain me?" he asked, his voice dark.

I nodded. "I want to torture you. Make you beg."

He growled, lifted his hands over his head voluntarily.

I moved so I could work one cuff onto his wrist, then through the headboard slats, then to the other wrist, taunting him with my breasts some more. He definitely was a boob man.

I checked they were secure and that he wasn't coming loose, but that it wasn't too tight.

Straddling him again, I kissed him. "Ready for the torture?"

His eyes darkened. "You want me to beg?"

I shrugged, kissed down his body again, hovered just over the crown of his cock.

"Mate," he groaned, looking down his body at me. My hair was a curtain that fell over his thighs, his cock, his balls. Yeah, torture.

I kissed the tip, tasted his salty essence.

"Destiny," he cried, his body going taut, the restraints clanging against the headboard. I kissed down his length and kept on going, sliding off the bed and standing at the end.

"Mate?" he asked, eyeing me. He looked gorgeous, naked and virile. Potent and so mine. He trusted me enough to allow me to restrain him, control him.

Yeah, well, I'd trusted him, too.

"The torture begins now, *mate*. That meeting you're going to without me?"

His eyes widened, all at once realizing I'd somehow heard.

"Yeah, well, looks like you're not going at all."

I grabbed my clothes off the floor as he protested.

"Destiny. Mate. It's for your own protection. I won't see you hurt. Let me go. This is not funny. Be reasonable. You'll get hurt. They want you dead. Destiny!" He shouted the last as I shoved my foot into my boot and moved toward the door, fully dressed. I'd even grabbed his utility belt, fully loaded with weapons, and put it about my waist. He wouldn't need the ion pistol or anything else while naked and tied to my bed.

I spun about, gave him once last glance. The look on his face was murderous. Oh, he hated having the tables turned on him. Every line in his body was taut. Furious.

Served him right.

I pouted my lips and gave him the best version of puppy-dog eyes I'd ever thrown down on anyone, accentuating carefully chosen words to make sure he got my message loud and clear. "Don't worry, Nix, you'll be nice and *safe* in my bed. I wouldn't want anything to happen to you. Since you're my mate, you're my responsibility, and I know how *frightened* and *weak* you really are. So, I'm just going to have to protect you —*without permission*. It's for your own good. You might be mad *now*, but you'll *forgive me anything* after a *few hours in bed*. Isn't that right? Now you'll be as *I* want you, safe and naked and waiting for me to return from the *big, scary, dangerous meeting*."

Shoving the final blade in its sheath, I walked out the door, closing and locking it behind me with a very decisive click. I was mad and also very sad. We might have said we were mates, that we loved each other, but this... him intending to leave me behind, me restraining him to the bed, this wasn't love. This was manipulation. Lies. A power struggle.

A struggle I refused to fight. He either accepted me or he didn't. The end. I was not weak. Or foolish. And I didn't need his approval or permission to fight for what I believed in, or for whom I loved. He'd learn that soon enough. Starting now.

And if he didn't? Well, I was royal. I'd have his ass shipped to a continent—hell, even another planet—so far away I'd never have to look at him and hurt again.

"Destiny!" he shouted, although with my bat hearing I could hear him so loudly his bellow hurt my ears, making me wince.

I took a deep breath, sucked it up. It was time to go get my sisters and end this.

※

Nix

I LAY THERE, stunned and with a cock as hard as it had ever been.

Holy shit. She'd seduced me. I glanced down my naked body at my cock. Purple, dripping pre-cum. Aching. I could still feel the swirl of her tongue, the hot, wet suck of her mouth.

Tugging at the restraints, I knew I was caught. I wasn't getting out of them unless I somehow broke the headboard. I wasn't that strong, not since it was made with the strongest Aleran metal. Nothing but the best for the palace.

Fuck!

How the fuck had she overheard our conversation? We'd been down the hall and talking quietly. Had she gone to the door and eavesdropped? Even then, she couldn't have heard everything we'd said. But she had.

My mate had even repeated what I'd said to the others word. For word. For word.

Oh, she was angry. So furious she'd actually turned sweet. Sweet and sexy and alluring and had gotten me thinking with my cock.

She was good. Very good at seduction. Or I was weak when it came to my mate. My cock pulsed because I was even hungrier for her than before. My mate couldn't just take care of herself, she'd taken care of me, too. Stubborn. Beautiful. Willful...

I was going to get her beneath me in this bed, tie her down and make her promise never to do this again. Not that I didn't deserve the lesson. I'd spoken exactly the words she'd accused me of. Protecting her without asking permission. Lying and deceiving her. My mate.

Shame pulsed through me right next to the desire. I'd failed her on an elemental level. Would she forgive me? Would I be able to forgive myself? If she were injured because I was not beside her, I would never recover. Yet, she was out there, alone, because I had made my decision without considering her needs, or her strength.

She was not a princess as I'd always thought of one, soft, pampered and docile, a female to be sheltered, an innocent beauty to be protected at all costs. No, Destiny was a warrior. I'd filled her with my cock and my seed, reveled in her trust and her surrender. And I'd betrayed her at the first opportunity.

And now she was going to get herself killed. Because I'd failed her.

I tugged again, but there was no give. I had to lay here and wait.

And wait—regret pounding through my veins with every painful beat of my heart.

It took seventy-two minutes—I had nothing to do but watch the clock—for Thor and Leo to burst through the door. They stopped just a few feet inside the room and stood there. Stared.

Thor grinned. "Oh, this is perfect."

I frowned, tugged at the restraints. "Let me up so I can get to my mate."

Leo remained where he was, hands on his hips, but I couldn't miss the smile on his face. He was enjoying this, but not as much as Thor.

"Your mate is fine." He raised a brow, crossed his arms and laughed. "I thought Faith was vengeful, leaving me covered with just a small towel. But Destiny didn't bother to cover you at all."

"Stop talking and release me. I know where she's going. She's going to get herself killed."

"She's fine. They are, all three of our mates, well-protected," Leo said.

"You can't know that, let me up."

Thor moved closer, raked his gaze down my body. Oh, it was a clinical look, not something I'd seen on Destiny's face. I wasn't modest, not at all, but I didn't need Thor and Leo to see my hard cock. As he inspected the bindings on my wrists, he actually laughed. "Oh, she's good. Remind me not to get on Princess Destiny's bad side."

Fuck.

"I'm going to have to cut these off." He looked at Leo. "Do you have a blade?"

Leo tossed a dagger to Thor, who caught it in midair as if the motion were as natural to him as breathing. A businessman? Right. I'd have to investigate my new brother a bit more thoroughly in future. "Hold still. Destiny will have my hide if I cut you."

"Hurry up. I have to get to her."

Leo crossed his arms and leaned his hip against the tall bed as Thor just looked at my restraints. "They're with my father and the queen's guard. They're ahead of us by an hour, but they're well-protected."

"How did they get you?" I asked. Thor made no move to release me from the restraints and I wasn't too eager to beg. That was how I'd gotten in this mess in the first place with Destiny.

"Our mates stunned us with ion blasters and locked us in the armory," Leo said.

I grunted a response. It was amusing, but I was still naked and cuffed to the bed.

"But you," Thor began, spinning the blade in his palm, in no apparent hurry to set me free.

"Stop playing games, Thor."

He grinned at me, the fucker. "I think I should take a few moments to appreciate the irony. Payback's a bitch, isn't it?"

I frowned, then remembered. He'd been stunned at his family's mountain retreat and brought to the palace. *Under my command*—and the princess's bidding—he'd been stripped naked and restrained to Faith's bed. I'd watched them tie him up and I'd walked out the door.

He'd been there for hours. I hadn't thought much of it, once we'd left him there. He had been Faith's to punish and not my concern. Only now did I fully appreciate the torment he must have suffered. "My apologies, Thor. I was only following orders."

Leo chuckled. "Trinity did leave orders to set you free." He glanced at Thor, who shrugged.

"Did she give a time frame for the deed?" Thor asked.

"No, I don't believe she did." Leo was not helping my mood to improve.

Yeah, payback was a bitch. "Fine, you've both made your point. But it's your fault I'm here to begin with. You were the fools who decided to keep the truth from our mates in the first place."

"You agreed freely," Thor said.

I sighed. I had. Damn me straight to eternal hell. "I did. I never said I wasn't a complete idiot when it comes to my mate. Now will you let me up?"

Thor grinned. "No begging?"

I narrowed my eyes, hoping he'd notice I wasn't amused.

He sighed. "Fine. Fine." He had me free quickly, then reached down, grabbed my clothes and tossed them at me.

"Time to go get our mates," he said, heading for the door, Leo on his heels.

I tugged on my shirt. That's right. Time to get Destiny, keep her safe, then... fuck, I had no idea what. I probably would need to grovel. A lot.

I'd said I would not beg, but even that was a lie. For Destiny, I would do anything.

6

D *estiny*

THERE MUST HAVE BEEN something about midnight on this planet, because here I was again, sneaking around in the dead of night. Not alone this time, but with my sisters, at least thirty guards, and Captain Turaya hovering over Trinity like she was a piece of glass about to topple from a high shelf, and he needed to be ready to catch her.

My sister was tougher than that, and after our conversation earlier, when we'd all decided to teach our overprotective, bossy, alpha men a lesson, I knew she needed to be here. I'd left Nix shouting and swearing in our bed and had sent a comm to Faith and Trinity to have a secret girl meeting.

I got them up to speed. Fast. They'd been pissed as well, for their mates were just as bad as Nix. Although, they hadn't had to tie up either Leo or Thor. They'd only had to lie and say we were doing girl stuff and talking about periods and other female things.

Worked like a charm every time.

While we were pissed, but we weren't stupid. We'd gone directly to Leo's dad, gave him a good tongue lashing, and Trinity had ordered him to be ready for us to go to the secret meeting, without our mates. Trinity and Faith had grabbed ion pistols, set them to stun and headed off to visit their stubborn males where they awaited Captain Turaya in the armory.

Captain Turaya had looked at me in silence as we waited, but I'd just raised my eyebrow and kept my mouth shut. He obviously knew I'd done something to Nix, since my mate was nowhere to be seen, but the captain didn't ask.

Smart man.

Trinity and Faith had returned, both of their mates stunned and left to contemplate their sins frozen and immobile for about an hour, and we'd gone off with at least thirty queen's guard for protection and the captain for his expertise.

The guard would offer substantial protection, but my sisters and I had our own agenda. Trinity's citadel-given power was really quite handy. Turned out, she could see auras now.

Auras.

One look, and she knew if someone was good or evil, truthful or lying, sick or well.

Nice trick. And as she looked through the scope at the people entering the building where the meeting was to be held —per Elder Amandine's letter—the captain right next to her listing off names of every one, Faith was keeping the list. A large monitor of some kind was set up next to them. Captain Turaya aimed his scope, a mark appeared on his target, and Trinity stood beside him, looking at them through a scope of her own, calling off the status of each. I watched the monitor closely, trying to commit each face to memory. They would all die. Every single one of them. They'd betrayed my family, killed Trinity's father, tried to kill our mother and kidnapped Mom, dragging her from her own bed—screaming.

"Lord Vangar." The captain's voice was matter of fact. As was Trinity's answer.

"Evil."

Faith was scribbling names down as fast as she could. She sat closest to the door, saying that while I'd done years of martial arts, she was the new Kung Fu bad ass fighting princess and I just had to deal. The citadel had made her a skilled combatant in hand-to-hand fights. Which was pretty cool, considering she'd always hated my self-defense workouts.

I let her have her way, my blaster and knives loose in the holder I'd stolen from Nix. Faith had offered to make me a new one with the S-Gen machines when she made my black uniform, but I was feeling sentimental and stupid and I wanted a piece of Nix with me. Armed as I was, Faith wouldn't need to fight. Anyone came through that door, they'd be dead before they took their second step.

"Cleric Fergia."

"More evil."

"Optimus Officer Morson."

"Good. Don't kill him," Trinity ordered.

I looked up at that one. Good? "If this Morson is a good guy, what the hell is he doing here?" I asked, inspecting him on the screen. Long, blond hair. Gorgeous. But it seemed all of these damn Aleran males were too good-looking for their own good. Still, he would be easy to pick out in a crowd.

Faith shrugged and we both looked at the Captain. He didn't turn away from his scope.

"Don't know. Investigating a crime? Spying? Same as we are? That is the job of the Optimus Unit."

Oh, yeah. I'd forgotten about that, seeing how I was convinced they were holding my mother prisoner within the unit's walls, in the infamous Cell Level C. "They're like the Aleran FBI and judicial system all in one."

"Not sure that's the best arrangement," Trinity mused. I didn't much care. Not until we had Mom back.

But talking to my sisters earlier did make me feel better about one thing. My bat-like hearing. Knowing that I wasn't going crazy, that the citadel had made that change in my biology, set my mind at ease. It was a weapon. Without doubt. And a perk. It was my super-ears that allowed me to hear Nix's plans to betray me at his very first opportunity.

Oh, I wasn't really angry. Okay, I was, but it wasn't like he cheated on me with another woman or went around telling everyone I was a homicidal bitch. No, he just tried to coddle and protect me, treat me like a delicate piece of china. And I was not having it. This was my planet. My mother. My sisters. My mate. My future.

My war.

He could fight beside me, with my sisters, but not without me. And he obviously needed a little help getting that fact through his thick skull. Which was why he was tied to the bed —to think about the errors of his ways—and Trinity and Faith had stunned Leo and Thor and locked them inside the armory back at the palace. They left a guard with orders to set them free an hour after we left, if the stun had worn off by then. Which meant our three sexy mates would arrive any minute now. No doubt furious. Furious, but here. We could use them, and their expertise, but they'd needed to learn. We wouldn't be subdued. Or outmaneuvered.

The thought made me smile.

"Lady Tabitha."

"Wow, really evil."

Faith went back to scribbling and I checked the time. Again.

Served Nix, Thor and Leo right if they were livid, stubborn cavemen. All three of them. "Our mates should be here any minute."

Faith snorted. Trinity cursed. Captain Turaya chuckled with a bit too much glee. "I tried to warn them."

"I know you did, which is the only reason you're standing here next to us and not locked in the vault with your son." I'd overheard him argue on our behalf, tell our stubborn mates they were making a mistake. He'd been wrong about one thing, though. I was *not* going to torment myself with abstinence to punish Nix. Oh, no. I would fuck his brains out, take him hot and raw and dirty, and *then* he'd get the cold shoulder until he apologized. Over and over. Maybe on his knees.

Maybe with his mouth on my pussy. That idea sounded damn appealing right now.

Which was shocking, considering I'd just finished my Ardor.

I didn't smell like him anymore, and that was oddly disappointing.

"Jesus, I have it bad," I muttered to myself.

Faith snorted again, not looking up from her notepad. "We all do. They're fucking irresistible."

"Did you just drop an F-bomb, twin?" I asked.

"When it comes to our mates, I'm sure it won't be the last." Trinity's dry response made me laugh.

"Captain Yanlon."

"He's neutral. He's probably just playing the odds."

"Then he dies," I said.

"You are a bloodthirsty bitch, aren't you?" Faith asked.

"When it comes to someone hurting Mom, or trying to kill my sisters, then yes. I am."

"Agreed. He dies." Trinity's voice had gone cold, the voice of a queen authorizing execution. When it came to our family, none of us were feeling particularly forgiving. Thank god. I did not want to have to argue with my sisters. Stressing about my impending confrontation with Nix was already setting an entire hive of bees loose in my gut.

"I can't do anything from up here just watching. It's like watching the red carpet at the Oscars. I'm going in," I said.

"No! That wasn't the plan," Faith said.

True. But things had changed. "There weren't supposed to be any good guys in that meeting either. We need to know what they're saying. I can crouch outside a window, or on the roof, and hear every word."

"Seriously? Your hearing is that good?" Faith asked.

"This spot is too far away, but I'm a regular vampire now."

"Fine. Go but stay out of sight," Trinity said. "We'll comm you if there are any more good guys down there."

"Sounds good." I'd listen for her, but I had a feeling whoever this Morson guy was, he was flying solo. Suicidal, if you asked me. Which, obviously, not one male on this entire fucking planet would do. Neanderthals. All of them.

"Find out what you can," Trinity said. "I don't want to take down anyone who might be on our side."

"Agreed." I stood and rolled my shoulders to get the kinks out. I was wearing my usual night climbing gear, tight black pants, tight black shirt, black gloves, hat. Faith had been kind enough to do her S-Gen machine magic and make me what I'd wanted. I was a regular goth nightmare, complete with weapons stacked on top of weapons. I had enough knives on me to take out a football team. "I'm out. Tell your snipers not to shoot me, Captain."

"They can hear you through your comms unit. Just tell them where you're going."

"Got it." I left them behind and exited the residential building as quickly as possible. When I hit the street, I looked up at the darkened window six stories above me. I knew they were still there, watching. I whispered as I moved, telling the snipers where I was going. North wall. Up the tree. Onto the roof. I didn't get shot, so I figured that was good enough. I was also safely hidden, completely away from any danger. The captain had to agree if he let me go alone.

I made my way to the center and turned on my magical ears, zeroed in on the sound of talking. Movement. People.

Adjusting my position twenty feet to my right, I laid down flat on the roof and set my ear to the freezing cold shingles. They were odd, like clay, and I was shivering in a matter of seconds as the rooftop sucked all the warmth right out of me like cold cement would have.

"Mom needs to move the capital somewhere else. It's too fucking cold here." I was whispering that to my sisters, but I knew everyone on the channel would be able to hear me. I didn't care. It was the truth. I fucking hated the cold.

"Then you should not be out in it, mate." That ice-cold voice came from right next to me and I froze. Holy shit. I startled and bit my lip to stifle a scream.

"What are you, a ghost or something?" I hadn't heard my mate's approach. Not a whisper of breath. No scrape of his shoe on the roof. Nothing, and I had epic hearing. It was like he'd poofed into existence next to me.

He didn't answer, simply wrapped himself around me to warm me, careful not to break my contact with the roof. I melted into him. I had no problem accepting the heat he offered. No problem at all.

He remained silent, and as soon as my shivering stopped, I focused on the conversations I could hear coming up from below. The meeting hadn't started yet. There were multiple smaller groups talking about mundane things. Who had more money. Whose children were excelling. The weather.

Jesus. Really? It was freezing ass cold. End. Of. Discussion.

I rolled my eyes and lifted my ear from the roof, the side of my face feeling like a solid block of ice. "I need to get closer. I don't know whose voice is whose. I need to get inside." Morson was in there. And per Trinity's aura reading, he was one of the good ones. I needed to figure out what he was up to. Maybe help him if I could. Hell, maybe he knew something that could help us.

"No."

I turned in his arms and looked up at my gorgeous, sexy, stubborn mate. "You can come with me, or I can go in alone. Those are the options."

He didn't like my tone or my words. "It's too dangerous."

The sigh was real. "Fine." I pulled out of his arms and wiggled my way to the edge of the roof. "Snipers, if Nix tries to stop me, shoot him. Don't kill him, but shoot him."

"Destiny. Are you out of your fucking mind?" he hissed.

"What happened to *I want every stubborn, willful inch of you?* Huh? Were those just words? Or did you actually mean them?"

"You know I love you."

"Yes. And I love you." I crouched for the leap to the nearby tree. Jumped. Landed perfectly. We were on the opposite side of the building from all the arrivals, shrouded in darkness. No one would hear us, or see us, unless they were looking. "God I'm good."

"Destiny, no."

I stopped, looked at him over my shoulder where he was crouched by the edge of the roof, gave him one more chance. "Are you in, or are you out? I'll love you either way, but I'm not staying out of this fight."

"You're mine." It was a vow.

"That is not an answer, Nix," I said, confused.

"I'm in. I'm always in. But next time, you will be restrained to the bed."

I heard a muffled laugh through our comms units, but ignored it. "You're not leaving me behind."

"Oh, no. I'll be right there with you, I promise. The whole time I'm fucking you."

My smile was so big my face actually hurt. I was relieved. Thrilled even. A little kink would be fun. Later. "Good. Let's go." I jumped to the ground, landing in a crouch. Nix was on the ground next to me in seconds. Impressive.

I kissed him, hard and fast. I loved him more in this moment than I ever had before.

"You will look at me like that when you are riding my cock, mate."

"No problem."

"And you will not get yourself killed. Do you understand me?"

I didn't make promises I knew I couldn't keep. I knew better than that. So I kissed him again instead. "I need to get inside."

"That's what I said," he told me, running his knuckles down my cheek.

I rolled my eyes at him. "Let's go."

⋇

Nix

I COULD FEEL the eyes of at least two snipers on me, the hair on the back of my neck standing at alarm. I'd been hunted before, but never on the orders of a female I loved to distraction. My mate was going to be the death of me, but when she'd restrained me to the fucking bed, closed the door to our bedroom suite and walked away, I realized exactly how big of a mistake I'd made.

Huge.

I never wanted to see that look in her eyes again.

Disappointment. Resignation. Pain.

And I never wanted to have Thor find me like that ever again. Fuck, no.

Captain Turaya had tried to warn all three of us. He was older, mated for decades, and far wiser than we had been. I should have listened. Destiny was strong enough to walk away from me, and that scared me more than anything ever had. More than Hive Scouts. More than the Hive Integration units. More than being hunted by enemy assassins. More than death.

If I tried to control her, she would leave me behind. Which meant I would have to rearrange my thinking and fight my instincts every day for the rest of my life.

I leaped to the ground after her, amazed at her agility and

confidence. I'd never really seen her like this. The first night we'd met in the elder's office—the first night in the Jax-provided suite didn't count—I'd been too distracted by my newly awakened cock to appreciate exactly how light on her feet she'd been when she escaped me, or how quick and nimble she'd been climbing the vines to the old woman's office. She moved silently, her skill well-practiced. The knives lining her body testament to the threat she posed to her enemies.

When she jumped to the ground I realized this was it, that what happened between us this night would determine the course of the rest of my life.

And without her, it meant nothing.

I followed her around the building, both of us moving quickly through the shadows. When she reached a low-level window, she stopped and pressed her ear to the glass, just as she'd done on the roof.

Strange, but I would ask her about it later. Not now. Not when a hint of sound might get us both killed.

Whatever she heard appeared to satisfy her, for she opened the window and leaped up, pulling herself up as easily as any man. I followed quickly, knowing she would leave me behind without hesitation if I slowed her down.

Goddess, she really was magnificent on a hunt. And I had no doubts about what was going on, we were hunting. Together.

And I loved watching my mate move. I loved how deadly she was. I loved knowing she could fight her way out of here if we needed to. She was dangerous. A threat. A beautiful, sexy, passionate threat, and she was mine.

Pulling myself into the building, I landed on the floor next to her in a storage room of some kind. Shelves lined with boxes and supplies surrounded us. My eyes adjusted quickly, and I saw Destiny standing near the door. Listening.

The muffled sound of conversation came clearly through from the other side. A stream of light slipped just under the door itself, and I noticed Destiny was careful to keep the toes of her boots just out of sight. One hand was on the door, the other on a weapon. She was thorough, and ready for trouble, although I doubted anyone would get close to the door without her knowing.

I wanted to push her out of the way and listen myself. I wanted to open the door and peek outside, assess the situation. Decide on a course of action. But something about the way she moved held me in check. She wasn't just listening at the door, she was *listening*. Intent. She obviously had a plan.

My only plan was to protect her.

I'm in. I'm always in.

I had made my mate a promise just a few minutes ago, and I had no intention of breaking it now. When I found her freezing and miserable, alone on top of that roof, my heart had broken at my own stupidity. She was out there, alone, unprotected, because of me. I'd gotten exactly the opposite of what I'd wanted.

I needed to make her understand what she was to me. I wanted her to know I loved everything about her. I hadn't realized it until now, but it was the truth.

Unable to speak, I reached for her hand. When she turned to look at me with a question in her gaze, I kissed her. Really kissed her, with everything in me. Everything. Willing her to understand.

When I pulled back, she stared at me for long seconds, holding my gaze. Then she smiled. Nodded.

She understood. Thank the goddess. I never wanted to see her look at me with so much hurt in eyes again, not at my betrayal. And I had betrayed her. I realized that now. It took being secured naked—alone—to our bed to see it.

Never again.

She turned back to the door and I inspected the room, looking for anything useful. Exits. Weapons. I had plenty on my utility belt—a new one since she had mine—but it never hurt to be prepared.

There was neither. The window and the door were the only two ways in or out. And without opening the boxes, I had no idea what might be in them.

She pulled me down close, her lips pressed to my ear. She spoke so softly I barely heard her.

"There are twenty-two distinct voices. Six female. The nearest is about ten steps to the right of this door."

My eyes widened and I stared at her. *How the fuck did she know that?*

"Nix? Did you hear me?"

I nodded and squeezed her shoulder so she'd know I was listening.

"If anything goes wrong, we need to get Morson out. He's Optimus Unit, one of the good guys. The only one."

I squeezed her shoulder again. I knew who he was. How she knew what she was telling me, I had no idea. But I trusted her.

"Everyone else can fucking rot."

Awww, there was my female. I grinned, which made *her* squeeze *my* shoulder.

Then she froze.

"Do you hear that?"

I shook my head. What? What was she talking about? Just like that night in Elder Amandine's office. She'd said she'd heard something and I hadn't. And she'd been right.

"Oh, shit."

She pulled away from me and walked along the boxes, listening. Searching. Then she stopped and just stared at one in particular. "This one," she whispered as she pulled a box down off the shelf.

I saw the circuits and wiring a split-second before she could pull off the lid. Fuck, she'd kill everyone in the building!

Slamming my hand down on top of the box, I tore it from her arms and settled it back where it had been on the shelf. When she just looked at me, I pointed to the circuits and leaned in close. "It's a bomb." The timing circuit was clearly visible, counting down in a military style system of clicks I knew all too well.

She frowned. Stared at the odd dashes and lines on the display. "How long?"

I glanced at it again. "Five and a half minutes."

Her eyes widened slightly, but she remained calm. "Shit. There are twenty-two people who are going to be blown up. We have to get Morson out of here."

"Morson?" I whispered. Fuck Morson. He'd walked into this place, he could get himself out. There was a fucking bomb right in front of us. I had no idea if this was the only one or not. I needed to get my mate out of here.

Now.

She darted toward the door. I grabbed her by the elbow. When she turned back to look at me, I saw raw fury in her eyes.

"What?"

"Obviously, someone wants a lot of people dead."

"A bomb?" I heard a female voice clearly through my comms unit. Princess Trinity, most likely. Other voices came through as well, hearing our conversation. "Get out of there!"

If Destiny could hear a pin drop in the other room, then she could hear her sister's command, yet she paid her no attention.

"Mate, someone's been killing people off one at a time. Crayden was the latest."

I saw a shiver run through her, most likely as she envisioned coming upon his body.

"This bomb—" I pointed to the box. "It's a step up. No muss, no fuss, but a big explosion with a big body count. The mastermind isn't here, but he has been. Looks like he's cleaning house. Completely. Adding you to the list will just be a bonus. We need to get out of here. Now."

She shook her head.

"We need more intel. We need Morson alive," she murmured, her voice close to my ear. Her breath fanned my neck, but this was not the time to even consider how it made me feel. "Two minutes to listen and get Morson. Then I'll be out the nearest window or door. Are you in, or are you out, Nix?"

Fuck. She was right. If everyone in the room was worth killing off, we did need what we could get out of them before they were blown to bits. We couldn't storm in, arrest them all, and get them all to talk. That would take much longer than five minutes.

Fuck. *Fuck!*

"Two minutes and we're out of here. I *will* carry you out if I have to." I might be allowing her to remain, but on my terms.

"You're such a caveman." She stroked her knuckles down my cheek as I often did to her.

She turned toward the door and I let her go.

BOOK 9

ueen Celene – Optimus Unit Prison, Cell Level C

I STARED AT THE WALL, trying, once more, to use my power.

Nothing. I'd been too long from the citadel, the bond grown too weak to use as I once had.

The last time I'd truly used my gift, it had saved my life. It had often felt like yesterday when I'd had to flee, but now... it felt like a lifetime ago.

I needed to return to the citadel. Reconnect. Become strong, as I was long ago. My daughters needed me. Alera needed their queen. First, I *needed* to escape.

The cleric bitch who'd threatened my daughters was gone. Had been for days. I had no idea if she were dead or alive. I'd been well-treated since then, strangely so considering the misery when I'd first been taken. Not that it mattered. I had to get out of here. Time was ticking in my mind like the count-down on a bomb.

Something had changed, something significant. The

moment that cleric had murdered the guard I thought of as Scarface, everything had shifted.

My clothes were warmer.

There had been no more beatings. Before that even, if I thought about it, but it was as if I'd gone from a cruel gulag to the Four Seasons, by comparison.

I had shoes and thick socks to keep my feet warm and an extra blanket on my bed.

I wasn't hungry, either. I'd given in and eaten everything they brought me, which had been not only delicious, but nutritious as well. Fattening me up for the slaughter, perhaps? No. If they wanted to kill me with poison, it would have happened long ago. Besides, they didn't need to resort to such devious means to commit murder. If they wanted me dead, they could slit my throat and dump my body in the Western Sea. It was only a few hours away by EV, and the creatures that lurked beneath the waves on Alera were much more aggressive than the peaceful sharks on Earth. They were true predators. Piranha-like monsters the size of small boats, some of them with teeth longer than my arms.

Dead or alive, I'd be fish food in a matter of minutes. Seconds, even.

I'd been moved three times in the last two days, so when the door opened and I saw the two young guards holding handcuffs, I wasn't surprised. Their words, however, shocked me.

"Greetings, My Queen. We have been sent to escort you to your new home." One spoke. Both bowed.

What the hell was going on here?

They knew I was the queen. Greeted me formally. As Destiny would say, WTF?

"What are you talking about? Where are you taking me? To the palace?"

The second guard straightened and stood tall, shifted his shoulders back and puffed out his chest, as if he were *proud* to be holding his queen captive. As if locking me up against my will was a fucking *honor*. "Our king has returned, My Queen. He has instructed us to escort you to your new home where he will see to your safety and well-being."

The King? Again, WTF? What the hell were they talking about? "The king is dead."

The first guard, young and beautiful, and clearly so, so naive, smiled. "No, My Queen. He lives. He has returned, at long last, to take his place by your side."

"At long last?"

"Twenty-seven years is a long time to wait, My Queen. We had nearly given up hope." His dark blue eyes were bright with excitement, as if he were about to open a gift on Christmas morning. The look was genuine. Which meant this young idiot believed what he was saying. He hadn't even been alive all those years ago.

"The king has been gone for twenty-seven years?"

The second guard spoke. "Yes, My Queen. He disappeared when you did, and returned soon after your daughters appeared."

"He disappeared because he's dead," I countered. Dead was dead. I'd watched as my mate, King Mykel, was stabbed, killed in front of me. It was a memory I could never forget.

"He's alive and well and eager to see you, My Queen."

But... could he be alive? Could he have somehow survived? Surely, others would have had to know; he'd have needed a ReGen pod. Help to get there. Doctors.

And this guard used the word *eager*. No one was eager and waited twenty-seven years. Yeah, I just bet he was. If it *was* Mykel then why wait so long? Why now? It seemed the game had changed even more than I had realized. Or maybe it wasn't him. Someone else and that meant nothing had changed. I *still* didn't know who'd kidnapped me. Tried to have the girls killed. Now they were going to try to convince me to accept someone else as my dead mate? Did they believe that after nearly thirty years, I would not recognize him? True, our mating had been short, the attack coming soon after our mating ceremony, but I would know him. He had eased my Ardor, pledged his life and love to me. And died protecting me. Or had he?

"Then where is he?" I asked the guard. "Tell him to come down here and explain this to me himself." I'd watched a masked assassin in black drive a dagger through the king's heart moments before I'd fled. That hadn't been faked. Whoever these guards were following, he had to be an imposter of some kind. Surely. Mykel was long dead. My heart belonged to Adam now. Adam, who was far away on Earth, worried sick about his family.

"He can not yet reveal himself, My Queen. He has asked us to personally escort you to your new accommodations and see to your safety."

I'll just bet he has. "Then why the handcuffs?"

The first guard dipped his head in a show of apology. "Apologies, My Queen, but he was afraid you would not believe us and attempt to escape."

The mystery king was right. But I wasn't going to *attempt* anything.

I sat on the edge of my bed and took my sweet time putting on my shoes, hoping the guards would come closer and enter the room.

My patience was rewarded. By the time I was done, they were both inside my cell and the door left wide open behind them.

I stood and held out my wrists like a docile doe. The guard nearest me stepped forward with the cuffs.

"You know," I said, "the last person to stand where you are now threatened to murder all three of my daughters."

His eyes widened in a mix of surprise and horror, as if the idea was appalling to him. Strange, considering I was his pris- oner. "Our apologies for your mistreatment. It took us some time to find you. I assure you, that person will not hurt you or the princesses."

"Is that so?" The cuff drew near and I held back a smile when the second guard stepped closer, very close to the first. Two puppies, the bumbling fools. Kind, unlike the others, therefore, I would only incapacitate them, not hurt them.

Catching my escorts unaware, I grabbed the first guard's wrist and tugged him toward me. Off balance and leaning forward, I swept his front leg with my foot as if I were kicking a soccer ball to the side. With his leg lifted out from under him, he fell like a redwood tree and the wind was knocked from him. On the way down, I grabbed the handcuffs.

The second guard stood there blinking, completely stunned that I'd actually moved, and on top of that had taken his partner to the ground. I took the opportunity to snap one end of the cuff around his wrist. When his eyes met mine, I gave him a small smile. "Sorry."

I *was* a little bit sorry because they were sweet, but not sorry enough to stop.

Letting the cuff drop so it dangled from his wrist, I placed both hands on top of his hand and twisted. It turned his lower arm in a direction that wasn't all that comfortable—thank you Destiny for torturing the entire family with showing all of us what she'd learned in her Jiu-Jitsu classes way back in ninth grade—until he had no choice but to drop to his knees, then to the ground as I kept up the pressure on his shoulder blade. He went to the floor or his shoulder popped out of the socket.

This happened in all of two seconds, and I wrapped the cuff around the nearest leg of the simple bed, then connected it to his partner's wrist. The first guard was finally catching his breath and they flailed and tried to get up, but they didn't make it far since their arms were trapped beneath the bedframe which was affixed to the floor.

I looked down at the two, wondering if they were the worst guards on the planet or if they had truly felt I was a sweet, kind queen they'd envisioned their whole lives. I could be sweet, but not when someone threatened my daughters. Moving to the open doorway, I stopped and looked back at them where they moved awkwardly on all fours. "You'll be found soon."

Someone would come for them, eventually. Moving on silent feet down the hallway, I kept going until I saw another guard. This one armed.

Good. When I found this imposter king, I was going to put a very large hole in his head.

When he saw me, he raised his weapon, but I played the weak woman card. "The guard, he's hurt." I pointed anxiously down the hallway and gave him an Academy Award winning performance. "Hurry, I think he needs a ReGen pod."

He came close to me, his weapon forgotten since I hadn't portrayed myself as a threat. As he was walking past me, I grabbed his ion pistol, quickly set it to stun and shot him.

He crumpled to the floor, remained still. Leaning down, I patted him on the shoulder. "You'll live." He'd be incapacitated for a while, but I had no idea the strength of his stun setting, so I didn't linger.

Goddess, it felt good to be doing something, to be assertive instead of meek. Offensive instead of defensive. I was grateful they'd moved me to a less secure cellblock. They'd transferred me every day, as if they were barely keeping one step ahead of someone who was *looking*.

Well, the queen was out of the cage now, and the whole world was going to know about it. I'd lure this imposter king to me. And if it was Mykel after all these years, he was going down.

Alarms pealed, the sound harsh on my ears after so many days of near silence, alone in my cell. I might have been able to take down three guards, but it was impossible to disable cameras. Eyes on the walls saw everything. Saw me take down a guard. I ignored the shrill sound. I had to get out of this area of the prison, find guards who were loyal Alerans, not minions of my enemies.

The third guard station was manned, based on their uniforms, by three members of the Optimus Unit. Two females and one male, they all looked up when I blasted the lock on the door and stepped through to their station, their mouths hanging open in shock.

"You're the queen." The young female guard gaped and stood, her chair sliding across the floor in her haste. She was younger than my twins. Obviously, she hadn't known I'd been here, which had me believing I'd been kept isolated, a secret.

I nodded. "I am. I demand to speak with Captain Travin Turaya, of the royal guard on a secure channel. Then you three will personally escort me to meet him."

The all stared. Unmoving.

"Now."

I wasn't sure if it was their queen issuing a command or the ion pistol I aimed at them that got them moving. It didn't matter. They were following my commands.

I smiled. The queen was back.

1

D*estiny*

Morson. Morson. Where the hell was this guy?

Nix searched the other side of the room, moving from shadow to shadow along the periphery, unnoticed by the attendees. I had no idea how that was even possible. He was six-foot-plus of pure power and raw sex appeal, but then, maybe since we were in a room full of traitors who were plotting to kill my mother and my sisters, they had other priorities.

Most in the room were powerful in one way or another. Clerics. Lords. Ladies. I hadn't been on Alera for long and even I could tell. Members of the Optimus Unit, too. Talk about the fox watching the hen house. The Optimus Unit was like Earth's FBI and judicial system all in one. Not the brightest setup, in my opinion. Civics class taught me about separation of powers and yeah, they didn't have that here. I meant separation of powers, but Civics, too.

I scanned the faces, searching for the man I'd barely caught a glimpse of on the monitor before coming down here. Morson.

The only person here who, according to my sister, Trinity, was worth saving.

With my bat hearing, the ticking noise of that bomb was still echoing in my ears, despite the fact that it was more than one hundred steps behind me, in another room. It appeared my strange superpower had locked onto the sound as a constant reminder that I was running out of time.

Tick. Tick. Tick. Worse than a metronome. Infinitely more annoying.

Die. Die. Die. That's what I heard. The sound made my blood pound and my head hurt. Someone wanted everyone in this building dead. Someone wanted to destroy everyone who knew the truth about what happened to my mother all those years ago. Whoever it was held onto a grudge. Twenty-seven years. *Twenty-seven!*

People had been dropping like flies. One after the other, some psycho was killing people off. Fortunately, Trinity, Faith and I had survived. And Mom, too, since her spire was still lit. And now, this fucker—yeah, he was a total fucker—was planning on getting the rest with one bomb. A bomb was ticking down and here I was, looking like I was mingling at a cocktail party.

The risk didn't bother me. No. What bothered me was knowing Nix was still in the building. My death? Not the end of the world. But if anything happened to him, I'd never forgive myself.

Was this what love was supposed to be? Gut wrenching anxiety?

I thought about how I felt any time I imagined Mom rotting in chains somewhere, or the times my sisters were hurt growing up.

Yep. Gut wrenching anxiety. Worry. Fear. Helplessness.

Love sucked. Why did we spend our whole lives chasing it?

"Morson, good to see you here. I knew you wouldn't disappoint me."

I wrenched my neck in the direction of that voice and spotted my prey, Morson, talking to an older woman who also wore the uniform of the Optimus Unit. I had no idea who she was, nor did I care. She'd be dead soon. And so would Morson, if I didn't get him out of here.

But Nix. How would he know I'd found him? He was on the other side of the large room, dozens of bodies between us.

"It has been a long time," Morson replied. "I am looking forward to hearing what the next steps are in taking the throne."

If Trinity hadn't said he was one of the good guys, I would have had a very hard time controlling myself. But this meeting said it all. The person who'd killed the king and tried to kill Mom was back at it. I didn't linger to find out who the woman was. Clearly, she knew Morson well. But why was he under-cover, and for how long? It couldn't have been since the attack on my mother.

I looked at him one more time.

No. Too young. Maybe Leo's age. He had probably been a child when Trinity's father was killed. Still, he could have been at this for years.

Poor bastard. I could never pull that off. I was too impatient, and I knew it. Too prone to take risks. Sometimes, stupid risks. Like riding Nix's cock in the high cleric's office while she spoke to a warrior on the other side of a door.

But god, what a magnificent cock.

I looked for Nix. Found him. His eyes met mine and I dipped my chin so he'd know to start moving closer. And those eyes. Intense. Beautiful. Focused on me.

That was the answer. That look. That was what made love worth the pain.

The woman talking to Morson crossed her arms, her booted foot tapping the floor in obvious annoyance.

"I expected to be patient and wait for another attempt, but twenty-seven years?" the woman said, thinking the same as me.

"I have to wonder if the king is actually dead. It would be just like him to pull a stunt like this, although I never knew him to wait this long for anything."

That had me stopping in my tracks. *The king might be alive? That meant... Holy shit. If it had been him behind the attempted coup, why wait so long to try again?*

Morson looked as stunned as I felt. "Did you know him well?"

"Oh yes. We grew up chasing each other through the citadel gardens. He was just a few years younger than I. Always a selfish bastard. A bully. I never did understand what the queen saw in him."

With my feet like steel welded to the floor and my brain in overdrive, I turned to look for Nix, my mate, the only man in the universe I cared about right now. Well, Morson, too, but not in the same way. Duh. But once he was safely away from this exploding building, he could do whatever the hell he wanted and Nix would still be mine.

Nix's gaze bored into mine as he moved closer. Intent. I saw the same anguish I'd been feeling moments before in his gaze. He didn't want me here. He was only in this room for me. Because I asked it of him. Because he respected me enough to give me what I needed even if it placed me in danger, although I'd probably be handcuffed to my bed if he'd known a bomb was involved.

I hadn't understood what it cost him, until now. What letting me be reckless and wild on Earth had cost my sisters and parents. Danger meant nothing to me. Pain meant nothing. Death? Well, I'd prefer not to rush toward my end, but even that held no true cost to me. Until now. Now, I understood.

Fuck me six ways to Sunday. I was in love. Head over heels, do anything to keep him safe, anything to make him happy, love. With the gorgeous, growly guy moving through the room like a wild animal hunting his prey.

"Your timing sucks, Des." I was talking to myself as I moved toward Morson, but I tilted my head at Nix, this time clearly indicating that I'd found our target and to get moving. He didn't take his eyes off me, but changed direction, heading for the closest exit, which was a good twenty paces away. And Morson was big. If he didn't cooperate, I'd have a hell of a time getting him out of here before the bomb went off.

Tick. Tick. Tick.

"Excuse me?"

Morson looked down in shock as I looped my small hand under his elbow and tugged him toward me. I offered a brilliant fake smile to the older female with whom he'd been speaking. Who'd shared some interesting intel.

"Excuse us for a moment?" I said, using my Trinity-diplomat voice. "I really need to speak to Morson about a"—I ran my fingertip down the front of his uniform, over his chest. I could practically hear Nix growling—"a very personal matter." I tugged at him, my cheeks starting to hurt from my ridiculously big smile. "If I could have a moment of your time before the meeting begins?"

He blinked, eyes rounded with a mix of suspicion and surprise. He glanced at the elder out of respect and that seemed to be enough to put her at ease.

If he *was* working undercover, he was good. I had to give him that. Very, very good. That one glance had preserved the woman's trust, despite the fact that something unexpected and strange was happening. Mainly, me. Maybe he was nudging information out of her and I'd interrupted. Well, it was break up the gab fest or die.

Her head tilted to the side like a cobra about to strike, but she nodded. "Of course."

Morson allowed me to pull him away, and I moved toward the exit doors a good five steps before he stopped me. Cold.

Damn my small size. Why wasn't I six-foot-six and two-hundred-fifty pounds? Then I could just throw him over my shoulder and make a run for it. It wouldn't be subtle, but it would work.

"Who are you and what do you want?" While he spoke softly so as not to draw attention, he was rigid and uncooperative. I flicked a glance over my shoulder. Nix was moving closer, but still not close enough to help. Not yet.

I turned back to find Morson's gaze drifting over my face, the look in his eyes one I would have equated with desire, if not for the lack of a rise in his pants. These Alerans and their dormant cocks. Made them much more difficult to bullshit or seduce. False flattery and flirting was going to get me nowhere, except over Nix's knee for a hot, toe-curling spanking.

Reaching up, I wrapped my hand around his neck, up to the back of his head, and pulled him down so my lips were pressed to his ear. He allowed my bold touch, but it felt wrong. Wrong man. Wrong scent. Wrong face too close to mine.

Whatever. This was the only way I could talk to him without fear that someone would overhear.

"My name is Destiny, and this building is going to explode in less than a minute. You need to leave with me. Now." I grabbed his arm once more and pulled him toward the door.

He didn't move. Not one freaking inch.

"Interesting claim from a beautiful woman," he countered, not swayed. "How do I know you are speaking the truth? You could have an ambush set up outside those doors."

"Don't be an idiot," I countered with a wave of my hand. "Move before we're blown to bits."

When he just stared, I took a deep breath and calmed the bitch rising inside. Tried to temper my need to flee. *Tick. Tick. Tick.* I could hear the bomb as clear as I could hear him.

"Fine," I huffed, sounding like an annoyed teenager. "Stay here, get blown up. I'll tell my sister I tried. She's the one who told me you were one of the good guys and to save you."

His dark brow arched. "Sister?"

"Trinity." I slapped him on the shoulder and walked quickly toward the exit. "Not too bright, are you?"

I reached the doors. Tall. Thick. Made of some alien metal that reminded me of the vault doors in the basement of the cleric's fortress. I had my palm on the handle when he came up beside me. "Who are you? Truly?"

Nix moved into place on my right and saved me from responding. I hated to repeat myself. Especially when I'd already told Morson once, and he was just being thick-headed. Perhaps, cautious. I couldn't blame him in his line of work, but right now there was no time. Nix wrapped his arm around my waist and I leaned into him. Just for a moment.

It was enough. I was home.

"We have seconds, Des," he murmured, his fingers tightening. While his words were calm, he was anything but. "Hurry."

Morson glanced at Nix over my head and whispered, "She is truly the third princess?"

I tugged at the door handle. It didn't budge. *Houston, we have a problem.* "Nix, it's locked. Shit."

I lifted my hands and Nix took my place, straining against the door as he applied his entire body weight to the handle.

"Check my comm," Nix ordered.

I did, the screen plainly visible to me once I lifted it from his pocket. "Thirty-two. Thirty-one. Thirty."

Nix pushed harder, his entire body straining. I looked around us, searching for windows. Doors. Any possible way to get out of there.

"Fuck. It's not moving," Nix said. His breathing was ragged, his eyes a little wild.

"You were serious. About the bomb?" Morson looked from me to Nix. "And what are you doing here, Vennix?"

"Later, Morson. We have to get the fuck out of here."

"Twenty-six." Not that I wanted to interrupt, but we didn't have time to chat. "We could go back." The room we'd entered was an option, the window still open.

"Too far. We'd never make it." Nix was right. It was on the other side of the building, and we were starting to get some odd looks, and I could hear quiet murmurs. Well, not *we,* Nix. He was kind of famous on this planet, his face plastered all over the news every time my sister or Faith was broadcast, standing behind them. Watchful. The ever faithful guard. That notoriety was not helpful at the moment.

"They recognize you, mate. Know you aren't on their side. They might start shooting any second." I hissed the words to him as I slid my own weapon free from its holster and stood just behind him, protecting his back. "Get the door open. Shoot the lock."

"That won't work." Morson shoved Nix aside and pulled an oddly shaped key from his pocket. "The door will absorb the ion blast. You need a key to get in or out."

Nix looked from Morson to the key. He was wondering why he had a key just as I was. But I wasn't taking the time now to figure it out. "Hurry the fuck up. If my mate dies in here, I'll kill you myself."

Morson grinned.

Inappropriate. At least I thought so. But Nix grinned back. *Men.*

Morson inserted the key and the door's locks clicked open with a very loud series of pops, thunks and sizzling noises, like lightning bolts were moving along the frame.

I checked the comm. "Twenty. Nineteen."

Morson opened the door. Nix tried to shove me through, but I got behind Morson and shoved him. "Trinity said to save your ass, so get out. Now."

He had the sense not to argue. Nix held my gaze as I shouted as loudly as I could over my shoulder, "There's a bomb. Everyone get out!"

I didn't like any of the people in the room, knew they were evil, but I couldn't just let them die. They deserved justice, not death.

Morson hadn't gone very far, waiting for us, but took off again when we followed.

Nix and I sprinted. I heard commotion and heavy footfall behind us, but didn't take time to worry about the others. They had warning. They could get their own asses out. We bolted through the front doors and dove to the ground at the first loud rumble behind us. I heard it first, diving on top of Nix, covering his body with mine. I didn't think. Just dove, taking him down, my small frame wrapped around his upper body, protecting his torso and head the best I could. Any NFL linebacker would have been proud of my take down.

The boom blasted through me like I'd been hit full speed by a semi-truck. My eardrums ruptured and I screamed, covering my ears as heat scorched my back through my uniform and hot blood filled my ears.

It was all over in less than a second because Nix kept rolling, his big frame covering mine completely as he cradled my face to his chest.

Another blast rocked the air and moved through the ground beneath us like an earthquake. I clung to Nix, in so much pain I could do nothing else, every sound like a cannon blast inside my skull.

The rumbling stopped. Fire blazed into the sky behind Nix's outline where he hovered above me. His large, warm hands were gentle on my face and he turned me so that I looked up at him. His lips were moving, but my ears hurt. I couldn't hear a word he was saying, but could read his lips. "Destiny, what have you done?"

My back burned, the uniform sticking to my flesh where the explosion had seared my skin. Contact with the ground under me added to my misery, but I felt the welcoming cold numbness of shock setting in, and I didn't even try to hold it off. Numb meant bliss at the moment.

Nothing mattered. Morson didn't matter. He had been in front of us, far enough away to survive. And if he didn't, well, we'd tried. I looked Nix over the best I could from my position. Satisfied that he would survive relatively unharmed and with just a ReGen wand pass or two, I smiled with relief. Mission accomplished. I loved him. And I protected the people I loved. The list wasn't all that long, and Nix had somehow clawed his way to the top. "I love you, Nix."

"Goddess damn it, Destiny."

That one I knew. I read his lips easily, he'd said it often enough.

I was still smiling when I lost consciousness.

2

N *ix*

Six hours. Destiny had been beneath the glass of the ReGen pod for six fucking hours. I knew she'd be fine; the initial scans had proven her injuries to be extensive but, thanks to the ReGen pod technology, not life threatening, but still.

Fuck!

I'd missed the explosion cleanup, skipped Morson's debriefing, the fear and upset of Destiny's sisters sounded like the chattering of angry birds in the background when we'd arrived at the medical center.

None of it mattered to me. Someone else could deal with a bunch of dead bodies. Someone else could question the traitors who'd survived, arrest and interrogate them. Make them bleed.

As upset as Trinity and Faith were over Destiny's injuries, I had no doubt Leo and Thor could oversee the process just fine without me. They were well motivated, their mates' pain affecting them in ways they'd never before imagined.

As seeing Destiny unconscious beneath the glass affected me.

I couldn't breathe. I'd never felt terror before. Not facing down a Hive Soldier. Not sneaking through enemy territory or organizing a strike deep in Hive space. Death had seemed like a distant friend, and if he had come calling, so be it.

There was no escape from this. From her. From the dagger-like strike inside my chest with each beat of my heart.

She'd sacrificed herself to protect me. Suffered. Burned. Her eardrums blown out. Blood dripping from her gorgeous body to cover me.

And then? She'd smiled. She'd fucking smiled and looked at me like I was a god. Told me she loved me as she lay dying in my arms. I'd seen that love in her eyes. Pure. Raw. Free of desire or lust or laughter. Deep and true.

I'd never seen anything like it. Never felt a punch to my gut so powerful.

Everyone had become a blur around me, the only thing I saw was Destiny. All I heard was the blood pounding through my body as the doctors treated her. I listened to her ragged struggle for each breath. Winced as they peeled the burned pieces of clothing from her open wounds, explaining to me that they would be enclosed by the new skin if they were not removed.

I died a hundred deaths before they tucked her into a pod and began the healing process.

And so I sat. Touched the glass. Willed her to breathe. Willed her skin to heal. I would have peeled the flesh from my own bones to provide for her, but the doctors assured me that was unnecessary. She was young. Strong. Her body resilient. She would heal.

They promised me and I had to believe them. The alternative was not acceptable.

I hovered near her, a ghost of a male, and realized this is

what I would become without her. Nothing more than a shell.
Empty. Lost.

So I willed her to open her eyes and smile at me again.
Waited as the seconds ticked down, just like the bomb that put
her here. Three, two, one. A beep sounded, the blue glow that
filled the unit went out and the seal broke on the lid, the hiss of
air like an electric jolt to my body as the lid slowly lifted.

I stood. Stared at my sleeping mate. Waited. They'd cut the
clothes from Destiny's body, careful to remove the fibers that
had been caught in her burned skin. She was naked beneath a
thin sheet that covered her.

The doctor returned, probably alerted by the pod somehow, and checked his gadgets and the pod's readouts. I stared at
the man. I knew I probably looked half feral, but that was how
I felt. "She is healed?"

His face was serious, lips thin and taut, and I was grateful
that he did not try to jest or put me at ease in that odd way
medical professionals had, as if they were uncomfortable
unless they were trying to ease another's pain.

I didn't care about being in pain; I cared about my mate.

"Yes. The pod took care of her injuries. She might be sensitive to touch for a few days as the newly regenerated skin
adjusts, but she is fine."

My knees would have collapsed, so I leaned on the edge of
the strange pod's bed and locked them under me. "Inform the
princesses."

"Of course. Of course." He turned on his heel and hurried
away, leaving me alone with the only person in the universe I
cared about at the moment.

Carefully, I lifted the sheet and inspected her skin. It
appeared normal. Healed. At least what I could see of it.

"Destiny, wake up," I said, my voice rough with unspoken
emotion.

After a few seconds, her fingers twitched and her eyes
opened. She blinked a few times, and I knew the second she

focused on me. A brilliant smile spread across her face. That smile. Goddess, I would kill for that smile.

"Nix! Are you all right? Not hurt?"

"Thanks to you mate." I sounded angry, I could hear the rumble in my voice. Instead of cringing from me in fright, she smiled brighter. Stubborn female.

She lifted her hand to my face, cupped my cheek, and I leaned into the delicate touch. I *needed* to feel her.

"And you? How do you feel?" I asked. I had to be sure before I touched her, before I did anything. "Are you still in pain? The doctor assured me all your burns have healed."

It was then she realized where she was and sat up. The sheet slipped and she tugged it up to cover herself. She looked down, as if she could see herself through the covering. One hand reached behind her, touched her back, then her ear.

"I'm... I'm fine."

I knew she was, for the pod had analyzed and checked off completed diagnostics on specific parts of her body. The advanced healing system made sure injuries were healed and finalized before moving onto the next. I'd spent many hours in a ReGen pod myself, during the war. Taken them for granted.

Never again.

I was relieved she was whole, but I'd had hours to calm myself to that. Now, now I was furious.

"Good," I said evenly, reaching into the pod and scooping her up, sheet and all.

"Nix!" she cried as her arms went around my neck. Her body was warm and soft in my hold. I felt her breathing, her heartbeat against my own. Thank fuck she was alive and mine. *Mine.*

But that didn't lessen my determination to set her straight. My mate would not behave in such a way again. In a few minutes, I would ensure it.

"I can walk," she commented, trying to wiggle out of my hold.

I was having none of it, so mid-pace, I shifted her, tossed her over my shoulder.

"Nix!" she cried again, pummeling my back with her fists. The sheet was twisted, so I wrapped it over her back—her bare ass was mine to see, mine to spank, mine to fuck—and gripped her thighs.

"Settle, mate."

She must have heard the tone of those two words, for she fell silent. For all of twenty seconds.

"Where are you taking me?"

"Fortunately, the palace medical team has a ReGen pod and you were brought here directly after the explosion." I thought of her beneath me, unconscious, bleeding. "You are well?" I asked her again.

"Nix, I'm fine. Put me down."

"No." I kept walking, my stride long as I took the stairs two at a time to the second floor, to the family level of the palace. I turned right onto the corridor that led to Destiny's suite of rooms. *Our* rooms.

Trinity and Faith came out of nowhere, walking toward the medical station. They stopped as we approached. The look on their faces was pure happiness and they opened their mouths to stop me, but Leo joined them. "Not now," he murmured. "Let Nix deal with his mate."

I couldn't help but grin. Yes, I was going to *deal* with Destiny.

"Deal with her?" I heard Trinity ask Leo. "She was hurt!"

"There was a bomb, mate. A bomb. And she covered Nix with her body. Risked herself to protect him"

"I would do the same." Trinity's defiance was clear, and I felt my own spine stiffen in response. These females were trouble. Every. Single. One of them.

"Perhaps you need to be reminded who protects who in this mating." Leo sounded as I felt. Frustrated. Worried that his mate would do something crazy. Reckless. Dangerous.

For him.

For me.

For the males they loved.

The knowledge of their combined defiance was terrifying and I wondered about the queen. What female raised such fierce daughters?

Trinity said something in reply, but I was too far down the hall to hear. I opened the door and kicked it shut behind us as I heard her squeal. Not in terror. She was laughing. And I had no doubt she'd be beneath Leo soon. Just as Destiny would soon be submitting to me. To my hands. My mouth. My cock.

"Nix!"

I ignored Destiny as I carried her directly to the bathing room and slapped my hand on the wall to turn on the shower tube. It was pre-set to Destiny's desired water temperature, so I opened the door and carefully lowered my mate to her feet. Now, I tugged the sheet from her, already sodden in parts from the warm spray.

"Nix!" she sputtered. "What are you doing? You're acting like a caveman."

I didn't close the door, just watched with satisfaction as the dirt and blood washed away, swirling down the drain. The pod had healed her, but it hadn't done anything to clean the remnants of the explosion from her. Grabbing the soap, I washed her myself, having her turn so I got all of her.

"Settle, mate. I will ensure every inch of you is well."

She lowered her hands to her sides as I gently but thoroughly cleaned away the horror of those few seconds. My fear settled into a hard lump in the pit of my gut. I wasn't afraid any longer, but the emotion clogging my throat hurt even more.

Relief. Despair that this would happen again. Anger at myself for being so weak and needy when it came to her. I was a warrior, not a simpering idiot. But when it came to Destiny...

Fuck. I wiped the wetness from my cheeks while her back

was turned, so she would not see how weak she made me. How desperate and lost I'd be without her.

"Nix." So soft, my name on her lips. I was down on one knee before her and she leaned over, pressed her wet lips to mine. Gently. When she pulled back, her own cheeks were streaked with tears. "We're a mess, aren't we?"

Her hair was now an electric shade of purple, a striking contrast to her pale skin. She pulled me under the water, next to her, and stripped me naked. She took her time, washing me as I'd washed her. I leaned my head back against the wall and let her touch me. Let her soothe the pain still swimming in my blood like acid. "Don't ever do that again, mate."

Eyes closed, I felt her lips press to my chest. My neck. Her hands slid around my waist and she leaned her entire body along mine. Skin to skin. Making us one being. One body. Her cheek rested over my heart and I wrapped my arms around her. Squeezed. Couldn't stop.

"I need you, Nix. You can't die. I love you too much."

Goddess help me, she was trying to kill me.

My cock, always hard for her, took control of my mind. I needed her. Now.

Lifting her in my arms, I turned us until her back was to the wall and entered her in one long, hard thrust.

She was hot. Wet. Ready.

"Yes! Fuck me, Nix." Her legs lifted and hooked at my lower back. "I need you."

Never able to deny her, I thrust hard. Fast. Pumping into her with all the fear, worry and relief coursing through me at once. Never had I felt so adrift. Too many emotions swirling inside me like a storm. But she was right here with me. Her body my anchor. Her hands in my hair. My name on her lips. I held onto her. Made her my center. And fucked her. Hard. Deep.

"Mine."

"So hot," she moaned as I thrust, grabbing her ass, lifting her hips so I could go deeper. "...so hot when you go caveman."

That was not the first time she'd used that word. I would ask for clarification later. If my mate preferred a caveman, I would act as a man in a cave for her.

Too fast, it was over. Both of us riding the edge before we'd begun. I rinsed my seed from both of us and turned off the water. Holding her close, I activated the drying feature. As warm air circulated and dried us from head to toe, my fear for her life swam back to the surface, turned to anger.

How dare she place her life at risk for me? I was nothing. A soldier. A warrior. She was everything.

When the dryer setting turned off, I opened the door.

Her gaze raked over my body, took in my still hard cock, then moved higher so her dark eyes met mine.

"You're mad."

I laughed, which was ironic because I wasn't amused at all.

"You are well?" I asked a third time. "The doctor said your skin might be sensitive for a few days."

She nodded. "Perhaps you could take a nibble and we can test it."

"I want to hear you say it, mate. Are you well? Are you in pain?"

"I am fine."

I nodded once, then took hold of her hand and tugged her out of the bathing room and to the bed. I picked up the restraints she'd put on me earlier, to keep me from following her into danger, dangled them between us.

"I should tie you down, mate. Then you couldn't be hurt. Wouldn't be able to do stupid things like get blown up."

"Nix," she began, but I tossed the restraints onto the bed, picked her up and had her over my lap, ass up, in two seconds flat. Now, when she called out my name, I followed it with a nice hard spank on her ass.

She bucked and wriggled and I hooked her ankles with

mine. When her hands went back to cover her ass, I gripped them together in one of mine.

"You said you love me." *Spank.* "You shield me with your body."

"I didn't want you to be hurt!" she cried.

Spank.

"If you love me, Destiny, you will let me protect *you.* You are my life and I will protect you."

Spank.

"And you are mine," she said. Her muscles went lax over my lap and she moaned. I could smell her arousal, calling me. Mocking my attempts at a punishment. Goddess damn it. She *liked* this.

I spanked her twice more, but without any intensity. I rubbed her reddened cheeks, my thumb dipping between the lush swells to find her pussy nearly dripping.

"Mate," I groaned, sliding two fingers deep. "You like my palm on your ass." She clenched her inner muscles around me, bit my leg. Not hard enough to hurt, but to let me know she wanted to devour me. That the wildness in her rose to meet my own.

"Yes," she replied breathlessly. "It burns. So hot."

That was it. I needed to be balls deep. Now. Right fucking now.

I scooped her up, tossed her into the center of the bed, then crawled over her, my forearms planted on either side of her head. Settling between her parted thighs, my cock was right at her entrance. I looked down at her, met her dark gaze.

Our breaths mingled. Her soft skin touched mine. Her heat seeped into me. Her heartbeat thrummed in time to mine.

"Mine."

Lifting her hips, she took an inch of me into her. I hissed. She gasped.

"Mine," she repeated. "Can we both agree to never go near

a bomb again so we can move on to the super-hot make-up sex?"

I groaned again, settling my forehead against hers. "Can we both agree to never go near any kind of danger ever again?"

While I was too close to see much more than a blur of her face, I couldn't miss her smile.

"No danger. Ever. We shall stay here in bed forever." Every word was a lie, and neither of us cared. Her inner walls clenched about my tip.

"Liar."

"We shall stay in this bed forever." She nibbled on my lip, her hands reaching down to smack me on the ass. Damn, the burn went straight to my balls and I moved deeper inside her. Another inch. "And fuck."

I groaned, her sex talk making my mind go blank. My body took over, my hips thrusting into her of their own accord. I wanted more of her heat, more of that wet, snug fit. I was home with her. *Inside her.*

"Yes. Bed. Fuck. Forever."

That was all I could say once her legs wrapped around my hips, her heels in my ass as she pulled me in deeper.

Our mouths met and we kissed and fucked, hot and heavy. This wasn't going to be fast and furious like we had been when the Ardor and Awakening were upon us. This was going to be fast, and it was going to be furious, but it was proof that we were alive, that we were whole, that we were together. That we loved each other.

I couldn't hold back. Could only fuck her harder, deeper, to match her begging, her cries of pleasure. She would come first. I could feel my orgasm tingle at the base of my spine, knew I was close when my balls grew tight, heavy with cum.

Reaching between us, I found her hard little clit and brushed my thumb over it. One, two gentle brushes and she clenched down, gushed all over my cock as she screamed my name.

Yes! This. Fuck, this was heaven. The feeling of my mate's pussy as she took her pleasure. To know I was the one who had her heart as well as her body.

I didn't hold back, just gave over to the pleasure I found in her in return. Shouted as I filled her with my seed, marked her and someday, from a moment just like this, would make our child.

When it was over, I started again, the ride far from over. But slowly this time. Hands clasped. Lips melded together as we moved. Climbing to the peak again.

I had no idea how long it took us to recover our breaths, for me to slide off her and tuck her into me, her head on my shoulder. I had no idea how the covers ended up over us. I was mindless, boneless, sated. Happy. And Destiny was asleep in my arms, where she belonged. Where she was safe.

I must have dozed as well, for a knock on the door startled me. My mate tensed in my hold. "Come back later!" she shouted, clearly annoyed, the demanding fighter back again.

I kissed the top of her head and she snuggled into me, throwing her thigh over mine. Claiming her territory. Which was just fine with me. Until she went stiff as a board...

"Destiny. Marie. Jones. Open this door right now. I assume, since you two have quieted down, that play time is over."

Destiny bolted upright, tugging the sheet up to her chest. "Mom!"

I didn't have time to process that one word before the door opened and Queen Celene walked in.

Holy shit.

The woman before me truly was the queen. I recognized her at once. I'd seen vids of her when she was younger, but her resemblance to Trinity was obvious in every line on her face. Her golden hair. Her eyes. Even the way she moved.

Goddess damn it. I was meeting the queen. My mate's beloved mother. Naked.

The fucking queen.

And she was the queen who'd obviously heard me fucking her daughter.

"Mate, we need a new room," I said to Destiny. "I'm sick and tired of people finding me naked in your bed."

"At least you're not handcuffed this time," she muttered, a huge smile lighting up her face as she stumbled off the bed, dragging the sheet with her as she ran into her mother's arms.

Me? I was left naked, again, in Destiny's bed.

I would not meet my queen naked, on my back.

Stripping the bottom sheet off the bed in one vicious tug, I wrapped it around my waist and looked out from behind the canopy to find my mate wrapped in the queen's embrace. Sobbing.

The sight made me stop in my tracks.

The queen looked over Destiny's shoulder at me and I knelt, bowing my head. "My Queen. I am Captain Vennix Bryndar. It is an honor to meet you at last."

"You are my daughter's mate?"

"Nix is mine, Mom." Destiny's laugh struggled past the sobs and she turned, wiping her cheeks to smile at me. "He's totally mine and I'm not giving him back."

The queen looked down her regal nose at me, assessing my worth. I stayed down on one knee, but I held her gaze. I was a warrior. And Destiny was mine.

"Very well." She bent her head to me and I rose. "If Destiny chooses you, I respect her choice."

Destiny's smile widened as her gaze traveled over my bare chest. "He's hot. Seriously. How could I say no to that?"

I had never, not in my entire life, been embarrassed. Never felt my cheeks heat, turn red. Until that moment. My face was on fire as the queen's gaze meandered down my bare chest to my waist and back to my face, her look assessing. "Indeed."

Thank the goddess she turned away quickly, hiding a grin. Destiny didn't even try to hide her amusement.

I'd spank her ass for that later.

"Get dressed, both of you. I have summoned the others as well. Meet me in the queen's solar at once." The regal queen was back, all amusement gone.

"But where have you been? What happened to you? Who kidnapped you? How did you get away?" Destiny fired off the questions so quickly no one would have been able to answer. The queen didn't even try.

"Get dressed. You know I hate to repeat myself. I will tell all of you, together."

"Okay." Destiny was still smiling, practically glowing with happiness as her mother turned and walked out of our rooms. When she turned that radiant smile on me, my cock responded. My heart leapt. My entire body on fire for her. Beautiful. She was so fucking beautiful. "That's my mom."

"I figured that out on my own." I smiled as she walked toward me, as she pushed me backward toward the bed. When my knees hit the edge, I sat, unprepared for the seductress who pulled the sheet from my hips and climbed, naked, onto my lap. She took my cock in her small hand and positioned it at the entrance to her warm, wet core.

"You're mine, Nix. I meant what I said. I'm not giving you up." She slid down, taking me deep. Claiming me in the most primitive of ways.

"Your mother is waiting." Fuck. I grabbed her hips, arched up into her. Deeper. Harder. She arched her back and I leaned forward, taking her nipple into my mouth just so I could hear her moan my name, feel the harsh tug of her hands in my hair.

"She can wait ten minutes. I need you."

I need you.

I gave up arguing. Celene Herakles was my queen, but Destiny was mine. If she needed me, who was I to argue?

3

D

estiny, *The Queen's Solar*

"I can't believe you just walked into the palace like you own the place," I said, for the first time taking my seat at the big table in the queen's suite used for group powwows. The queen's *solar*. Such a fancy name for a living room with comfy chairs, couches and a huge oblong table in the center surrounded by twelve high-backed chairs. The table could easily squeeze in half a dozen more.

After Mom had completely stunned me—and Nix, and I managed to tear myself away from my mate's hard body—it had taken about an hour for the four of us, Mom, Trinity, Faith and myself, to stop hugging and crying once we were all in the same room.

Between sobbing and holding on to each other like we might be separated again, we'd managed to confirm to our mother how we'd arrived on Alera. And that our Ardors had passed. And that Trinity had been acting as ruler. And where we'd been and what we'd been up to, Trinity at the palace,

Faith in the Jax household, and me with the clerics. And all three of us had found and fallen in love with our mates. And. And. *And.* There were a lot of *ands* to fill the time.

All three of our mates had stayed in the room with us, Leo's father a stoic guardian at the door, watching over all of us like he'd just won the lottery. The men had remained silent, probably equal parts content that the hunt for Mom was over and equal parts horrified at what four females sounded like when we were finally together and all talking at once.

To me, it felt like I was finally home. All I needed now was for Dad to walk through the door, hug Mom and plant a big fat kiss on her lips—just like I'd seen him do a thousand times before. Earth. Alera. I didn't care where we were, as long as we were all together. A family. Plus Nix.

He was mine now, too.

I patted the seat next to me at the large table, but there was no need. He was already making a beeline for me now that I'd stopped moving. It was time to get down to business and finally solve the mystery of who took Mom and who was trying to kill all of us.

I was thrilled—over the moon—that Mom was safe, whole and alive, but the threat was still out there. Knowing that made my muscles tight and my jaw clench. I wanted to know who was behind this... and I wanted them dead.

Our mother looked lovely. I wasn't used to seeing her in long, flowy dresses that were the popular style on Alera—she'd been a jeans and blouse kind of dresser on Earth—but it only accentuated the fact that she really *was* Queen of Alera. Growing up, we'd known, but now...

She *looked* like a queen. She *talked* like a queen. A badass, regal, no-nonsense queen wearing an ion blaster on her hip. Which was really fucking weird, since I'd seen her cleaning toilets, doing laundry, and covered in flour while baking cookies for school fundraisers. The whole situation was surreal.

Queen of the whole damn planet.

As if she could sense my thoughts, she moved to the head of the table and met my gaze, pinning me in place. I'd seen that look before, too. She was happy. And happy usually meant we were in for some serious mischief from her.

God, I'd missed her. So much.

My eyes burned again and I blinked back a fresh round of tears. Jeez, I was a mess.

"What are you looking at, Destiny? I do own the place," Mom finally replied to my statement. My thoughts were moving so quickly I'd forgotten what I said.

Captain Turaya, who looked at least as happy as we were that the queen was alive, pulled out her chair for her. While the look on his face wasn't infatuation—he wasn't in love with Mom—he moved with a depth of loyalty and reverence I hadn't really seen before. He clearly loved her. Not the way Nix looked at me, but it was still love. Dedication. Absolute loyalty.

I remembered being told he'd been one of two—and the only one still alive—who had helped her escape the attempt on her life all those years ago. He'd helped her make it to the citadel, where she'd disappeared. Until now.

With Mom at the head of the table, Trinity sat at her right, Faith on her left. Their mates sat beside them. I took the foot of the table with Nix beside me. Captain Turaya sat in the open chair on my other side. There were two empty seats on each side, but I had no doubt that they would be filled soon. I would suggest to my mother that one of the seats be offered to High Cleric Amandine.

It was time to unite the planet once more. And my mother would need everyone to feel like they had a seat at the table to make that happen.

I slapped my forehead with my palm and shook my head. God. I sounded like fucking Trinity with my diplomatic thinking. What was happening here?

"There is much to discuss. Shall we start at the beginning?"

Mom asked, although since everyone remained silent, the question was rhetorical. The only ones alive at the *beginning* of all this were Leo's dad and the queen, herself.

"Twenty-seven years ago, not long after my official mating ceremony to King Mykel, we were suddenly and brutally attacked by a band of masked assassins during a dinner event with my mate's family. The king was stabbed in the heart right before my eyes. I saw the dagger pierce his flesh. Watched him fall. His parents were murdered as well." My mother placed a hand over her chest and looked at Leo's father. "Would you continue from there, please, Travin."

Holy shit. I didn't even know Leo's dad had a first name. But I had no doubt only Mom would be allowed to use it.

"Of course, My Queen." Captain Turaya stood behind her chair, one hand on her shoulder. A friend offering comfort. "I was there. I, too, watched the attack unfold. A fellow member of the queen's guard assisted me in fighting off some of the attackers. We could not save the king, but we dragged the queen from the room. She was defiant, even then, and wanted to stay and fight."

"I do not bow down to traitors, Captain."

"No, you do not." His hand tightened on her shoulder and he released her, pacing along the length of the table as if the pain of his memories made it impossible for him to remain still. "As I said, we pulled her from the room. Then took her through the secret tunnels to the exit nearest the citadel. We were all bloodied, hurting. The guard with me did not survive the night. But we managed to escort the queen to the citadel, where she disappeared."

Mom looked to the older man. "I am sorry for leaving you. For disappearing like that. I trusted you, but I could not risk your life by revealing my plan."

"Plausible deniability," Captain Turaya said with a nod. "I understand and you did what was right. Your spire remained lit all these years and has given us all hope. We remained faithful, ready for your return."

Mom smiled warmly at the man, cleared her throat and nodded. "I stayed on Earth for all these years. I was selfish. First, I convinced myself that my daughters were not ready, but that was a lie. I was not ready. Our life on Earth was good. Peaceful. I am ashamed to say that I was not in a rush to return."

"Did you notice anything amiss during your time on Earth?" Leo asked.

Mom shook her head. "Nothing. The kidnapping was a complete surprise. One minute I was sleeping, the next I'd been transported."

Leo looked to his father. "And in all these years, you never figured out who was behind the attack? Who killed the king?"

Captain Turaya sat, at last, his shoulders slumped. "No. It was as if the attackers vanished into thin air. There was no trail. No DNA. No comm traffic. No abandoned EMVs. No vid records. Nothing. It was as if the entire incident had never happened."

"They left behind corpses, Captain," Mom said.

"It's not possible." Thor spoke up. "My mother spent decades in the Optimus Unit. Their tech is everywhere. They track every transport. Every message. What you are saying is not possible."

"But it's the truth." Leo's father leaned back in his chair, suddenly looking his age, which was several years older than my mother. "Whoever orchestrated the attack was a genius. It was no random or hasty action. The plan was executed perfectly. They murdered the king and his parents and left absolutely nothing for us to trace."

"Perfect, except for Mom's escape," Trinity added.

"That's because she's a troublemaker, like me," I tossed out there. I had to grin at Mom, break up the tense mood. All this talk of death was making the air too thick to breathe. I had heard the stories before, but it had never been real. Not until now.

I looked around, felt the blood drain from my face as an idea occurred to me. "Wait. Here? It happened here? In this room?"

Mom looked around, her eyes taking in everything, but seeing the past. "Yes. I am not pleased to be back, but at least the décor has been changed." She looked at the dark green silks on the windows, the pale green sofa cushions, the dark marble table. "It used to be dark brown and burgundy. The cushions on the couch were like red wine."

"Okay." Faith waved her hand through the air. "Enough of this bullshit trip down memory lane. If everyone died, who was looking for you all these years? And how did they find you?"

Trinity squirmed in her seat and I leaned forward, my hand on Nix's thigh squeezing tightly. I didn't notice, until his warm touch covered mine. I let up, but didn't lean back. Whatever Trin was about to say was going to be good.

"I think that's my fault, actually," Trinity said.

Oh, hell yeah. Called it.

Faith's head looked like it was about to explode. "What?"

Trinity looked from Faith to Mom to me. I was nodding in agreement. I'd figured it out a while back. "You contacted Warden Egara, didn't you? Asked about Alera. The Ardor."

Mom offered Trinity a small smile.

"Yes," Trinity continued. "My stupid Ardor. And less than two days later, Mom was gone and we were running from the CIA."

"I don't think they were CIA, Trin." Faith leaned to the side and into Thor's shoulder. She processed fast. We all did. "Those Men-In-Black were probably NSA or some other way-top-secret organization that doesn't exist."

Nix went stiff next to me. His glare focused solely on me. "Are you in danger? Are these males from Earth hunting you, mate? Do we have more to worry about than just a ruthless killer on Alera?"

I sighed. God, he was so damn cute. "No. They were after us, but we ditched them at the Bride Processing Center. You should have seen those big Atlan guards back them down."

"God, they were huge," Trinity said with a laugh.

"And hot," Faith added, waggling her eyebrows.

"Enough." Mom interrupted before we could go into a full-out assessment of the Atlan warriors and their big... everything. Not that Faith was wrong, but I had Nix now, and absolutely zero interest in any other man, or alien, touching me.

"How they found me is irrelevant. I was transported using a mobile transport beacon. I have no idea how they acquired such rare technology from the Prillons, but they did. They slapped the beacon on me and transported me right out of our house and into a prison cell aboard a spaceship orbiting Alera. They held me there for several days, beating me, starving me, demanding the jewels. Once the spires lit for you three, I was transported again, to the planet, into the custody of Lord Wyse."

"That bastard. I knew it! If he wasn't dead, I'd kill him again." Trinity, in a full rage, was a sight to behold, so much like Mom it was scary sometimes. "We saw signs of a struggle, heard you scream, but nothing more," she said. "We immediately went to the Interstellar Brides Program because we knew that was the nearest transport center on Earth. We had to get to Alera."

"And your father?" Thor asked.

"He said you two had talked about things before," Faith replied, looking to Mom. "He said he had a safe place to go until we could send for him." Faith reached across the table and offered her hand to our mother, who took it. "He's fine. He's smart as hell and not afraid. The Men-In-Black were after him, but I know Dad. They'll never catch him."

"Yes, you're right. Good." Mom sighed in relief and leaned back, breaking Faith's hold. "So, Lord Wyse is dead?"

"As a doornail," I said. Nix looked confused by the term, but he could figure it out. Context was key. Although, now that I thought about it, a doornail... dead. Yeah, it was stupid phrase, but Wyse was dead. Sooo dead.

I thought back to how our house on Earth had been trashed. Not a lot, but enough to know something had happened. Mom had warned us about the possibility of someone eventually finding her. We'd heard her scream, but by the time we got upstairs, she was gone.

But we were ready. Our entire lives, she'd told us what to do. Still, we'd only imagined the scenario. Then it had become real. All of it. The stories of a faraway planet. The strange language she'd forced us—and Dad—to learn. The culture and customs she'd drilled into us but we had never used. Until now.

The car chase on the way to the Bride Processing Center felt like a lifetime ago. Earthlings. God, it had been so simple. Just a car chase. No ion blasters. No transport technology. No aliens. Or assassins. Or thirty-year plots to unravel. It had been like the Wild West, now that I looked back. Some of my last moments on Earth.

"So, you were treated poorly. Questioned about the royal necklace." Trinity was back in analyst mode. "What else?"

Faith's eyes widened and she leaned forward. "Someone wanted the necklace? Did they find it?"

Mom shook her head. "That night." She tipped her head toward Captain Turaya. "When I went into the citadel, I hid it. No one knows of its whereabouts, but me."

That was a lie, of course. Mom knew where it was, but so did we. We'd made sure it was still in that hidden compartment inside the citadel when we'd first arrived. We had all agreed it was safest to leave it where our mother had kept it hidden all these years. And we'd been right to protect it. Someone kidnapped Mom to get the necklace. "If they want the necklace, then someone thinks they can take the throne."

"But what if..." Leo lifted his chin. "I beg your pardon for speaking plainly, but what if your spire had dimmed? The necklace would have been lost forever."

She shook her head. "No." Her gaze flicked to each of us, nearly too quickly for anyone to notice. But Nix did. His hand still rested over mine on his thigh, and I felt his muscles tense.

"The royal jewels will remain hidden until I decide to retrieve them." She said nothing more, and I glanced around the table. It didn't answer Leo's question, but he didn't point that out.

"Why would someone want the royal necklace? What use is it without the queen herself?" Thor asked. "With no spire lit, there is no heir. The jewels are worthless without an heir."

Mom looked to him, smiled. "A common belief, but not correct. The citadel chooses who shall rule. How the ancients created such a gift, I do not know, but the citadel is more than a building. More than stone. The citadel is alive. Intelligent. If the royal line were truly to die out, I am sure the citadel would choose another to rule in our place."

"So if someone wanted to rule, but wasn't the queen or a descendent, they would need the necklace," Thor offered. "And what? Hope that by having the necklace the citadel would make him or her the true ruler of Alera?"

"Correct."

"What?" What the hell was Mom talking about? I'd never heard this before. "Mom, are you telling me that if they actually managed to wipe us all out, they could actually take over and rule the planet?"

Mom thought for a moment, tilted her head. "It is possible. But not likely. The citadel sees all, and would likely not reward such dishonorable behavior."

"It really is alive?" Thor seemed fascinated by the fact. Me? I was not amused. Not in the least.

"Not alive, as we are," she answered. "But an ancient intelligence dwells within. I cannot explain it or tell you more."

Well damn and double damn. I was going to be spending some time in the citadel. See what I could see. What Mom was describing was the most amazing artificial intelligence ever conceived, and it was millennia old. Five millennia, at least. No. More. That was more like ten... ten thousand years.

Holy shit.

"Then the person who kidnapped you wanted you dead and the necklace for himself," Nix said. He'd been quiet until now, but clearly analyzing everything. "Or herself."

"I've had a lot of time to consider the possibilities," Mom said. "Years. You said there have been attempts on your lives as well since you've been here. I was found... after all this time. I was kidnapped and brought to Alera and questioned after the necklace. But then—"

"Oh my god," I said, cutting Mom off, everyone's heads whipping my way. "But then we arrived. Whoever wanted the necklace never expected the queen to have kids. Daughters to take over."

"Very good, love," Mom said, beaming. She looked to Captain Turaya. "I was pregnant with Trinity when I fled."

The older man's mouth fell open as he processed the words. "I never knew. Then Trinity is full Aleran, King Mykel's daughter?"

"My true heir." She took Trinity's hand in hers and gave it a squeeze.

Trinity looked to me and Faith, then stuck out her tongue. "The heir and the spares," she singsonged, but I knew she was only playing around.

"Trinity can be queen," I said, looking to Nix. "I don't like people that much."

Nix leaned forward hooked his hand behind my neck in a very possessive gesture. "You like me."

"All right, you two," Faith complained. "We had to wait forever for you to come up for air."

"Like you weren't well-occupied," Thor said in a low voice. The way Faith blushed, I had to assume they'd made use of the time in very pleasurable ways.

Captain Turaya was the one who cleared his throat, yet smiled.

"Someone wanted to take over the throne by getting the royal necklace from you, then killing you," Leo said, clearly not into the teasing. "But when it was discovered you had heirs, when the three extra spires lit, their plans went to hell. They had four females to kill, not one." His gaze darted around the table, between us girls. "And they had one hell of a time finding you. Nicely done."

"We are badass princesses, after all," I offered. "Daughters of a badass queen."

The captain looked confused. Stammered. "I don't understand this phrase. You all seem to have perfectly good backsides to me."

Trinity laughed, which was so unlike her, but seeing the uptight and formal captain so flustered was fun. Leave it to Faith to be having opposite day. As usual.

"But who could it be?" Faith asked. "None of this makes any sense."

"Who's left alive?" I added. "Or, who can we rule out because they're dead?"

"My parents," Thor said and Faith leaned into him, took his hand in hers and kissed the back of it.

"Almost everyone in the building that blew up," I said and Nix grumbled to himself.

"We have a list of names. It is extensive. There was also Zel," Leo added, and explained to Mom about the queen's guard who had tried to kidnap Trinity during the fancy reception. Another bit of excitement I'd missed because I was busy pretending to be a nun.

"As we all know, Lord Wyse," Faith offered. "He arrested me and tried to have me taken to a scary prison. And poor Radella," Faith said, looking down at her and Thor's joined hands. "Her dad's dead, her mate is dead and her son is in prison."

Apparently, Trinity agreed. "I can't imagine having that creep for a father. Lord Wyse was vile. And so was that scarred jerk who was always following him around." She shuddered. "He disappeared. Maybe we should start looking for him."

"No need." The queen spoke immediately as she held up one hand. "He's dead. Killed by the clerics who took me from Lord Wyse."

"Killed by the clerics?" Captain Turaya asked.

"Yes," Mom replied. "The last few days, I've been held by clerics."

"And you are certain he's dead?" he wondered.

"Yes," she repeated. "They killed him in my cell and dragged his body out after. He's dead as a doornail." That small grin on Mom's face was for me. I grinned back.

The clerics had had her for days. Shit. I'd been soooo close. So damn close. "Contact Amandine," I said. "She's a good guy. I know for sure. Maybe she can help."

"Amandine? Is she still alive, then?" Mom asked. By the smile on her face, she seemed pleased with the news.

"You knew her?" I asked.

Mom nodded. "She and my mother—the previous queen—were very close friends. She was Aunt Ama to me when I was young."

I was glad to see at least one happy memory of this planet existed in Mom's head, but this wasn't helping us get anywhere. "There's no way it was the clerics. At least not officially. Amandine sent her best to search the Optimus Unit prison. She'd heard there was an unauthorized prisoner there and she was determined to find out what was going on."

"What happened to that cleric? Where is he?" Leo asked.

"He's dead," I replied. God, everyone was dead! "I found his body the next morning when I followed him out of the main hall. I was questioned and taken to Amandine. That's how I know she's one of the good ones. We can trust her."

Mom nodded, chin resting in her hand. Thinking. "Where is my cousin, Radella? How was it that her father, her mate *and* her son were all involved and she knew nothing?"

4

D *estiny*

"SHE'S NOT my favorite person, but she was a total wreck when everything went down," Trinity said. "I don't know if she's that good of an actress. She had a total meltdown when we locked up Pawl—her son." She added the last since Mom probably didn't know anything about him. "And while I feel bad that her mate is dead, the guy was a jerk."

"Once an asshole, always an asshole," Mom clarified. Faith covered a laugh with her hand over her mouth. "The same goes for his father. You might need to be diplomatic, sweetheart, but not only did Lord Wyse try to hurt Faith, but he came to see me while I was being held prisoner. He took great pleasure in gloating. He really was an asshole. He wanted the necklace, he made that abundantly clear."

"For himself?" Trinity asked, eyes wide. "The necklace would do him no good."

"Lord Wyse was my cousin, and so was Radella, obviously,

as his daughter, therefore of royal descent. It would explain the need for the necklace. Without it, they had no power."

"But with you gone, he and Radella had already lived in the palace for over two decades," I considered aloud. "Why bother with kidnapping you now? They were living it up with you gone. It doesn't make sense."

Mom shrugged. "Powerful, but not *in* power. Plus, my spire remained lit. No one would ever accept them as true rulers with me still alive."

"Wyse wanted the necklace and he wanted you dead. It took him all this time to find you and then he kidnapped you to get the location of the necklace and then planned to kill you." Captain Turaya stood and paced behind Trinity and Leo. "It makes sense."

"But he's *dead,*" Faith reminded everyone. "If that was his plan, which makes sense and proves he was ridiculously patient and a little insane, it didn't work. And since he's dead, he wasn't the one inviting everyone to the great big, explosive party to wipe them all out. We're still under attack. It's not something he can organize from hell."

Everyone was quiet after that because what she said was true. It was possible Wyse had been searching for Mom for all that time, found her and kidnapped her to get the necklace, only to kill her and take over the throne with Radella. But that couldn't be the whole story, because we *were* still under attack. I ran my free hand over my hair and sighed. God, my brain hurt trying to figure all of this out.

"During my captivity, there was mention made of King Mykel," Mom shared.

Trinity's head whipped toward Mom, her mouth open. "My father?"

"We heard that, too," I added, leaning my forearms on the table. I glanced at Nix, who nodded. "Before the bomb went off, I overheard Morson with an older woman who mentioned the king. She implied that he might not be dead."

Mom tapped her finger on the table. "Yes, that matches what the guards were saying to me right before my escape. They claimed the king had returned and that I was to be sent to our new home where he was waiting for me."

"What? Holy shit balls, Mom," Faith said, straightening her spine as if she'd been prodded by an old biddy who didn't like to see someone slouch. "You mean your mate is still alive? What about Dad?"

"I should have mentioned this earlier, but as soon as Mom showed up, I got in touch with Warden Egara back on Earth," Trinity said. "I told her to have Dad brought to the IBP building and transported to Alera. She was going to look into it and get back to me. It might take a while. He can be a hard man to find."

"Wait, the king... your *mate* might still be alive on Alera? Mom, you're a... you have *two* husbands?" Faith seemed to be really bothered by this. "What are you going to do about Dad? Did you really love your mate?" Faith looked at Thor and I understood the tormented expression that crossed her face. It was what I, too, was thinking. I could never imagine giving up Nix. Even if we'd been separated. For years. For twenty-seven years.

And knowing Dad, he was *not* going to be into *sharing.* What a mess.

"Who cares if she's married to two men at once? That's soooo not the point," I reminded her. "If the king is still alive, then where the fuck has he been? I mean, it's been *twenty-seven years!*"

Nix spoke so everyone could hear, but looked directly at me. "I would have searched the universe for you."

"As I would you," Thor said to Faith, but I wouldn't have torn my gaze from Nix if I was given a million dollars.

Leo murmured something, but I was already leaning in, kissing Nix.

We all looked to Mom when she cleared her throat.

Grinning at Nix, I focused back on the reason we were all sitting here, not the way Nix squeezed my thigh, and then slid it higher.

"It is possible he wanted me dead," she said plainly, although she didn't answer my question about where he'd been all this time. She looked at Leo's dad. "Is it possible, truly possible, that he survived the attack that night?"

Now it was Captain Turaya's turn to freak out. "No." He slashed his hand through the air. "I don't believe it. I saw him take a dagger to his heart. Watched him bleed as we struggled to free you. I find it difficult to believe he faked his own death... to what end? He was your mate. Your king. He had nothing to gain."

Mom shook her head. "I don't know. Perhaps I wasn't supposed to flee. Perhaps my escape to Earth ruined his plans."

"If that were the case, what *were* his plans?" Leo asked, rubbing a hand over his face. "This is insane. All of it."

No one said a word because who could argue with that?

"All right," Thor began. "We talked about who is dead. My parents. Wyse. Radella's mate. Zel. The king, until we discover otherwise."

Trinity added to his list. "Everyone who died in the blast."

"Scarface," Mom said. I didn't know the man's name, but is seemed irrelevant and the nickname the perfect description.

"Right," I added. "Then who's still alive? Dead people don't kidnap someone from Earth. Dead people don't orchestrate mass homicide or plant bombs or call meetings." I said. "I've been out of the loop since I was with the clerics for most of the time everything went down. Who's *not* dead?"

"Lord Wyse was alive at the time of the queen's kidnapping. He was also still alive when Zel attempted to murder Trinity and when Lord Jax's parents were killed." Leo's fingers were playing a steady beat on the top of the table.

Thor spoke up. "The only person who we know committed

treason, who was involved in all of this, that we know for absolute certain was involved, is Pawl, Lord Wyse's grandson."

Leo nodded. "Right. We have his recorded confession, the confession that you *pulled* from him. He's in jail right now."

"I guess it's a good thing I didn't kill him," Thor offered, but he still didn't seem pleased with the choice.

"You did the right thing, love." Faith leaned up and kissed him and when she pulled back, the haunted look was gone from his eyes.

Did I have that effect on Nix? Did I have that much power?

I remembered his tears in the shower... and what came after.

Yes. Yes, I did. But he had the same power over me. *That* was love.

So be it.

"Then we start with Pawl," Captain Turaya said, moving to stand behind the queen, ever the guard. "We talk with him again. We know more now, the rumor that the king is still alive, the information we gathered from Morson and from those who survived the explosion."

"Which isn't much," Leo complained.

His father ignored him. "And now, the queen has been found. Perhaps he will share more. I will have guards bring him here."

Captain Turaya moved to the door, then stopped. Nix stood. "No, we will collect him."

Pawl would come. I looked to Nix and saw skepticism, yet fierce determination, in his eyes. Would Pawl talk? And if he did, would he have the answers we needed?

🌾

Nix

. . .

THE TRIP to retrieve Pawl from his detention cell was uneventful, but every moment I thought of the female I'd left behind at the palace. Leo's father and I barely spoke, only because we were both lost in our own thoughts.

When they pulled the traitor free from the depths of the prison and he saw me standing next to Captain Turaya, his face paled, but he straightened his shoulders and walked stoically to an unknown end. He probably expected us to kill him. Perhaps I would. Depending on his answers.

He was not completely spineless. I had no idea of the possible extent of his crimes other than that he'd admitted to being one of a few who went to Earth and kidnapped the queen. I'd assisted in his capture, when Thor left him tied up and helpless for us in the Jax family mountain home. But I'd left the art of investigation to the experts.

I did not enjoy interrogations. I didn't have the required patience.

I preferred quick and clean. Killing the enemy had always been easier than talking to him. And Pawl was no exception. Just looking at him made me ache to take his scrawny neck in my hands and twist.

He was a threat to my mate, to my queen, and to everything I'd come to value in this life. When I'd served with the Coalition Fleet fighting the Hive, I fought to protect my people. But mostly, I fought against evil.

And this plot against my mate and her family was an evil of the worst kind.

Vile. Murderous. Patient. A master strategist waiting to take Destiny away from me.

If killing Pawl wouldn't have made Destiny angry with me, I'd have done it anyway, and damn the consequences. As far as I was concerned, and from the crimes he'd admitted to, he'd more than earned a quick death.

"Stop scowling like that or he'll have a heart attack on the way to the palace." Captain Turaya stood next to me as Pawl was escorted to the back of a prisoner transport EV. Two additional guards would accompany us back to the palace.

We didn't need them.

Pawl did.

"He should be dead already," I murmured, watching him walk to the vehicle and take a seat in the back. He didn't look remorseful.

I could fix that.

"Goddess damn it, Vennix," Turaya swore. "Get your head back in the game. You aren't doing Destiny any good like this."

"I know." I did. This was not normal for me. Normally, I was calm. Cold. Emotions did not rule my decisions or my life. But then Destiny had ripped my soul wide open and exposed all the rough edges. I was raw and it seemed, irrational.

When I was with her, my lips on hers, my cock in her sweet pussy, her skin touching mine, this rawness was bliss.

The rest of the time? Fuck. I was a wreck.

Captain Turaya slapped me on the back. "You'll get used to it."

"Get used to what?"

I glanced at the other male and he grinned. "Loving your female."

I didn't deny his words. There was no point. Every cell in my body belonged to my mate. Every part of me.

"Come on." He stepped toward the EV. "Let's get Pawl back to our queen and end this."

I didn't argue and the ride to the palace was over in just a few minutes. We ordered the guards from the prison to wait at the palace while we questioned the prisoner and they hurried toward the kitchens, no doubt eager to put their feet up and enjoy the food in the palace.

Pawl walked between us, his wrists connected by a pair of large cuffs. We didn't bother with his feet. Were he to get free, I could kill him with my bare hands in seconds. He was a spoiled young lord. Never properly trained.

As we approached the queen's solar, High Cleric Amandine approached the doors from the opposite direction. The captain and I stopped. All three of us bowed to the elder, and I was pleased I did not need to cuff Pawl on the back of the head to force him to show the proper respect.

"High Cleric. It is an honor to see you here," Captain Turaya spoke.

"The queen summoned me," she replied, her voice soft but filled with awe. "Is it true? Has she returned at last?" The elderly woman had tears in her eyes and a sadness that shocked me. But then I remembered the queen calling her Aunt Ama, saying they had been close.

"It is true," the captain confirmed. "She is eager to see you."

"Then let's hurry, shall we?" Amandine's step was much lighter as she closed the distance to the double doors. Two guards, good men I knew and trusted, flanked them. They nodded to the elder, then the Captain, then me as they pulled the doors open on silent hinges.

Pawl they ignored completely.

"Aunt Ama!" The queen's cry was clear and the elder had not walked more than two steps into the room when Destiny's mother embraced her. "I missed you so much."

The elder didn't even try to hide the tears streaking down her face. "Me, too, child. Me, too."

5

N *ix*

No one corrected the old woman, referring to our queen as a child. None of us dared say a word to ruin this reunion. It was quite obvious the queen loved her and that they had been close once. It was hard to imagine being separated from those one cared about for so long. The queen quickly made the introductions. Leo and Trinity. Faith and Thor. And when she got to my mate, the elder walked to her and hugged her as well. "It is good to see you again, young lady."

Thankfully, the elder hadn't *seen* us when I'd been balls deep in my mate in her office.

Destiny hugged her back, briefly, then scowled. "You had me kicked out of the fortress. I know it had to be you."

Amandine chuckled. "You were the one caught fornicating on sacred ground."

Or maybe we had. No, that was a different encounter, later, in Destiny's rooms. After she abandoned me in that tower and thought she'd escaped. So much fucking to keep straight.

"But..."

Amandine's laugh filled the entire room. "Not that I blame you." The old woman looked over her shoulder at me, her eyebrows raised. "He is a very fine choice for your mate."

Destiny's cheeks turned pink. "But why did you have to get me kicked out? Sure, *fornicating* wasn't part of the rules, but he is my mate. It's a given we'd be doing that." Destiny waved her hand in the air. "I was onto something. I was really, really close to finding Mom."

She nodded. "Yes, you were. And had you remained, they would have killed you as they did my best guardian. The walls had eyes and ears, I'm afraid. The moment you climbed the vines and sneaked into my office, you became a target."

"The vines? What? You?" Destiny was at a loss for words. "You knew we were there?"

My mind went back to that moment when Destiny and I had first met, when my body had awakened for her, a stranger in the dark. Me, buried balls deep in her wet core, Destiny's back pressed to the wall in the cleric's office. My hand over her mouth as she came all over my cock, holding in her cries of pleasure so the elder would not know of our presence.

It was my turn to blush. All this time, we'd thought she hadn't known of our presence. It would appear we had not been nearly as stealthy as we had thought. I rubbed the back of my neck and looked away. It was one thing for everyone to know we couldn't keep our hands off each other, another to be doing it just out of someone's view.

"I shall not answer that," she replied. "You managed to escape, did you not?"

"I—" My tough female looked to me for an answer. I had none.

A corner of the older woman's mouth tipped up and I decided it was time to change the subject.

"Shall we get on with questioning our prisoner, My Queen?"

I shoved Pawl forward toward Captain Turaya, drawing the attention of everyone in the room. Pawl had been behind me, hidden by my taller frame until I knew he would pose no threat.

As Pawl moved, I met my mate's gaze across the room. The sweet smile she gave me was my reward. For now. Later I'd have that soft mouth around my...

"Pawl? You're Pawl?" The queen paled and swayed on her feet. Captain Turaya shouted in alarm, but he was not about to release the prisoner to go to her.

Trinity caught her mother and helped her into the nearest seat, the queen's gaze never leaving the prisoner.

"This is impossible," she murmured. "I don't understand."

And neither did we understand her reaction. She'd never seen Pawl before from what we knew.

Pawl shifted from foot to foot, waiting, as we all were, for some kind of explanation for the queen's reaction.

"What is it, Mom?" Trinity straightened to her full height and looked at Pawl. Eyes narrowed, as if assessing how she could kill him herself depending on what her mother said.

Queen Celene had her head in her hands. "This can't be happening. I don't believe it. I can't."

"What?" Faith moved too quickly, nearly too fast for me to see, and I determined to ask Destiny about it later. These females all seemed to have odd—abilities. Faith had her fist raised in a fighter's stance. "What is it?"

"Jesus, Mom. Stop being a drama queen and tell us what the hell is going on." Destiny's fist slammed down on the table to accentuate her words and I held back a laugh.

Oh yes, she was mine. All. Fucking. Mine. And she was magnificent. Only my mate would dare insult the queen of our planet and make demands of her at the same time.

For whatever reason, it worked. The queen recovered instantly, standing and walking toward Pawl, her face an expressionless mask. "Where is he?"

Pawl frowned. "Where is who?" He tried to take a step back, but Captain Turaya's grip was too strong.

"Where is your father?"

Pawl looked from the queen to me. "He's dead."

Queen Celene stood before him like a goddess from hell. She was shorter than Pawl, but much more formidable. "Don't lie to me, boy. Where is your father? Where is Mykel?"

That stopped everyone in their tracks. Faith gasped.

The king? The dead king? She was saying King Mykel was Pawl's father?

"Mom, you must be confused," Trinity said. "This is Pawl. He's Radella's son. Lord Wyse's grandson. His father was Danoth."

"Bullshit," she replied, not looking away from Pawl. "I want to see the DNA on that. This boy is the son of King Mykel. And he looks *exactly* like his father." She turned away from Pawl and looked for Amandine. The elder had taken a seat at the table and was examining Pawl as if she'd never seen him before.

"Mom, he's one of the guys who went to Earth and kidnapped you," Trinity explained.

"My grandfather arranged it," Pawl said. "I didn't know why we were going. He only mentioned bringing an Aleran back from Earth. I had no idea it was a female until we arrived. And then we all had the portable transport beacons. Mine returned me here, to Mytikas. Everyone else"—he dipped his head indicating the queen—"went somewhere else. I had no idea."

The queen pursed her lips and studied him, then looked to the elder cleric. "Aunt Ama? Do you see the resemblance to Mykel?" She ignored Pawl's explanation.

"Yes," Amandine replied. "I see it now. I can't believe I was so blind."

"He admitted to trying to seduce my mate, then kill her," Leo said, stepping forward, hands in fists.

Pawl took a step back, as if the little bit of distance would keep Leo from pummeling him. "My grandfather spouted threats about my mother, told me if I didn't help, that our enemies would kill her."

"Who?"

"You!" he shouted. "He said *you* would kill her. I see now... and I've had plenty of time to think of it; he was twisted, mentally insane. He wanted me to fuck my..." He looked away, paled. "He wanted me to fuck and kill my half-sister. He knew... *knew* who she was."

Bile rose in my throat and Trinity just stared wide-eyed. Yeah, that was a little gross.

The queen's voice gentled, but not much. "I don't think so, Pawl. No one knew the I was pregnant when I escaped. No one. Not even Mykel."

"And we had no intention of hurting Radella," Trinity added.

Pawl looked destroyed, now more than ever. Knowing Trinity was his half-sister had pushed him over the edge. "I see that now. All of it."

Trinity stepped to Leo, took his arm. "Do not harm him. He is just another pawn."

"I interrogated you," Thor said, pointing at Pawl. "You admitted to helping in the kidnapping of the queen, of attempting to kill off all of the princesses."

Pawl licked his lips, lifted his chin. "I did. I also admit to being used. My grandfather, my father, they were ruthless and cunning. Evil. I succumbed to their strength when all I wanted to do was protect my mother."

I didn't know if he was lying or not, but I had to believe Pawl would never intentionally fuck his half-sister, or kill her.

"Um, guys, we have a problem," Faith said. I wasn't sure when she'd picked up the small comm tablet, but she was looking down at it, Thor glancing over her shoulder. She glanced nervously at her mother. "Remember when Trinity said she'd reached out to Warden Egara, to have her find Dad and get him here?"

Mom nodded. So did Trinity.

"Warden Egara responded. From Earth." She bit her lip and looked confused.

"Well? Did they find Dad or what?" Trinity asked.

"Yes." She drew out the one syllable into two.

Destiny let out a whoop. "I knew the stupid feds wouldn't catch him."

I didn't know who the stupid feds were, but it seemed people were unskilled on Earth.

"Is he on his way?" the queen asked.

"No. Not exactly." Faith looked at her mother and the expression on her face was both confused and apologetic. "Warden Egara said Dad's already here. She said he transported to Alera a week ago."

The queen's Earth... mate... husband had been here on Alera and no one knew? Destiny's father was... where exactly?

Silence descended. Cold. Hard. Deadly.

The look on the queen's face when she turned back to Pawl was murderous. "Where is he? What have you people done with my husband?"

Pawl flinched, but remained stoic. The look on his face wasn't of defiance, but confusion. "I know nothing of this, Queen Celene. I have been in prison since the day Thor interrogated me."

I was afraid I would have to step between the queen and our prisoner, but Destiny beat me to it, cutting off her mother's advance and saving me from the difficult choice. With her arm out, she halted the woman's steps. "Mom, calm down. We need him alive. Dead men tell no tales, remember. That's why he's here. Everyone else is dead. And we learned some stuff. A little incestuous and creepy, but still, new stuff."

Queen Celene's gaze held a combination of rage and terror

I well understood. I'd felt the same anytime Destiny was in danger.

As my queen, I would have been honor bound to let her pass. Allow her to slice Pawl's throat, if she so desired. But as Destiny's mate, I had a duty to discover the truth so I could protect her from our enemies. Not *her* enemies. Ours.

If they threatened my mate, I would destroy them all.

But we needed Pawl alive to find them.

"Princess Destiny is correct, My Queen," I offered. "We need him alive."

And I felt a tiny bit sorry for the fucker.

After several tense seconds, the queen walked back to the table and sat down. "He's not the only one. I want Radella brought to me." She poked her finger at the table, her voice full of command. "Now. I don't care if you have to drag her out of her bed, drag her naked through the streets, put her in chains. Bring her to me. Now."

Captain Turaya shoved Pawl in my direction and I took hold of his upper arm, holding him motionless so he posed no threat to anyone in the room. He couldn't do much with the restraints, but I wouldn't put it past him to try, even as broken as he appeared to be from the latest revelations.

Before he could move, a loud boom sounded behind my mate. She turned, weapon drawn. Thor spun, shoved Faith behind his back. Leo grabbed Trinity and pushed her to the floor. Captain Turaya jumped in front of the queen.

We stood, weapons raised, facing the newly forming opening in the wall.

No, the secret tunnels. Fuck. We were under attack.

"Not again." Captain Turaya had his weapon drawn, his face grave, and I realized this was how the attack on the queen had happened all those years ago. They'd used the tunnels. Just as Zel had used them to try to harm Trinity.

"We should seal those fucking tunnels," I told the captain.

"Too late for that now." He moved forward and I'd had enough. I shoved Pawl to the ground, set my knee in his back.

"If you move from this spot I will kill you myself." Pawl nodded his agreement and remained still as I moved closer to the queen. In this moment, I had to trust Destiny to take care of herself. I had a job to do. I was a queen's guard, and even being Destiny's mate did not release me from that duty. "Stand behind me, My Queen."

6

N^{ix}

A SMALL WHITE garment placed on the end of a stick emerged from the door. Captain Turaya fired and struck true. The fabric caught on fire.

"Wait!" Destiny yelled the order and we all froze, unmoving. "They're waving a white flag!"

"What the hell?" Trinity peeked out from behind Leo's back. When he put his hand on her head and shoved her out of the line of danger, she weaved and popped out the other side. I heard his growl of protest.

"What is this *white flag?*" I asked.

"It's an Earth thing." Destiny spoke loudly, but didn't take her eyes, or her ion blaster, off the gaping entrance to the room. "All right. White flag. You surrender. We won't fire. Come out with your hands up."

Lady Radella walked forward with her arms raised, palms forward. She lumbered awkwardly, one high-heeled shoe on her left foot, her right foot bare. Her fine yellow gown was stained and torn, as if she'd been shoved to the ground many times over. Her face was tear-streaked, but her gaze was defiant and filled with hate. Irrational. Burning hot.

Lady Radella? What the fuck?

Behind was a man I'd never seen before, but based on Destiny's reaction, I knew instantly who he was. Her father. Adam. From Earth.

He shoved Lady Radella farther into the room and she stumbled. She didn't look happy. In fact, she looked miserable. I wasn't sure where the danger rested with the duo.

"Dad!" Destiny put her gun down and ran toward him, leaping into his arms as she'd never leaped into mine. Jealousy reared its ugly head, but I bit it back. He was her *father*. Of course, she loved him. He had raised her to be strong. A warrior. He had helped her become the perfect female for me.

Lady Radella kept walking, moving slowly toward the table. She collapsed into a seat next to Amandine as if she had every right to be seated there. As far as I knew, she did.

"Adam!" The queen stepped forward, but I put out one arm to stop her progress, keeping her close enough that I could place her behind me in an instant if things went bad. The shocked look on her face as she looked at her mate had me far from relaxed. She did not look nearly as happy, nor as accepting, as her daughter. "Adam?" she repeated. "What is going on here? Why are you with... Radella? Why are you with her in the *tunnels?*"

"Mother, are you all right?" Pawl shouted from the floor, but there was no way he was getting up to help her. His concern for his mother was evident, but my threat held, and he was smart enough to know I'd meant what I said. If he moved, I'd blast him.

Destiny released her father and he set her gently aside.

The man looked to the queen. "Celene, babe, I can explain everything."

Babe? Was that an earth endearment? Because the queen was a female fully grown. She was not an infant.

Celene pursed her lips, clearly displeased. Ah, I'd seen that look from her daughter as well. "Don't babe me. You've been on Alera a week. Start talking."

He moved forward and the queen nudged my hand, the one holding my blaster. "Nix, if he takes one more step, shoot him."

"Yes, my queen." I raised the weapon, held it steady, despite Destiny's strangled cry. She moved her body to stand between her father and my weapon.

"Nix, no!"

"Move, Destiny," I replied, my voice steely.

"Mom! This is Dad we're talking about here! What the fuck?"

"Move, Destiny." Her mother issued the order this time, and Destiny put her hands on her hips in refusal.

"Nix, can you still take the shot?" the queen asked.

Faith and Trinity hadn't moved, only gasped when they saw their father. But they seemed as stunned as I was with all that was happening. The queen said Pawl looked like the long-dead king. The tunnel door was open and hanging from its hinges. Radella looked like she'd seen better days and then an Earthling appeared. Not just any Earthling, the queen's Earth male and my mate's father.

I judged the distance, the margin of error, the placement of Destiny's head in proximity to her father's. It would be close. Goddess damn it. "Yes." If I had to. If it was life or death.

"Excellent," the queen replied, clasping her fingers together in front of her. Captain Turaya moved to her side, ready to defend her in this room yet again. Leo hovered by Trinity and Faith still. Thor had his hand on his mate's shoulder, who had come out from behind him when she discovered the threat was her father, but Thor looked ready to tug her behind him once again if needed.

"Now, Adam, start explaining." She looked at Radella. At

Pawl, who was still on the floor. Back to her Earthling mate. "All of this."

But it was Amandine who spoke. I'd completely forgotten her presence. "Well, I can start," she said. "His name isn't Adam. He is Lord Buchan Adamos Cray. Born and raised on Alera. He is Aleran, Celene. I knew him as a boy. Knew his father."

That completely deflated my mate. "What?" She stepped out of the way of my shot and stood facing the man she'd known only as her father for her entire life. Her *Earth* father. "What? Dad? You're Aleran?"

"Dad!" Faith yelled, narrowing her eyes in a mix of hurt and confusion.

Holy fuck. What was going on here?

Destiny looked lost. It was in her eyes. Nowhere else. But I knew. When she moved across the room to stand next to me, she nudged Pawl on the floor with her boot as she moved behind him, blaster aimed at his face. "Sit up. Your Mommy is here, and you all have some fucking explaining to do."

Pawl wiggled about, but it was near impossible for him to do as commanded with his wrists restrained. I reached down, grabbed him by the biceps and hoisted him to his feet.

Trinity stepped in front of him, poked him in the chest. "You should be *very* thankful the consort got in my bed instead of you."

"No kidding," he muttered and actually shuddered. The idea of what he'd almost done had settled in.

Leo came up to her and tugged her back, his gaze murderous on Pawl. I didn't blame him one bit. I was also impressed with his restraint. Punching a guy with his arms restrained wasn't honorable.

The queen motioned to Captain Turaya. "I agree. Put them together. Send guards down that tunnel. I don't want any more surprises."

In less than a minute, a full contingent of guards had disappeared down the secret tunnel and all three of our captives were seated on one of the sofas, Pawl next to his mother on the small sofa and Destiny's father, Lord Cray on an ottoman several feet away from the other two. They were surrounded, and every single one of us was armed. Even Trinity, who just glared at Leo when he tried to talk her out of holding an ion blaster pointed at her stepfather.

I knew women who'd been scorned were quite angry, but four of them? And with ion pistols? I almost felt sorry for the male. *Almost.*

Destiny's father held up his hands, palms out, and attempted to placate his mate. I could see no evil in his eyes, no darkness. Only a mate who had done something wrong and had to grovel to get back in her bed.

This should be entertaining.

"Celene, babe, there is so much you don't know."

"Start talking." The queen paced around the entire group in a circle, firing off questions. "Where is King Mykel?"

"Dead."

"Bullshit," she said, pointing at Pawl. "His son is sitting right there."

Beside me, Destiny tensed but said nothing.

"Conceived a full month before Trinity, babe." I noticed he didn't disagree that King Mykel was Pawl's father. "Radella was already pregnant during your mating ceremony to Mykel."

"What?" Trinity's outrage spoke for all, all but the queen, who looked coldly furious. "Oh shit, Pawl really is my half-brother."

"Wait," Thor said. "I thought he was born a few years *after* the queen disappeared. That's what I'd heard."

Everyone looked to Pawl, who obviously had no idea since he'd been a baby, then Radella.

"Mykel was dead. My father married me off to Danoth and we lived far from Mytikas for a time. If anyone questioned

Pawl's age upon our return, and it was only off by less than a year, no one said anything."

Holy. Fuck. I looked to the prisoner who looked just as stunned.

Lord Cray, Adam from Earth, Destiny's father, shifted and looked at Lady Radella. "Tell the truth, or by the goddess I will flay you alive and enjoy the killing." His tone of voice was one I recognized. Deadly. "And then I'll do the same to your son."

That broke her and the woman began to cry. "I hate you. I hate *all* of you."

"There's a shocker." Faith's arms were crossed, her foot keeping time to some invisible rhythm only she could hear. Thor still stood directly beside her, but seemed to recognize her "hands off" vibe. "So, what? You were having an affair with the king, got knocked up with his kid, and then decided life would be great if you could kill off Mom and keep the leftovers?"

"It wasn't an affair, we were mated!" she wailed. "My father wanted the throne. He knew Mykel was my mate. He'd been awakened by *me* and he'd soothed my Ardor. And he knew *you*"—she looked at the queen with pure hatred—"you wouldn't be able to resist him. He was so handsome. So skilled in bed. You had your own Ardor to ease and you fell in love with him like a stupid little girl."

"And what was your father's plan, Radella? Tell them the rest." Destiny's father taunted her now. She was enraged, but knew she was caught. Venom was spewing from her lips in her final attack.

"I was pregnant with Pawl. We knew you would be too young and stupid to see the truth. So he was supposed to kill you, Celene." She pushed her tangled hair back from her face. "It was going to be an accident, of course."

"And after I was dead, what?" she asked. "You were going to step in and claim him as your mate? Steal my throne?" The queen leaned down close. Too close and I took a step forward.

"The citadel didn't accept you, cousin. No spire lit when you went within and it tasted your blood. The people never would have accepted you."

"They already did." Radella lifted her chin and glared at the queen. Then she looked to Destiny's father. Her gaze turned feral. "But *he* ruined everything! He was supposed to be dead. Mykel promised me he was dead."

"He who?" Celene asked.

"Your mate. Your *real* mate."

"Me." Destiny's father rose to his feet and none of us stopped him. "You were mine, Celene. I was in the palace on a training mission and my body awakened for you. One look and it was over for me. You were mine. Mykel was my commander in the royal guard. I told him first, too young and stupid to keep my joy to myself."

Destiny's mother looked shaken to her core. "Mykel was not my mate?"

He shook his head. "No. He faked his awakening as part of his plan to put Radella on the throne."

I had to think this through. King Mykel had been awakened by Lady Radella, the haggard, hate-filled female before us, and got her with child. At the same time, he pretended to be awakened and in love with Queen Celene so he could be king. That had worked. But a guard in the palace, Cray, *had* been awakened by her and he knew the truth, knew that the king was faking.

I could imagine how Cray had felt. I'd have killed King Mykel, too. Faking love? Duping Cray's mate? It must have been excruciating to watch. The laws of Alera had extenuating circumstances for murder and protecting a mate was one of them.

"You are mine, babe," Cray said. "You've always been mine."

Captain Turaya looked confused. We all did. "Then who killed the king? Who orchestrated the attack that night?"

"I did," Cray answered immediately.

What? Holy shit.

I knew what it was like to be awakened, to be obsessed with my mate, of getting inside her, making her mine. If there was a male who was untrue, someone so duplicitous as to fake an awakening to my female, I'd want him dead, too.

"I discovered Mykel's plot to murder her, to take over the throne with Radella by his side. I could accept Celene's choice to love another, but I could not allow him to harm her. She was never in danger that night, Captain." Cray looked to the elder Turaya. "Not for a moment. It was my blade that took Mykel's life, and I'd do it again to protect what's mine. *Mine.*"

Radella rose and approached Queen Celene. "You. You took Mykel from me. I just wanted a family. A quiet life with my mate. Nothing more. But he had to want *you.*"

The queen looked sad. "He didn't want me, Radella. He wanted power. He wanted the throne. So did your father." Queen Celene raised her finger and pointed it in Radella's face, her voice going deadly quiet. "And so did you."

"He loved me! But he had to fuck you. Had to claim the pussy of the virgin queen!" Radella's eyes were wild, almost feral and she raised her arms as if to choke the queen. Captain Turaya blocked her, gripped her arms and tugged them behind her back with one hand, the ion pistol in his other aimed at her head. Still, she struggled and fought his hold.

Her words were irrational. Mykel didn't want Celene, he wanted the throne.

"You knew, Radella," the queen said. "Knew of his intentions."

"You think I wanted my mate to fuck another?" she spat. "Every time I saw you together, I couldn't miss the way he looked at you. The smiles, the lover's touches. Even if they were fake, they were meant for me. He was mine."

"Would it have been worth it if you'd become queen?" Trinity asked her.

"He died. You came back. It was all for nothing," Radella countered. "But my son. Don't hurt Pawl. He's innocent."

The queen stared at her, wide-eyed. Thinking. "Did you know Mykel's intentions all along?" she asked.

Radella shook her head, her hair flinging about, tears forming in her eyes. "He wanted the throne and intended to take it." The female sobbed outright now.

Pawl shifted on the couch, somehow got himself to standing even with his arms restrained. Thor moved to his side. "Don't hurt her!" Pawl shouted.

The queen raised her hand. "No, she will not die. No one else dies because of this. Have the guards take her away. She will be questioned more later, but her life has moved from the palace to more... humble accommodations. Take her to the prison."

7

D estiny

THIS WAS like watching *Dynasty* and *Dallas* and every daytime soap opera rolled into one. But this was my life.

All I knew was that my mom and sisters were safe. Nix was by my side and Dad was here.

Dad. An entirely different dad than I knew.

"You're not from Kansas?" I asked Dad.

He looked to me and shook his head and held out his hand to Mom, but she stepped back, shook her head. The anguish in his gaze was horrible to see. I'd never seen them fight, or argue or even bicker. Their love had been obvious at all times.

Dad sighed. "I didn't expect you to flee that night." He looked to Captain Turaya. "You did the right thing, protecting her. She surprised us all, leaving the planet. It took me a month to track her transport and I went to Earth. There was nothing on Alera for me anymore without you here, Celene. *You* were my life."

That was romantic.

Pawl dropped back down on the couch, probably glad the attention was off of him.

"I found you and wanted to keep you all for myself. The attraction was instant, wasn't it, love?" Dad's voice had gone soft in the way he always spoke to Mom.

"Why didn't you tell me?" she asked. "We could have gone back to Alera."

He shook his head. "I admit, I was selfish. On Earth, I had you all to myself. Mates together. No throne, no enemies. I knew Mykel was working with others. At least Radella. Most likely her father."

"Lord Wyse," Thor said.

Dad looked to him, nodded.

"You were safe on Earth and that was all that mattered. For twenty-seven years, we were safe."

"You didn't know I was pregnant," she replied.

This time, when he stepped toward her, she let him. He took her hands, held them both. "No. I hated the baby you carried, a living sign of Mykel, of the man who'd played you falsely, who'd wanted you dead."

Trinity turned into Leo, who wrapped his arm around her. The queen tried to tug her hands away.

"But one look when she was born, those blue eyes, I was hooked. I couldn't put the sins of the father upon an innocent child. She was a part of you."

Trinity turned in Leo's hold, looked to Dad.

"You know I love you, Trinity. As I do all my girls. All *four* of my girls."

"Because you're Aleran, you weren't too stunned when I told you the truth, that I was from a far off planet."

He laughed. "I remember that conversation. It was just like out of a movie. No, I wasn't surprised. I tried to be, but I'm not a great actor."

"You faked learning Aleran," she added, starting to see a pattern to their lives. *Our* lives.

I remembered Dad learning Aleran right along with us when we were little.

"I protected you, Celene. With my heart, my body. I'd do it again." He shrugged. "And I have."

It was as if a big ass light bulb went off over my head. "You put the bomb in that building."

"Yes." He didn't seem the least bit sorry. "They were all loyal to Mykel, could have harmed you all again. My mate. My daughters. I protect what's mine."

"And the others?"

"There is much to take in, but Pawl here made it clear who wanted you dead... who wanted you *all* dead. Not twenty-seven years ago, because there never was an actual coup."

"The kidnapping," Mom stated.

"You were safe, we were happy. But then you were found."

"Wyse," Pawl said from the couch.

I moved to one of the chairs, dropped down in it.

"Wyse found Mom," I said.

"After all that time?" Mom asked.

"He was an evil asshole, but I ensured we were well-hidden," Dad added. "Until we weren't."

"Until I contacted Warden Egara about my stupid Ardor," Trinity said.

Dad's mouth opened and he stared. Obviously, he never knew about that. "After all three of you didn't get your Ardor at the time most females do, I just thought it wouldn't happen on Earth."

Nix came over and sat on the arm of my chair, ever protective.

"Wyse found me and wanted me dead. Wanted the necklace... that's why he kept torturing me for it," Mom said.

Dad tried to pull her in for a hug, but she evaded his touch with a skill I admired. These Aleran males were not easy to evade. Not that I wanted to get away from Nix, but still, I was taking notes.

Dad sighed and dropped his hands back to his sides. "If Wyse weren't dead, I'd kill him all over again."

"He wanted the throne for my mother," Pawl said. "Kidnap the queen, get the necklace. When the queen never returned, the people would have accepted my mother. She was already ruling."

"Only we came looking for you, Mom," I added. "Wyse learned there had been another transport from Earth and sent the group to have us killed that night. He didn't know we were the princesses, just that we were from Earth. Which meant trouble."

"And that's when we first crossed paths," Nix said, tugging on my hair.

"When I was awakened," Leo added, kissing Trinity.

"Then we sneaked into the citadel and our spires lit. He had *four* people to kill before Radella could rule, even with the necklace."

"He kept me alive so I could tell him where the jewels were," Mom said.

"So he set out to have me killed," Trinity replied.

"It seems that's where he got me involved once again," Pawl admitted.

Leo growled.

"Zel," Captain Turaya said.

"By then, we were mated and well-protected," Trinity said, glancing up at Leo. "Wyse couldn't get to me."

"So he went after me," Faith continued. "He tried to take me away, to that Optimus Unit special prison. But you stopped him." Thor wrapped an arm about her, held her close. "It was your mom who almost killed me. It wasn't just Wyse!"

Thor shook his head. "She tried to poison you because she didn't want you to be my mate, remember? She wanted power, not a maid for a daughter-in-law. Her attempt had nothing to do with all this."

"But she conspired with Wyse," she countered.

He gave her a squeeze. "I think she fell for his evil, but she truly wanted power. And if she'd known you were a princess, she'd have had it all along. Her greed killed her."

That was so fucking sad.

"Wyse tried to kill Trinity and then stopped?"

"Yes, because I killed him," Dad said.

Holy shit, Dad had killed *a lot* of people. All for Mom.

"Who else did you kill?" Mom asked.

"My family knew we would return eventually. When I arrived, I contacted warriors I could trust among the clerics and the Optimus Unit. They found where Wyse was holding you prisoner. I sent the clerics in to kill the man with the scar on his face, Wyse's second. I tracked an evil female cleric when I heard she had threatened your life, I summoned Mykel's supporters to the meeting where I planned to destroy them all with a bomb. The list is long, Celene." Dad looked to the males in the room. "I did it to defend my mate, my daughters. I do not apologize. I feel no remorse. My family was in danger. I did what had to be done. You must understand."

Captain Turaya went over to Pawl, removed the restraints from his wrists and lowered himself into a chair across from me. He suddenly looked old.

"You killed King Mykel in defense of your mate. You went to Earth to be with her in peace. Wyse found her after all these years and wanted her for the jewels and then to finally give his daughter the crown he thought she deserved. But the princesses ruined his plans by just being alive. He attempted to kill Princess Trinity, but you arrived and took him out, and everyone else involved in hurting your family. Past and present."

Dad nodded. "That is correct. When I located my mate, I decided she was safest remaining in the prison cell, under my people's care, where I knew no one could harm her. But she derailed my plans once again, with another escape." Dad looked at Mom, a smile of apology on his face. "I shall never underestimate you again, mate."

"Holy shit," Leo muttered.

Mom stood, stunned. Processing. Thinking. Something. "The warm blankets. The food. Those stupid guards promising to take care of me? That was all you?"

"Yes, babe. I couldn't show my face until I had Radella under control. Until after the meeting that would destroy what remained of Mykel's plot."

All at once, she launched herself at Dad. He caught her, lifted her into his arms and she wrapped her legs about his waist.

Holy shit. Mom and Dad were kissing. Like serious, make out kissing.

After a *very* uncomfortable minute, Mom lifted her head. "Alone. Now."

Dad grinned, and playfully swatted her ass. I could never unsee my dad spanking my mom, even if it was over her clothing. "Yes, My Queen."

He turned and carried Mom out of the room.

I looked at my sisters. They looked at me.

"Holy shit." Trinity collapsed on the chair Dad had vacated. "I can't believe this. Any of it."

"Me neither." Faith pulled Thor close and burrowed into his chest. "I think I need a margarita."

"Amen to that," Faith said.

Nix looked at me, a question in his eyes.

"Alcohol, Nix. It's alcohol."

Captain Turaya chuckled and slapped Pawl on the shoulder. "Come on, boy. No one is dying today. And we've got plenty of fine Aleran wine downstairs in the kitchens."

Pawl left with the captain, and I didn't much care where they took him. Trinity probably felt differently, for she watched the two men leave with a thoughtful expression on her face. "What do we do with my brother?"

"Our brother," Faith said. "If he's yours, he's ours too. That's how this family works."

"The captain will sort him out."

High Cleric Amandine stood for the first time since she'd entered the room. "I must return to the cleric's fortress and report this. We will send out a formal announcement and make sure the entire planet knows the queen has returned. The people will expect a ceremony of some kind. At the very least, she must introduce Lord Cray as her mate, and also Destiny as her daughter."

Me? I forgot. No one knew I existed. Not yet, anyway. But I was in no hurry, and apparently, neither were my sisters.

"Wine first." Trinity stood and pulled Leo behind her out of the room. "Dinner in bed. Breakfast in bed. Let's spend a week in bed. I need some sleep."

Leo was on her heels and scooped her up into his arms as they left the room. "Anything you want, mate."

Thor pulled Faith close and she tucked herself against his side like one of the zebcats I'd heard so much about. "See you later, Des. I want to go home, and I know Mom and Dad won't come up for air for days."

"True." She was right. On their last anniversary, they'd kicked us out of the house and told us to stay somewhere else for a full week.

A warm hand settled on the back of my neck and I recognized my mate's touch, leaned into his strength. His heat. Just... him.

Faith and Thor disappeared and I turned in his arms. "Let's get out of here before they get loud enough for me to hear them through the door." I already could, if I were being honest, but listening to my Mom's moans of pleasure was too creepy, so I pretended it was rats in the walls and walked as fast as I could out of the room. Just... ewww. "Parents are *not* supposed to fuck like rabbits."

Nix left the doors to the queen's solar open behind us and

issued orders to a nearby guard to gather six men and stand guard both at the entrance here, in the hallway, and inside, at the mouth of the secret tunnel.

I hid a grin just imagining what those guards might hear later.

Better them than me.

Nix pulled me along behind him once the guards returned and took up their positions. "So, mate, what, exactly, is a rabbit and how do they fuck?"

I choked on my laughter, his expression so serious there was no ignoring the question. "Rabbits are very small, furry, adorable creatures that are well-known for making a lot of babies on Earth."

"And you think your parents are like these rabbits?" His raised eyebrows were evidence that he was about to argue.

"No. Not really. It's just a saying. We say it when two people like to have sex constantly and can't keep their hands off each other."

He grinned and wrapped his arms around my waist as he backed me into our room. "Then I would very much like to fuck you like a rabbit, mate."

"God, you're adorable."

"I am a rabbit set to fuck you for days without ceasing." I was half naked before he was done with the sentence. He dropped to his knees and pulled the rest of my clothes from my body. "But first, I am hungry, female."

His mouth. My pussy.

Oh, hell yeah. We both were starving for each other.

Always would be.

8

D estiny

I'D BEEN to the citadel before, but it had been at night. Pitch black all around, the citadel and the single spire that was lit a beacon. Sure, it had been all aglow, austere and yet beautiful at the same time. Brilliant white that seemed to come from the inside out. A perimeter of gorgeous flowers, grass and a park-like setting. But it was also ruthless, an invisible barrier that kept all who were not chosen from entering.

We'd stunned Leo with an ion pistol and run past the guards to gain entrance that first night. We sisters had separated then, putting our plans into motion. Faith headed for the Jax house. I disappeared within the clerical order. Trinity faced the world, became *Princess* Trinity and led Alera until Mom was found.

That had been the plan, and it had worked. Despite all the insanity, our plan had worked.

And now? Mom was here. So was all of Mytikas, spread out before the citadel like a crowd at the Capitol Building when the

US swore in a new president. The weather was perfect: bright skies, a warm breeze... perhaps the powers of the citadel affected the warm weather. The sun was setting, the building becoming brighter, the spires glowing more fiercely by the minute. As for the mood of the crowd? They cheered. Chanted. Everyone was boisterous and full of joy.

That was all because of Mom.

Their queen.

I was so proud of her. I always had been, the woman I'd always looked up to, listened to. Sure, we'd argued, fought. She hadn't liked it when I'd pierced my own ears at eleven—after I'd thrown up in the bathtub because I had a needle in my ear and realized I hadn't liked it either. She'd driven me to karate class after Jiu Jitsu class after Tae Kwon Do class without complaint. She'd even rolled her eyes but bit her lip when I'd dyed my hair purple.

But that was all nothing. Just... stuff. Mom offered love unconditionally. Was fiercely protective. Brave. Kind. Ruthless. And not just to me, Faith and Trinity. Not with Dad either. She was all those things for an entire planet.

She'd fled to Earth not to save herself, but to save the baby she'd carried. To save the next ruler of Alera. She'd spent our entire lives preparing all of us to one day return to Alera, but I doubted she'd ever imagined it would be like this.

God, the mess... all of it, had proven our blood bond was so strong. Royals or not, we were a family. And growing. Trinity, Faith and I now had mates. Not just husbands, but pretty much DNA chosen males that belonged to us. They were ours and we were theirs.

Just as Mom and Dad were mates. True loves. I'd seen it all my life, but never understood the depth of it until now. Until Nix.

What Dad had done to protect Mom... it made me weepy. And I was *never* weepy.

And now, Mom stood before the citadel, inside the invisible

barrier but before her people, in her white flowing gown, the royal necklace about her neck. She'd gone within just a little while ago to the place the jewels had been waiting all these years and retrieved them. She didn't look like the woman I knew who went to the corner store in Snoopy pajamas to pick up milk and eggs. She looked... like the fucking queen.

The crowd before her cheered, chanted her name. *Celene, Celene, Celene.* So did those who watched this moment from afar, from the most distant corners of the planet. To those on other planets as well. Leaders like Prime Nial from Prillon Prime had spoken with her, welcomed her return. She smiled, waved, indulged. Some had waited twenty-seven years for this moment, for their beloved queen to return. Some had never seen her before, except in images.

Trinity, Faith and I stood outside the perimeter, our mates behind us, as we, too, waited. This was Mom's moment. All of Alera's moment.

"Did I mention how beautiful you look?" Nix murmured. His breath fanned my neck and I reached back, grabbed his hand. I flushed from head to toe at his words, at the deep tone. He'd helped me dress, then helped me undress as he showed me just how much he liked what he saw. Then, after the quickie that had left me wilted and very, *very* sated, he'd fastened the small buttons up the back of my purple dress.

I gave a slight nod as I looked over my shoulder at him. From afar, everyone would see him so handsome in his uniform, in his military bearing, yet his eyes held heat and love just for me.

Mom held up her hands and the crowd instantly fell silent. She smiled brilliantly and nodded, as if giving thanks for their attention.

"My Alerans, we have all waited for this day, for this moment to arrive. I have dreamed of returning to you, to lead once again. You were never far from my thoughts. While I lived on Earth, a planet so far from here, know that your blood, Aleran blood, flowed through my veins and not a day went by that I did not think about you, my people, my home."

Wow, Mom had helped me with my English papers in high school, but sheesh, she'd downplayed her skills.

"These past few weeks, you have heard rumors. You have heard lies. Yesterday, I shared the truth. I am sure you have heard it by now through every news feed, read it for yourself. Know that every word came from my pen, from my hand. I will not go over all of the details, salacious, cruel and sad as they may be. I can't speak for those who have died. I can't hope to understand or explain their motives and intentions."

She paused, let all of that sink in.

"I would like to take a moment now to honor those who have given their lives in protection of me and Alera. Nothing I can say will match the depth of my gratitude for the sacrifice that was made, or for each individual's integrity. Whether they fought to free me, or are, even now, out there somewhere fighting the Hive menace, they are true Alerans, every one."

Mom lifted her hand and wiped at the corner of her eye.

Nix squeezed my hand again. He'd been one of those men. Him and Leo. They'd gone out and served in the Coalition Fleet. I couldn't begin to fathom how many friends he'd lost, or how many people had died hiding the truth about my mother.

After a minute of silence, Mom smiled once again. "It is time to formally introduce you to my family." Mom looked to Dad, who stood beside Captain Turaya and Pawl across from us. It was like we were at a wedding, bridesmaids on one side, groomsmen on the other.

Mom walked through the invisible barrier where many had died in their attempt to take all she was born with. She walked over to Dad, took his hand and moved so they were front and center for the entire world to see.

"My people, this is my mate, Adam, Lord Cray. I met him on

Earth, but he, too, is a true Aleran. He protected me, cherished me and saved me just as a mate should. He left the planet all those years ago to watch over me, to belong to me as I did to him. On Alera, he was born as Lord Buchan Adamos Cray. Since our mating, he has, unknown by everyone, been your king. King Adam."

Dad smiled lifted their joined hands to his lips and kissed her knuckles. The crowd went wild.

I'd read what Mom had sent to the media, a thorough yet simple outline of... everything. King Mykel's betrayal, Radella, Pawl. The plan to kill Mom and take over the throne. Her escape. Lord Wyse's long desire to have Radella rule, the kidnapping and attempted murder of Trinity. Dad's arrival and his ridiculously alpha male plan to protect his mate. All of it.

The truth had been shared. It was out. The true traitors were now a part of history, to learn from and never repeat.

"The Herakles legacy continues with my daughters. Trinity, Faith and Destiny."

Mom looked to us, curled her finger so we would join her. I didn't release Nix's hand as we went, stood in a line beside Mom and Dad.

"I have been gone a long time. In the few short weeks my daughters have been on the planet, they have become worthy princesses. Princess Trinity has ruled in my place and you have embraced her. She is a worthy future queen."

Again, the crowd cheered. Trinity smiled and waved her hand like the Queen of England on the balcony at Buckingham Palace.

Mom looked to Dad, who nodded, before she gazed out at her people. "My spire has been lit while I have been gone. Your hearts have held me well. But I am the past... and Trinity is the future. That future is *now*."

Trinity stared at Mom, wide-eyed.

Oh shit. This was like the time Mom told us she had a

surprise for us. We'd waited on the couch, all three of us side by side, and held our breaths. Of course, then, it was to say we were going to Disney World for spring break. Yeah, I had a feeling we weren't going off on a family vacation.

"I, Queen Celene Herakles of Alera, do hereby relinquish the throne to my heir and successor, Trinity Herakles, your new queen."

A gasp came from Faith. Trinity said, "Mom!" and the entire crowd started murmuring. This was huge. Like... holy shit huge.

Mom came over, stood before Trinity. "You've proven your-self to me, to the people of Alera. They need *you* to lead. I stopped being their queen all those years ago. I've just been their *hope*. They've been waiting for you."

Tears streamed down Trinity's cheeks as she hugged Mom. They stood like that for what seemed like a full minute. Mom was stepping down as queen? She just got back! But Trinity *had* been leading the planet. She had been raised to ultimately take over. And Dad had done everything he could to make sure she was ready. Law school. Debate club. Ethics and philosophy and all that fucking *talking*. I loved hitting and kicking and playing. Trin? She really was born for this.

What Mom had said was true. She'd been gone for so long. Her spire had been the hope the planet needed to keep going during her absence. And now, they didn't need Mom anymore. They needed a queen and duh, that was soooo Trinity.

Nix wrapped an arm about my waist and I leaned into him. He was my anchor, and I knew no matter what happened, no matter how things changed, he would be there.

Leo took Trinity's elbow and had her step back. He leaned down and whispered something to her, something no one could hear. As she wiped her face, she nodded, then nodded again.

When he was done, he kissed her temple.

Then she turned to Mom, lifted her chin, rolled her shoulders back and nodded.

"Come," Mom said to Trinity and started walking back toward the citadel, once again back in full royal mode. God, the two of them had that down pat.

I could barely walk in my long dress and yet the two of them appeared to be floating. I had no idea what Mom was up to... some things Aleran she'd never mentioned to us growing up. I glanced at Dad, who smiled indulgently. He'd grown up on Alera, *left* Alera when he was about my age. But he knew what was happening. I had no doubt Mom had talked with Dad, worked it out with him.

The barrier accepted them both.

In front of the large doors, they stopped and turned to face everyone once again. The crowd fell silent. Not even a baby cried or a bird chirped. Nothing. It was possible the wind ceased to blow just for this moment.

Mom reached up behind her neck and undid the clasp on the necklace. She moved to stand behind Trinity and put it about her neck, fastened it and moved back beside her.

No one said a word. I held my breath.

Mom looked up at the pale glow of the citadel, the spires. It was dusk now, the sky almost black, but Mom and Trinity were easily seen in the brightness. So were we, even outside the barrier.

As one, everyone tilted their faces up just as their queen did. One last time, they followed her silent command to look, to watch.

Slowly, the white glow changed, grew darker. Within seconds, the citadel was bathed in a royal blue—god, no pun intended—and the spires, the four that were lit, changed from bright white to cobalt beacons in the night.

It was stunning. Beautiful. Like something out of a fairy tale.

Magic. It felt like magic.

The silence was thick, as if everyone present couldn't believe their eyes and didn't know how to react.

Nearby, Captain Turaya hugged Leo's mother close, a contented smile on his face. When he caught me looking, be beamed. "Your grandmother's spires were a pale green, like buds of fresh grass in spring."

"You're such a poet, my love." Leo's mother was cute. There was no other word for the petite woman, or the way she looked up at her mate like he was her sun and stars. No wonder Leo turned out to be a keeper.

Mom turned to the crowd and I tore my gaze from Leo's parents. I didn't want to miss this, whatever this was.

"The ascension is complete. The citadel recognizes the new queen." And now, she radiated pride, joy, contentment, just as she had at all of our graduations. But this... holy fuck, this, even I was a little weepy. "Alera, welcome Queen Trinity."

The roar of the crowd was unlike anything I had ever heard. No football stadium could compare. No rock concert. All of Alera was shouting for joy in this moment.

They cheered for the past returning, for the present, for the peaceful, beautiful and very traditional hand-off from mother to daughter. They cheered for the future, which looked so bright. And so *very* blue.

Trinity and Mom walked back through the barrier to join all of us. Dad was the first to approach them and hugged Trinity fiercely. He might not be her father by blood, but definitely was her father in the heart. That was all that mattered.

Faith raced over to Trinity and Nix let go of my hand so I could join them. "Did you have any idea?" Faith asked Trinity.

Trinity shook her head and was beaming, like practically glowing and vibrating with energy. I had to wonder if her reaction was from being stunned or being excited, or if it were the necklace itself. I knew I could hear like a flipping bat by entering the citadel and having my spire light up the sky, but what powers did the necklace hold?

And what did the auras of an entire crowd look like all at once?

I'd get the details out of Trinity. But not now. I'd pin her to the ground and pinch her just like when we were young if I had to. I had my ways.

"Glad it's you and not me," I told her when it was my turn to get a hug in. She looked at me and rolled her eyes. We both knew I spoke the truth.

"You just don't like wearing dresses," she replied.

"And that's all the excuse I need," I countered.

"You must address your people," Mom interrupted.

I turned to go to Nix, but he was right there. God, yes. He would always be *right there.*

He tugged me a little to the side as Trinity stepped forward, Mom beside her. They were speaking quietly to each other, but I was more interested in Nix.

"You're happy for your sister?" he asked.

I frowned. "Of course."

"Jealous?"

My mouth fell open. "God, no. She can have that necklace and all the crazy power that goes with it. I just want you."

"I wonder what Leo's opinion of this will be. He was not ready to be king. Trinity will need more protection now."

"She'll be fine. She's strong." I swiped the air. "He can handle it. God, King Leo. That's insane."

"And Princess Destiny is not?"

I shrugged as I thought of it. "I am okay with that. Mom raised us to someday be right here, just like this. I never envisioned it quite like this. Never imagined Mom would hand off being queen to Trinity. Actually, I always thought of it like the end of *Star Wars* where Princess Leia gave medals to Han Solo, Luke Skywalker and Chewbacca."

Nix frowned. "I do not know that princess."

I laughed then. "I will have to introduce you to her. Tonight, when we are alone."

His eyebrows went up. "Is she kinky?"

My mouth fell open at the idea of Princess Leia being into wild sex. "No, but I am."

He grinned. "Yes, you are. Later, my princess. Later I will bow down before you."

I went up on my tiptoes and whispered in his ear. "As long as you bow down between my thighs."

He growled just as the crowd went silent. His arm banded about my waist and he pulled me back against him. I wasn't sure if it were to hold me close or hide his erection from the entire planet.

"My fellow Alerans," Trinity said, repeating how Mom had started her speech. "I am not as eloquent as my mother, nor as wise, but I promise with time and hard work, to earn your respect and your trust. I am proud to be an Aleran. Proud to be here with my sisters, my parents, and my newfound brother."

Trinity looked to Pawl, who stood beside Captain Turaya. After what he'd been through, he was content to stay in the shadows, as much as could be for being part of the royal family. The captain had worked out a deal with the Optimus Unit and Pawl's testimony was being used to lock away the survivors of the building blast. In exchange, he had been offered a post in training under High Cleric Amandine's supervision. I had no doubt the older woman was up to the task.

Nix's cock was pressed to my back. So hot. So distracting. And *Queen* Trinity was still talking. Talking. Talking. "I am now your queen, but I am also a mate. You may look to me in times of joy, in times of difficulty, but I look to Leoron Turaya in those same moments."

Trinity looked to Leo with all the love I knew she had in her. She held out her hand and Leo strode to her, took it. "I am not the queen without my mate, without my love. Without King Leoron."

She held up their joined hands and again, the crowd went wild. Leo looked to Trinity with the powerful bearing of an insanely alpha male. Protective, bossy and above all, loving. He leaned down and kissed her... the Queen of Alera. In front of everyone. He liked to stake his claim on her and he'd done it. The ultimate claiming.

Captain Turaya beamed. He'd been there through it all. Helping Mom to escape, helping to find her when she'd been kidnapped, and ending the almost thirty-year discourse that could have destroyed the planet. And now his son was king. He may have protected the queen, but little did he know that he'd raised a future king.

I looked to Faith, who was leaning against Thor. She was smiling, at peace. The calm one... or so we'd thought. But now, she could live her life with Thor, make all those babies she'd always wanted. The man of her dreams was beside her, their future wide open before them.

And then there was Mom. Dad was whispering in her ear and she was nodding. Both of them looked content. At peace. And finally, completely together. No secrets. Nothing but forever.

Mom looked my way, winked. She gave the shooing motion with her fingers and Dad followed the motion. He brought his fingers to his lips and sent it my way.

I was loved all around. Peace reigned on Alera, and in our lives.

Tipping my head up, I looked to Nix. "Get me out of here," I said.

Nix bowed. "As you wish, Princess Destiny. Your wish is my command."

I went up on tiptoe again, whispered in his ear, told him my wish.

His eyes widened and filled with intense heat. A wicked grin spread across his face. He took my hand in his and tugged me away from the crowd. I didn't know exactly where we were headed, but it didn't matter. I had Nix and he had me.

The world was ours. We were rich as Midas. Royal.

Hell, the entire universe was ours.

But I didn't care about any of that. I already had the only thing I'd ever really wanted for myself—Nix's heart.

THE ASCENSION SAGA

Thank you for joining me on this exciting journey in the Interstellar Brides® universe. The adventure continues...

TRINITY
Book 1
Book 2
Book 3
Volume 1 (Books 1-3)

FAITH
Book 4
Book 5
Book 6
Volume 2 (Books 4-6)

DESTINY
Book 7
Book 8
Book 9
Volume 3 (Books 7-9)

www.AscensionSaga.com

LET'S TALK!

Interested in joining my not-so-secret Facebook Sci-Fi Squad? Share your testing match, meet new like-minded sci-fi romance fanatics!

JOIN Here:
https://www.facebook.com/groups/scifisquad/

Want to talk about the Ascension Saga (or any Grace Goodwin book) with others? Join the SPOILER ROOM and spoil away! Your GG BFFs are waiting!

JOIN Here:
https://www.facebook.com/groups/ggspoilerroom/

YOUR mate is out there. Take the test today and discover your perfect match. Are you ready for a sexy alien mate (or two)?

VOLUNTEER NOW!

interstellarbridesprogram.com

GET A FREE BOOK!

JOIN MY MAILING LIST TO BE THE FIRST TO KNOW OF NEW RELEASES, FREE BOOKS, SPECIAL PRICES AND OTHER AUTHOR GIVEAWAYS.

http://freescifiromance.com

CONNECT WITH GRACE

Interested in joining my not-so-secret Facebook Sci-Fi Squad? Get excerpts, cover reveals and sneak peeks before anyone else. Be part of a closed Facebook group that shares pictures and fun news. JOIN Here: http://bit.ly/SciFiSquad

All of Grace's books can be read as sexy, stand-alone adventures. Her Happily-Ever-Afters are always free from cheating because she writes Alpha males, NOT Alphaholes. (You can figure that one out.) But be careful...she likes her heroes hot and her love scenes hotter. You have been warned...

www.gracegoodwin.com
gracegoodwinauthor@gmail.com

ABOUT GRACE

Grace Goodwin is a *USA Today* and international bestselling author of Sci-Fi & Paranormal romance. Grace believes all women should be treated like princesses, in the bedroom and out of it, and writes love stories where men know how to make their women feel pampered, protected and very well taken care of. Grace hates the snow, loves the mountains (yes, that's a problem) and wishes she could simply download the stories out of her head instead of being forced to type them out. Grace lives in the western US and is a full-time writer, an avid romance reader and an admitted caffeine addict.

ALSO BY GRACE GOODWIN

Her Viken Mates

Fighting For Their Mate

Her Rogue Mates

Claimed By The Vikens

The Commanders' Mate

Interstellar Brides®: The Colony

Surrender to the Cyborgs

Mated to the Cyborgs

Cyborg Seduction

Her Cyborg Beast

Cyborg Fever

Rogue Cyborg

Interstellar Brides®: The Virgins

The Alien's Mate

Claiming His Virgin

His Virgin Mate

His Virgin Bride

Other Books

Their Conquered Bride

Wild Wolf Claiming: A Howl's Romance